EARTH PUBLICATIONS
PRESENTS

Children of the
Wronged

Bernice

a novel by Reign

CARTEL PUBLICATIONS
PRESENTS

PUBLISHER'S NOTE:
This book is a work of fiction. Names, characters, businesses,
Organizations, places, events and incidents are the product of the
Author's imagination or are used fictionally. Any resemblance of
Actual persons, living or dead, events, or locales are entirely coin-
cidental.

Library of Congress Control Number: 2011905436
ISBN 10: 0984303030
ISBN 13: 978-0984303038
Cover Design: Davida Baldwin www.oddballdsgn.com
Editor: Advanced Editorial Services
Graphics: Davida Baldwin
www.thecartelpublications.com
First Edition

Printed in the United States of America

What Up Psycho's!

Before we unleash the craziness that is "Shyt List 4" to you, we wanted to say thank you to ALL of you who have supported, continue to support and will always support The Cartel Publications! We are proud to say this is our 20th novel and every time we drop a new project, we do so with you all in mind, ALWAYS! With that said, we'd like to personally and especially thank our new and improved *Cartel Street Team*! Our street team is not to be fucked with! We are a movement and they are a big part of spreading the word out about us. Thank you *Ms. Metha Coleman* for heading up our team and showing through your leadership how to rep The Cartel Publications officially!

The time has come again for us to take you on an insane ride with Ms. Yvonna Harris! She's back, with help and plenty of foolishness to keep you on your toes! I PERSONALLY guarantee you will LOVE this fourth installment maybe even more than all the previous parts! This book will have you laughing, loving and cringing with every page!

In keeping with Cartel Publications tradition, allow us to pay homage to an author who is trailblazing in the industry: We would like to recognize:

"Eva Bottier"

Eva Bottier is the author of the phenomenal novel, *"The Year it Snowed In April."* This was a raw, vivid and descriptive tale that left your heart bleeding for the son with sympathy. Do yourself a favor, make sure that you check it out, you will not be disa

On your mark, get set...Go!!! You on your own! We know you will love the ride! Enjoy!

Much Love!

Charisse "C. Wash" Washington
Vice President, The Cartel Publications

www.thecartelpublications.com
www.twitter.com/cartelbooks
www.facebook.com/publishercharissewashington
www.myspace.com/thecartelpublications
www.facebook.com/cartelcafeandbooksstore

Acknowledgements

I acknowledge every Cartel Publications customer who picked up the first installment of this series and stayed with it throughout. Because of you, and your excitement, I take joy in finding many different ways to disgust, excite and keep your attention.

Reign (T. Styles)

Dedication

I dedicate this to crazed Shyt List fans everywhere!

Note To The Readers

Since the real Gabriella has been introduced in Shyt List 3, we have decided that in Shyt List 4 **we will always** refer to the Gabriella in Yvonna's mind in italics as such: *Gabriella*. And the real Gabriella will appear without italics.

Thank you.

Prologue

In A Bind

The temperature was chilly in the extremely dark room that held Yvonna captive. It smelled of mold and motor oil and the odor, coupled with the fact that she was hungry, made her stomach rumble. She was lying against a cold concrete wall and one of her wrist was tied with rope that looped into a rusty latch that was embedded into the wall.

"Awww," Yvonna cried out holding her bruised neck.

When she placed her hand in front of her face, she couldn't even see her fingers wiggle.

Dropping her hand to her side she said, "Where am I?" Someone in the world wanted her dealt with and had ceased an opportunity to catch her ass slipping. "I need to get out of here! I need to leave! Please! Let me out!!!"

Silence.

"You know, if it was that easy we'd be gone already." A female voice said.

"Who is that?"

Silence.

Yvonna outstretched her arms trying to touch the person who had just spoken. But the pitch-blackness provided no direction. "I said who the fuck are you?"

"It's me. Gabriella."

Hearing her name Yvonna's raspy laugh filled the room. She immediately noticed her throat was dry and that she was extremely thirsty. She didn't know how long she'd been there without water, or how much longer she'd be able to live without it, but felt if she was going to die, she'd at least get the answer to a question she always wanted to know.

"So they got your ass too, huh? After everything, you right in here with me."

"If that's what you want to call it."

"That's exactly what I call it."

Loud rumbling outside of the room caused them to swallow any upcoming words. Sure they hadn't been given any orders to remain quiet, but until they knew what was going on, neither was taking any chances. After a few more minutes of silence Yvonna felt bold enough to speak again.

"Are you there?" She whispered into the darkness. "Can you hear me?"

"Yes."

"I wanna ask you something, and this time I want you to be honest. After all, what do we have to lose? Right?"

"We're both about to die, so what is it, Yvonna?"

"Why did you leave the home when we were kids? I mean, why did you leave us knowing we needed you? And why didn't you take me with you? I was being raped and tortured, too. It ain't like I didn't need an escape. You were all I had."

"We are about to die, and you want *that* question to be your last?"

"Yes." She paused. "I guess I gotta know."

Irritation sounded off in her tone. "Yvonna, I can't remember that far back. We were kids, and all I wanna do now is make it out of here alive. And that should be all you're worried about, too."

"I'm worried about a lot more than that. I can't help but believe that if you took me with you, that I would've had a chance at a real life."

"Whatever, Yvonna. I'm thinking about my life right now. All that other shit you saying don't make a difference to me anymore. We adults, get over it!"

Her words hurt. "Well it should matter to you. Because for each day you were gone, during that time in my life, your absence mattered to me."

"Well it doesn't matter to me." She was cold.

"It should."

"Why?"

"Because if we are able to get out of here, alive, I'm going to kill you myself."

"Is that right?"

"That's mothafuckin' right."

"Well what if we don't make it out of here alive?"

"Then I'm gonna meet you in hell."

Silence.

"Whatever," she said brushing her threats off, "We'll worry about that bridge if we get there." She paused. "Do you have any idea who would want you this bad?"

"You mean other than you? And them?"

"Yes."

Yvonna searched her memory and unlike some folks who didn't have enemies, there were too many people who wanted nothing more than to see her ass dead, but most of them were in their graves and unable to do anything about it. After all, she'd seen to it herself.

"Could be anybody, but it's probably Swoopes. I mean, he was in the room with us, too. Why isn't he here?"

There was a brief silence before they heard another movement. Both of them sat up straight in fear that someone inside the room with them had heard their conversation.

"Naw…bitch. Wrong again. 'Cause whoever wanted your ass dead got me wrapped into this shit, too."

"Swoopes?"

"What you think?"

THURSDAY

**Three Wild Ass
Days Earlier**

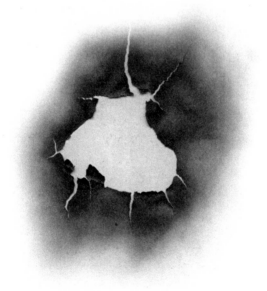

Shyt List IV

Sin City

Yvonna Harris

The sweat forming on Yvonna's forehead immediately evaporated after she stepped into the Aria hotel's revolving doors in Las Vegas, Nevada. The heat outside was unbearable but the air conditioning was exactly what was needed to put her and Ming at ease.

Yvonna's heart thumped in her chest, after all, she never left her hideout in a quaint part of town in Virginia. People were trying to murder her and it had gotten so bad, that any move she made, including going to the grocers had to be thought out in advance. She knew Swoopes was trying to kill her, and whoever else she'd done wrong. Always feeling threatened, she had to leave her fly pad overlooking Baltimore City because of the death threats on her life and the firebombs placed in her cars. Had it not been for Uncle Yao and Bricks she would be dead by now.

The hotel was packed this Thursday night as it played host to several celebrity parties. The fight between Urban Greggs and Armando Santiago was taking place Saturday and anybody who was anybody was attending the event. Oh yes, the best of the best was in attendance until Yvonna and Ming walked in. Five Asian men clad in black suits with wired ear sets tucked into their ears, disappearing into their blazers, looked at everyone through their dark shades as if *'they wished a mothafucka would'* touch either one of the ladies.

Yao sent his best men to guard her, after all, he had a mission *he needed* completed and only his best assassin, Yvonna, could handle the job. He knew that without the men, Yvonna's life was in danger. Outside of Bricks she didn't feel she could trust anyone enough to bare her soul and express her fears. But just like Bricks, Yao proved capable of protecting her.

Yao would not have pulled out all the stops if she wasn't worth it. The best security for his best assassin. But although he knew no one could kill a mothafucka as smoothly as her, he also knew that when he sent her on prior missions, she always managed to kick up a little shit along the way.

Like the time he sent her to murder Bandwagon Sade at a picnic. When on the way to the hit, a little girl unrelated to Sade said her ass was *way too* fat in the undercover Parking Attendant uniform she wore. Yvonna got so mad she slapped the shit out of the child sending her crying to her mother. Then there was the time she had to kill Brash Billy in a convenience store parking lot. Instead of things going as planned when she pulled her rental car up towards an available parking space, a lady stole it from her and refused to move. Her mind went into overdrive and she forgot all about the mission Yao had given her.

In a blinding rage, she opened the lady's car door, pulled her to the ground and threw her car into drive. Both watched as the woman's car crashed into ten parked vehicles totaling her Honda beyond repair. The mission was foiled and Yao had to get someone else to kill Billy and he was angry about it.

No this time had to be different, Uncle Yao told her. He demanded that she remain focused or else the consequences could be dire.

Shyt List IV

"Complete the mission I've assigned, get out and get paid, Yvonna. Don't let that temper of yours get you into trouble with me." The only thing was, he forgot he was trying to direct one crazy ass bitch.

Yvonna moved swiftly through the lobby bumping into anyone in her way. Her walk couldn't be fucked with as she was clad in a black one piece BCBG short set which displayed her perky breasts, phat ass and firm thighs. A pair of dark shades rested on her face, and a brand new cognac colored MCM bag swung from her arm. Her short spiky hair was flyer than usual because she loved all eyes on her. Oh yes, the bitch was back and she was bad.

To her left was her best friend, the sexiest Chinese bitch in the DMV (DC, Maryland & Virginia). Five foot two inch Ming Chi sported a tight red shirt, which led to her brand new phat ass, courtesy of Dr. Ryan Martin, plastic surgeon to the ghetto stars. She even had to get her True Religion jeans tailored because they didn't make them for the body of black girl, which thanks to several thousand dollars, Ming now possessed. Her brown eyes sparkled like the diamonds on her neck and fingers as she gave eye contact to those who had chosen to be her audience.

"Ming hopes you know she's gonna get some dick while she's here." Ming said. "Just cause that wretched uncle of mine has you out here on business, doesn't mean I'm not gonna have a good time. What are you doing for him anyway?"

"Nunya," she paused. "And you get dick all the time. Why should coming to Vegas be any different?"

"Well Ming is getting more dick than usual this weekend. We are in Vegas and what goes on in Vegas stays between Ming's legs."

Although they were in Vegas on a mission, they both had all intentions on getting fucked and having some fun before they boarded their plane back to DC on Monday. They were rich, evil and horny…three dangerous combinations.

When they walked up to the reservation counter, all side bar conversations ceased. *Who are these bitches?* A few girls said to themselves. Watching the women approach the counter followed by their bodyguards.

"I don't know why Yao insisted on having them come with us. They making us hot. I need to be low-key and this ain't hardly low."

"Because he care about you," Ming said, "He care about you more than he do his own niece."

"Look, don't blame ya'lls fucked up ass relationship on me."

"Ming isn't blaming anything on you. Ming is just stating the truth." Almost to the counter, a nearby clucker checked her man for eyeing Ming's ass. Giving him what he wanted, Ming winked and the disrespectful ass nigga blushed.

"Take a picture it will last longer," the girl said causing Ming to roll her eyes.

"Ming hates jealous bitches," she said loud enough for the girl to hear. It didn't bother her that she was dead wrong for flirting with the man in front of his girlfriend to begin with.

"Ming, when will you realize, haters are good for the planet? That's how we know we keep the world turning."

Ming had succeeded in talking Yvonna's head off the entire flight. If she wasn't talking about all the new nail salon drug fronts Yao opened in her name, she was talking about her mother in China and how the family hated that she was still under Yao's control.

Most of the time, Ming held one-sided conversations because all Yvonna could think about was the fact that she hadn't taken her Clozaril and Lithium in four hours. And her bag with the meds was packed and under the plane. And although *Gabriella* came and went as she pleased, the medicine prevented the frequency of the visits. She also missed her daughter Delilah and wondered what time she would be landing with Terrell and Boy.

Her heart was filled with so much love when it came to Delilah, still she was in Vegas to do business and she would not have had her with her if Terrell and Quita weren't in town. Ever since someone had attempted to take her life, she made it her business to take Delilah everywhere she went when she was out of town, just as long as she provided the proper precautions. And because she was afraid of losing her, she felt bad for what she had done to Bilal Jr., when she poisoned him as a child. In fact that was the only thing she regretted in all her years of living, and she often said that if she could make things right with him, she would.

Pulling her phone out of her purse, she texted Urban, the man who she was in town to kill. There was no reply. Rolling her eyes she wished Ming would shut the fuck up for five seconds. She needed to get her head right for what she had to do...kill.

Yvonna had been seeing Urban Greggs, the heavyweight champion of the world, for a few months. She enjoyed his company even though their union was business, not personal and Urban had no idea. In the beginning he was doing everything possible to win her over to no avail.

The thing was, if she could take him seriously she wouldn't, her heart belonged to Bricks. But she was dangerous. If everyone she ever loved didn't end up dead, she'd be with him in an instant. Her life's history proved that whomever she adored, died shortly thereafter. So to protect him, in her mind it was best to keep their relationship friendly, even though it was hard work. The good thing about it was she didn't have anybody serious in her life and neither did Bricks.

And then there was Terrell, although she had feelings for him too, and he was doing a good job at watching Delilah when she was out and about, she didn't feel the way he did about their relationship. She liked him, but love, well love was another story all together. Of course since they lived together, she did reserved the right to fuck him from time to time.

"Can I help you?" The Check In Agent asked.

"You see that bitch over there still talking about us? Ming can't stand bitch!" She said ignoring the Agent.

"You should not have been trying to fuck her man."

"Ming wasn't trying to fuck him. He was looking at Ming's ass."

"Are you ready yet?" the Agent asked.

Yvonna threw her finger up at the Agent and said, "One moment." She turned to Ming. "Stop tripping off of bullshit. I mean, we ain't been here for five minutes and already you giving a bitch all your time."

"Look at the bitch gear." Ming shook her head. "She's a hot ass mess." Ming got louder ignoring Yvonna and egging the girl on. "Ming is five seconds from slapping bitch." The hater rolled her eyes and Yvonna ignored both of them as she wrestled inside her purse for her identification. "Yvonna, are you listening to Ming?"

"Not really."

"I miss *Gabriella*." Ming said, knowing in the past, the mere mention of her name ruffled Yvonna's feathers. "*Gabriella* would step to bitch and slap face."

"How you miss her? Even though I don't see her often, she calls all the time."

"I'm talking about the one in your head."

Yvonna rolled her eyes. "Well too bad for you my medicine working."

"Look, if I can't help you can you please move." The Agent said. "There are people behind you who are pre-pared."

They both looked behind them to see a line full of evil stares.

"Bitch, please." Yvonna said turning to the Agent. "I ain't moving until I check in." She slid her ID to her. "Now, I have two connecting suites and don't tell me you can't connect the rooms because I already called about it."

The girl rolled her eyes. "'Bout time you ready, what's your name?"

"Yvonna Harris, bitch. It's on the ID."

"Okay, Yvonna Harris Bitch." The girl keyed in the information. "Umm, I can't seem to find your last name, Ms. Bitch." she laughed at her own joke.

"You must want me to come across that counter."

The girl frowned and said, "Oh, I found the name. It's under Yvonna Harris."

"I bet."

"But what about her? Is she checking in, too?"

"She's with me," Yvonna said sarcastically.

"Oh...she's with you, huh?" She laughed looking at her co-workers. "Figures."

"Fuck is that supposed to mean?"

"Nothing really," she said tapping at the computer. "Just sounded like ya'll were *really* together or something."

Yvonna knew she was trying to make her embar-rassed by implying that she was gay. So she decided to fuck with her head instead. Grabbing Ming by the back of her neck Yvonna threw her tongue in her mouth and slobbed her down. Those who were doing regular shit stood in awe at the sensual scene before them. Ming got so excited thinking Yvonna was going to give her some pussy that she tossed her purse to the floor and pushed her up against the counter. Had Yvonna had on a dress Ming would've been five fingers deep into her pussy. Even the hater that had taunted Ming upon entry couldn't take her eyes off the performance.

When Yvonna was able to pry her face from Ming's lips by way of a gut punch, she looked back at the Agent and said, "Like I said, she's with me."

The Agent was filled with embarrassment. "Oh...uh...yeah...okay. Your Sky Villas are ready. You have room 1209 and 1211. They're right next to each other. Will you and your friend," she cleared her throat, "be needing anything else?"

Ming remained silent as she picked up her purse and held her stomach due to the punch Yvonna landed on her. "She won't be needing anything but I will."

"Okay. What is it?"

"If you ever see me again I'm gonna need you to be more respectful. Because fucking with me could be hazardous to your health. Remember I said that. Cool?"

"Yes." She nodded. "It's cool."

With that Yvonna grabbed her MCM bag as Ming followed behind her in pain. "Damn! Did you have to punch a bitch in the stomach?"

"Yes! You were about to suck my face in! The kiss thing was a joke, Ming. I really need you to get out of your mind that you'll ever be fucking me again."

"Whatever. You tell Ming that all the time, and each time Ming fucks that pussy. Ming just has to wait until you're drunk enough. That's all."

Ming and Yvonna went about their meaningless chatter until there was a loud uproar within the lobby. When they turned their heads in the direction of the noise, they saw Urban Greggs walking in with his entourage. Yvonna didn't know he was staying in her hotel and she was about to approach him but thought otherwise. Besides, she had members of the Mah Jong Dynasty behind her and she would have blown her purpose and cover.

"It's all you, champ!" One dude yelled.

"I got money on you, nigga! You betta drop his ass quick." Threatened another.

Urban walked in smoothly with his thick fighter's physique and tailor-made pants and shirt. Although his coordinates were simple, he still looked rich. He was a handsome man and his face was very youthful although he was in his early thirties. His dark eyes held a lot of mystery and he had a winning smile.

"Wow, look at all the girls on Urban. He may not know who you are after the fight." Ming teased, still salty that she got gut blasted. Ming was unaware of Yvonna's true mission to kill. "But don't worry, Ming will keep your bed warm if he doesn't come for you." She threw her arm around her shoulder.

"You want me to drop you?" Yvonna warned, before Ming removed her arm.

"Fuck you! You not all that anyway!"

Yvonna was just about to give her a piece of her mind when she saw someone who looked really familiar walking up to Urban with a white piece of paper. Urban took the paper and scribbled his signature on it. Then he pulled the girl closer and whispered something in her ear that made her smile. Her long black hair brushed her shoulders and her white teeth shined brightly.

As she watched the scene, the words of one of her psychiatrist played in her mind. '*Remember Yvonna, you're going to reach a point where you feel you can control your illness. But you should know there's no controlling schizophrenia.*'

Was she seeing things now? Seeing familiar faces always bothered her because she feared they were figments of her imagination, reminders that her illness was going to be with her for the rest of her life.

But how could it be a figment? Outside of seeing Gabriella ever so often, Terrell was doing a great job of managing her condition with medication. After all, they lived together and in return for his babysitter/doctor services, she gave him weekly blowjobs like he couldn't imagine. He slept in the bed with her; watched Delilah when she needed and took care of her if she was mentally unprepared. The truth of the matter was, if Terrell got a mind to leave, whether Yvonna knew it or not, she'd be fucked.

"Ming, do you see that girl over there." Yvonna pointed in the direction of Urban.

"Fuck you, bitch! You hit Ming in the stomach and now you want to ask question."

"I'm serious. Do you see that girl over there or not? The one with Urban."

Ming looked. "Yeah. So what?"

Yvonna was relieved. She texted Urban again and saw him reach in his pocket, grab his phone and frown. He didn't respond.

"You can have Urban but you better not be here for my man, bitch. If you are there's gonna be problems. For you."

Sin City

Bricks

The room was too cold when Bricks, his brother Melvin and his five-year-old son Chomps stepped into the 4,000 square foot Sky Villa. Bricks had reserved two suites side by side so that his friends and family could be together. He also had another room on another floor for Quita, his son's sitter.

The moment they stepped further into the room and saw the beautiful suite their mouths dropped. Bricks was accustomed to luxury but even he had to proclaim that the Sky Villa's were the best suites he'd ever witnessed. When the TV's turned on automatically with a welcome message saying, '*Welcome to the Aria Hotel Bricks,* Melvin grabbed for his gun before realizing he couldn't carry it on the plane.

He was noid thinking someone was in the room. "Damn, that's some fly shit." Melvin said after calming down.

"Yeah, but turn that shit down." Bricks said referring to the air conditioning. "It's cold as mothafucka in here."

"I'm on it." Melvin replied walking to the unit. "They got everything in here! Kitchen utensils and some more shit!"

"It's a suite! It's supposed to be like that!"

Bricks smiled at how nice the room was and already imagined how much pussy he was going to get over the weekend. Although the only pussy he wanted was Yvonna's, he knew he'd sooner have a chance at fucking Beyonce' than her. After all that time, years had passed between them and he still didn't hit.

His grey eyes looked around his lavish weekend setting and the light from the lamp caught his 8-carat diamond earring. His chestnut colored skin and husky build filled the room and screamed boss. Bricks was just the right size for the girl who wanted all man. He placed their carrying bags down at the door before placing a bag of beer in the freezer. *Yeah, I'm in Vegas!* He thought.

After turning down the air Melvin opened the automatic blinds and they all walked to the window. The beautiful windows spanned from the top of the ceiling to the bottom of the floor and provided a panoramic view of the city. The brothers absorbed the energy pulsating from Vegas' streets.

"Nigga, we 'bout to get it in this weekend." Melvin said slapping him on the back as they both continued to look at the view. "And you know I got that rental so we can run this city crazy."

"Nigga, fuck you rent a car for?"

"A truck, lil bro. You'll thank me for it later."

"I don't think this weekend will be like any one we've ever experienced in Vegas. This gonna be it, Mel."

"Daddy," Five-year-old Chomps said reaching up to him.

"You wanna look over the city too, homie?"

Chomps nodded and Bricks scooped him up and looked into his eyes. He loved the boy as much a father could love a son, despite him not being his blood.

"Man, I'm telling you, the fight between Greggs and Santiago gonna be crazy."

"You telling me." Bricks paused. "So when Forty and the rest of the fam coming? I got the other suite so we could have enough room. They just gotta roll out when I meet with Yao on that business shit."

Melvin checked his red G-Shock watch. "They should be here any minute. But some of them already got rooms. They brought bitches with them and everything. You know we twenty five deep this weekend."

"Twenty five deep?" he frowned. "Everybody ain't leave post did they?"

"Fuck no! Just the lieutenants."

Bricks put Chomps down and laughed. "Niggas stay bringing sand to the beach." When he said that Melvin cleared his throat and looked away. "What?"

"Nothing man. Just thinking about the sand to the beach thing."

"Fuck you trying to say?"

"Yvonna ain't here?"

"Whatever," Bricks said.

Melvin laughed and asked, "Exactly." He paused. "Where Quita?"

"She on her way up. Her room is on another floor. I ain't want the kids that close to us and around all the bull-shit."

He paid to have Chomps' babysitter Quita come to Vegas so he could be near him. Chomps was still having a hard time with the absence of his mother, Kendal, who was actually his father. He also missed his grandmother, Bet. So Bricks went over and beyond the call of duty to let him know he would never leave him. Ever.

Quita was an interesting character who ran a ghetto daycare center in Washington, DC and had a crush on Bricks since she could remember. In her warped ghetto mind, if Yvonna weren't in the picture, or in his heart,

Bricks would be all over her. She thought wrong. Quita also had a problem with lying and stealing which earned her a five-year bid. When she came home she opened the center under an alias and never looked back.

"Man, I'm telling you, I'm getting into anything wet this weekend. I'm all the way serious, B." Melvin said as he placed his bag down in the suite and move to the fridge to grab a Stella Artois beer, his favorite. "Fuck, Fancee's ass."

"Yeah, aigh't. You know damn well Fancee would fuck you up she find out you out here cheatin'. You betta slow your roll, nigga."

"Picture that shit," Melvin laughed before hearing a knock at the door.

When Melvin opened the door, Quita was on the other side. She winked at him and switched her ass into the room wearing earrings too big for her face, and jeans that were so tight a sack of rolls showed in the back of her legs. If that wasn't enough her stomach rolled over the front of her jeans and her little jean jacket sat on top of the large mound. She was a mess, in every sense of the word. Yet there was a strange sex appeal in her over confidence. Although her body was dumpy, her face was as cute as an angel, which often got men caught up.

"Hey, Bricks." Gum smacked in her mouth. "I like my room, it's real nice. *Real, real* nice." She looked at him sexually and placed her hand on her hip.

"Not a problem. What took you so long coming up?"

"Some niggas was trying to holla," she lied trying to make him jealous. Bricks looked at Melvin who appeared to believe her. "But fuck them, I wanted you to know that you can come over and help me use my room if you want to."

"All that in front of my kid?" He said looking down at Chomps.

She looked down at him and said, "He don't know what we talking about."

"First of all if I wanted to use the mothafucka I would. I bought it remember?" He refocused his attention back to Melvin. "Like I was saying about Fancee, you talking that shit now, but you been with her for how long?"

He was changing Chomps' shirt because he'd poured red soda over it on the flight. He kept Chomps fresh all the time and although Quita was there, he made sure he was hands on with him whenever possible.

"Long enough not to wanna fuck with her no more." He said eyeing Quita again.

"Bricks, can I use your bathroom right quick?" Quita asked.

He frowned. "Why you ain't use yours?"

"'Cause I came right over. I ain't know if you wanted me to get Chomps or not."

Bricks and Melvin wasn't feeling the bathroom thing. She was a thief who hadn't stolen from him yet, but he didn't want to take chances.

"Chomps almost ready," Bricks said. When he was done changing his shirt he said, "Take him to go get him something to eat. Don't buy him no greasy shit. Get him some fruit or something."

The thing about Quita was this, she was all hood and it didn't matter if you took her to Vegas, or back to jail, she was gonna act like a hood bitch acts. But when it came to kids, her price was right, she traveled, and baby-sat on the weekends. And because of it, she always got the business.

"Damn, you just fed him when we was on the plane. That boy always got something in his mouth." She started beating her feet in place and holding her hands between her legs. "You tryna make him fat or something?"

"Look, do what the fuck I asked 'fore I fuck you up."

Quita loved when he went off on her, that way she could submit to him and it would look like only he could tame the savage hood beast. "Alright, baby, damn. I got you." She said seductively. "But can I please use your bathroom?"

Since most of their luggage was still in the living room he said, "Hurry up."

She ran to the bathroom and when she came out she grabbed Chomps by his hand and said, "Come on baby."

"Wait, what time did Yvonna say she was dropping Delilah and Boy off to you?" Bricks asked. "I don't know if she know what room you in and I don't want you getting too lost."

"She didn't say, but I do know her and Ming flew together and Terrell was on another flight with the kids," Quita said. She wanted to fuck with his head by letting on that Terrell was coming. Oh yes, the bitch Quita had the T on all of the mothers of the children she watched.

"So that nigga coming too, huh?" He said with an attitude. A small frown rested on his face.

"Yep. I guess she don't go nowhere without him. Not even to Vegas." She walked toward the door with chomps. "Oh well, be back in a bit."

When the door closed Melvin walked up to Bricks. "That Quita bitch sexy as shit."

"Nigga, you tripping. That bitch sloppy as a mothafucka and a cumbag. Niggas bust in that pussy raw all the time." Bricks turned up his nose. "But I'm trying to figure out why Yvonna bring that nigga with her when I told her I hired Quita."

"Slim, why is you still tripping off of that bitch? It's been five years and you still on her hard."

"You don't know what you talking about."

"I know my brother." He paused. "Now I get that she fine as shit, but she crazier than she's worth and too much trouble. You took six bullets for that bitch. One in your arm and five in your chest. And you telling me she ain't trouble?"

"I ain't fucking with her no more. But I ain't gonna lie, she gonna always be my peoples and I'm gonna always have her back."

"Prove you ain't tripping off her no more."

"How?"

"By passing the test I got coming up for you." He paused. Bricks was irritated and it showed in his face. "I sent for Carmen, the shawty you met in Atlanta."

"What? Where you find her at?"

"I ran into her a month ago. She was out Maryland. I think she said her cousin was throwing her a party for graduating from college or some shit like that. And she said her cousin's boyfriend works in this hotel, and she could get a discounted rate for her room. So I asked her if she wanted to hang out with us and I'll take care of the flight and she was down. She got friends too, nigga!"

"Man, she was mad as shit at me for how I carried her for Yvonna. I remember trying to get up with her after all that shit went down and she wasn't hearing it."

"Well she listening now."

Although he could use some Vegas pussy, Bricks didn't want Yvonna to see her and he definitely didn't want her to see them together. He knew if that happened, there would be no way that they'd make it. It was discussed when they talked about deal breakers for any future relationship between them.

"You can fuck any bitch you want, but don't fuck with Carmen." She forbade. *"I'm not coming behind that Atlanta bitch."*

After all these years, Yvonna still hadn't fucked him. So what was he gonna do, keep playing sucka to a female who made it known over and over that they could never be more than friends? Or could he get with the Georgia peach he knew could handle herself in the bedroom? Whose ass looked like a perfect circle when she bent down. Who talked so sensual, he thought of her as the black Marilyn Monroe.

"Fuck it. Set that shit up." Bricks said.

He was just about to get in the shower when someone else knocked at the door. When he opened it he saw his best man Kelsi and Tina, his cousin.

Kelsi's chocolate complexion looked extra tan and his five o'clock shadow rested smoothly on his face. He was sporting blue jeans and a blue Hugo Boss shirt. The handle of his gun could be seen under his shirt.

"Hold up, you holding?" Bricks asked referring to his weapon.

"Yeah."

"How the fuck you get that? I know you ain't bring it on the plane."

"I met up with my peoples out here." Kelsi told him. "I don't go too many places without heat. I'm beefing with niggas in fifty states!"

"You so crazy," Tina said looking at Kelsi seductively. "Ain't nobody after you."

Bricks caught their stares. He knew they had been talking more on the phone but he turned a blind eye to the shit. Besides, he knew his cousin was having problems with her boyfriend, Greek and that Kelsi was having problems with his girlfriend, O back in Atlanta. So he figured what harm could come by them being a little closer than usual? He just hoped they didn't get too serious where someone got hurt, causing him to step in. His only rule for now, was that they not fuck each other in Vegas, not on his watch anyway. Greek was his man and he respected him yet Kelsi was his childhood best friend.

"Damn, nigga! I ain't seen you in forever," Bricks said dapping Kelsi. "I almost ain't think you was coming. My party Friday is gonna be off the hook."

Kelsi and Tina walked fully into the suite and Bricks caught him eyeing Tina's fat ass. Tina was in her early thirties but looked like she was twenty something. She was short, cute and could bust a gun better than half of the men in Bricks' crew.

"You know how we do in the ATL. We show up when something comes up."

"Hold up, did this nigga just say, *you know how we do in the ATL*?" Melvin said giving him some dap before both Melvin and Bricks hugged Tina. "You mean you done got up in that ATL pussy and changed sets?"

Kelsi grinned. "Picture that shit."

"Yeah whatever, nigga. Just cause you fucking them ATL bitches don't mean you ain't a Maryland nigga."

Kelsi laughed a little and looked at Tina out of the corner of his eye again. Something was definitely going down between them.

"Home is where I lay my head but I'm always gonna be a Maryland nigga."

"You know what, fuck all this shit, where's Chomps?" Tina asked. It was obvious that Kelsi's response about getting in some ATL pussy made her angry. "I hardly ever get to see my nephew now that you got Quita's ghetto ass watching him all the time. What, you don't need me no more?"

"Chomps with Quita."

"She here?"

"Yeah," he paused, "And you know I'ma always need you, but you been missing in action. And every time I holla at Greek, he telling me you out of town on business. The only thing is, since we work together, I never understand what the fuck he be talking about, because if it's pertaining to money, I should know."

Tina looked at Kelsi and said, "Fuck all that. You got our tickets for the fight right? 'Cause I ain't come all the way out here not to see Urban's sexy ass drop Santiago."

"Yeah...I told you I got you." He paused. "But look, let me holla at my mans for a minute." Bricks said. "We got whatever you wanna drink in them bags over there and some beer in the freezer."

"I took 'em out and put them in the fridge. You know beer freezes." Melvin said on his second already. He was sitting comfortably on the sofa watching the large screen TV.

"Ya'll do you." Tina said sitting next to Melvin on the couch.

"Kelsi, grab a beer with me, homie." Bricks said putting his hand on his shoulder as they walked to the kitchen.

Once there Kelsi jumped right to it. "Before you say anything about Tina, let me say we ain't all that serious. You know I got my peoples at home, but she be nagging the fuck out of me sometimes, son. I'm kinda sick of her shit and Tina helps get my mind off of things. It's nothing more, nothing less."

"You sure?"

"Yeah...I mean, maybe I ain't cut out to be a one woman man."

"Exactly...so why you fucking my cousin?"

"I ain't fuck her yet."

The idea of his friend fucking his cousin didn't go over too well with him. It wasn't that he didn't trust Kelsi, it was just that he knew how easily females wrap themselves into him, only for him to break their hearts.

"Let me set a few ground rules, outside of this convo right here, I don't wanna ever talk or hear about you and

Tina. What ya'll do, ya'll do." He said seriously. "But...don't hurt my cousin, that's family, man, just like you...and I love her to death. Fucking her over will be like you fucking with me."

"Then I'm gonna have to cut shit off with her all together."

"So you had plans to fuck my cousin over?"

"How you sound?" Kelsi said stepping closer to him. He was prepared to check him for the disrespect. "I wouldn't do no shit like that to you, but I can't promise it won't happen if we continue to see each other. I'm feeling her though but until I can be sure what I'ma do about O, I think it's best to leave her alone."

"When you let her down don't put that shit on me. Make sure she know you breaking shit off on your own."

"Naw when I break it to her, I'ma eat that. It's gonna be all my fault. Plus after the beef we had when I thought you was fucking my ex-girl, Keisha when we was kids, I ain't trying to let nothing come between this bond again," he said pointing at himself then at Bricks, "not even your fine ass cousin." Bricks and Kelsi embraced in a one arm hug and released.

"Same here."

"So what's up with you and Yvonna? She bringing her crazy ass down here?"

"Yeah. She here already."

"You still got it bad for that broad don't you?"

"Naw, I'm done with her." He paused. "But later for all that. You know shit ain't been too good between me and my connect, Cameo."

"I know, that's why you was fucking with the nigga, M."

"The nigga, M?" Bricks said not catching the name.

"Look, you call that nigga Moms if you want to, but I ain't about to call him that shit. My mother's name is Janet, nigga."

Bricks laughed. "Yeah well the Moms *was* fronting our product after me and Cameo got into a beef because Yvonna brought the nigga Darcus to his party one night."

"The party at the Topaz you was telling me about?"

"Yeah."

"But I thought ya'll squashed that shit. That was like five years ago."

"We fake cool and I cop from him now because I have to. But we not *real* cool, know what I'm saying? Anyway, when the nigga Moms showed up dead, we lost all access to his dope, too. So Yvonna arranged some shit with the bamma Yao recently. I think she runs for him or something. Anyway, he talking about giving us the product for lower than what Moms did. I don't know, young, but this looks like a win-win situation for everybody. I'ma have to drop Cameo."

"Yao? The nigga that be in the news all the time?"

"Yeah." Bricks said knowing Kelsi could feel death looming over his head, too.

"When you meeting him?"

"Tomorrow night. Right before the party."

"You sure you can trust him?"

"I ain't got no choice. I'm in love with this money, nigga. I can't turn back now and we need the price cut."

There was a knock at the door and Melvin got up to answer it. Bricks and Kelsi walked out of the kitchen and toward the door. When it was held open they were surprised to see who was standing in the doorway.

"What's up, Cameo?" Bricks was shocked he was there. "What can I do for you?"

Shyt List IV

Nevada Desert

YBM (Young Black Millionarz)

The rental truck was hot and smelled of weed and liquor as the threesome drove along the hot dusty Nevada roads. Growl was behind the wheel and Rook was in the passenger seat. Mike was in the back with a short girl with spiky hair, whose face was so badly beaten, she was hardly recognizable. They kidnapped her earlier in the day from the hotel.

"I'm telling you, I don't think this the bitch," Mike said looking at the woman who was slouched over hanging onto life. He grabbed a fist full of her hair to look at her face. When he got a good look he allowed it to fall back down. "What we gonna do with her now?"

"Nigga, shut the fuck up!" Growl said looking at him through the rear view mirror. "You talk too fucking much." He paused. "Just let me think."

Growl was trying to find the best place to dump her body. It was the second girl they'd picked up and killed from the Aria Hotel in an effort to snatch Yvonna. But once again their attempts ended in vain. He hated this bitch almost as much as their leader Swoopes did. After all, she killed Cane, and had something to do with YBM members Bobby and Reuse being murdered. As far as he was concerned, the world would be better off without her.

"Are you sure you know what this bitch looks like?" Rook asked looking over at him. "I mean, we can't keep snatching up bitches out of the hotel trying to get at her. We gonna get caught. Maybe we should get a positive identification first."

Growl was listening but he was growing tired with all this shit. They wouldn't even be in Vegas if Swoopes was still part of the YBM. But his absence meant no drug connect and no money. Their operation was worthless without him and there was no other way to say it. He had to come home to run shop and he couldn't do it as long as Yvonna was alive. The men were starting to believe he was obsessed with her.

"Call that bitch you fuck with at that hair salon," he said talking to Rook. "See if she can email us an up to date picture of this bitch."

"Email?" Mike laughed. "Who the fuck uses email?"

"Nigga, I got a mothafuckin' account!" Growl yelled. Then he looked back at Rook. "Make the call, cause do or die, I'm not leaving Vegas before killing this bitch with my own two hands. That much I can promise you."

Shyt List IV

Washington DC

Bilal Jr.

The small bed Bilal laid on was pushed against the cold yellow, dirty wall. Filthy cream curtains brushed the edge of his bed and from where he was laying, he could see dust piled up in the corners of the window seal, courtesy of the poor job he and his roommate did when they fake cleaned up.

Bilal Jr., who was now a teenager in high school, shared the room with his best friend James "Jukes" Sharps. Any other time Jukes would be there talking his head off about Tayla, his girlfriend from school. But tonight he needed the room alone to be with his own girlfriend Rozay, who had been acting funny at school lately.

It was his fifth time calling her and he was pretty sure she wasn't going to pick up, still he gave it a try. Dialing her number from his cell he listened to the boring sound of the ring when she answered.

"Rozay, you gonna tell me what the fuck is up or what?" He said shooting up straight in a seated position, his Nikes still on his feet. "I mean...why was you acting all funny at school?"

"At least you can do is say hi first, Bilal."

"Well I wanna know what's up first. Fuck all that other shit."

"If you gonna be that way I gotta go. I'ma holla at you later."

"Wait!" He paused. "Don't hang up. I mean...did I do something to you? Or is somebody fucking with you?"

"Bilal, I got two older brothers. So you tell me...who gonna check me, boo?" She laughed.

He laughed too and said, "There you go with that Real Housewives of Atlanta shit."

"I'm dead serious." She said making smacking sounds with her mouth. "Ain't nobody at school bold enough to fuck with me. You know this and everybody else know it, too."

Bilal played with the edge of the tattered bedspread. "Well come over here. We can go get something to eat from the carry out. And before you say anything you can get whatever you want."

Rozay sighed heavily into the phone. "Thought you said you ain't have no money, when I asked you to buy me the pink Louis Vuitton wallet I wanted. Remember?"

"I ain't got no money *like that* right now. But I got enough to buy you something to eat."

"You always crying broke. I'm so sick of your shit."

"You know I'm saving to buy a car, Ro."

"Bilal, I told you when we first hooked up that I liked money a lot. And you said you had it cause you sold drugs."

"Why you talking all wild over the phone?"

"Whatever, boy! Ain't nobody listening to us on the phone, you ain't that big time with that little bit of change you crying about giving me." She exhaled. "Anyway, if you got the paper to get me what I want, why you faking on me now?"

Bilal made money from a hotheaded drug dealer named AJ up the street from his apartment. Although the work AJ got from his connect wasn't enough to make it big, he was able to make his time worth it by dividing his work between Bilal and Jukes, this way he would have more time working at his Tow Company.

"I ain't faking it's just that," he paused realizing if he didn't bend he'd lose her, "you know what...how much is the wallet again?"

"About two...three hundred dollars." She sounded anxious. "Why?"

"I'ma give you the money."

"For real?" She said excitedly. The bitch had been dry begging from the gate and Bilal knew it but he was feeling her so much, that losing her was worse than the pleasure he would gain from calling her out on her shit. Plus her pussy game was tight.

"Yeah. Now you coming over or not?"

"Yeah...but leave something in the building door downstairs so it can stay open. I hate banging on that thing and waiting for you to come open it for me."

"Aight."

"I'm serious. If the door not open I'm leaving, Bilal."

"I said okay."

After hanging up with her, Bilal jumped up and got himself together. Then he put the brick they kept inside their apartment in the building's door. When he was done with that, he thought about all the freaky shit he would do to Rozay for making him short his shoebox stash by three hundred dollars. Yeah, she was gonna pay long and hard. He expected to get his dick sucked and everything. After he removed three hundred from his three thousand dollar stash, he put his slick shit on and called Jukes.

"What up, nigga? Where you at?" Jukes asked.

"I'm at the crib."

"What? I thought you were meeting me down Kristina's?"

"Man, I'm hooking up with Rozay later. I ain't got no time for all that shit."

"Rozay?" He said sarcastically. "I thought you said ya'll was beefing."

"We was. We 'aight now though."

"What you do press her out or something?"

"Naw. She called me." He lied.

"Man, the way that girl was acting at school, if I was you I'd leave that bitch alone. You saw how she was treating you after third period. Dump her and save your loot!"

"Nigga, kill yourself." Bilal said. "And whatever you do, don't come home early. I'm smashing that pussy and I don't need extra eyes watching my flow."

Jukes laughed and said, "Aight. Hit me when you done."

After Bilal grabbed something to drink, someone knocked on the door and he just knew it was Rozay. But when he opened it he saw AJ and a dude name Dirk who supplied and sold coke in southeast DC.

"What up, lil nigga." AJ said, pushing his way inside the apartment without an invitation. "Your peoples here?"

"Naw," Bilal said looking out of the door, and into the hallway. Only to see that since they came in, the building door was now closed. He hoped they left early enough so he could prop it open again. He didn't want to miss her. "What's up though? I got somewhere to be right quick."

"You got somewhere to be right quick?" AJ said, opening the refrigerator. "Picture that shit, Dirk." Then he turned his attention back to Bilal. "Fuck you gotta do, lil nigga that's more important than me?" He closed the fridge and without waiting on his answer, grabbed him by his shirt and said, "You work for me and when you work for me, that means whenever I come by, time stops. Feel me?"

"Yeah." Bilal said under his breath.

"Good." He released his shirt. "Dirk," he paused, "give this lil nigga the pack." Dirk reached in the bag he was holding and handed Bilal a package of dope. "I need you to work this off this weekend. You and your little boyfriend. "

"Okay, I'll start tomorrow."

"No, you'll start tonight."

"But my girl coming over."

Just when he thought of her, someone knocked at the door and Dirk, without asking, opened it wide. Rozay, who resembled Nicki Minaj, walked in with an attitude. Her skin was light and her cheeks were rosy and she sported a short banged bob, which moved with the slightest motions. She didn't bother to look at who opened the door because her glaze was fixated on Bilal who was front and center in the living room.

She stepped up to Bilal. "Fuck you ain't open the door downstairs for? I was banging for like five minutes and shit."

"Ro, we got company."

Rozay spun around on her heels looked at AJ and Dirk and said, "Soooo...fuck them!"

AJ not liking the girl's attitude walked up to her and said, "Fuck you just say to me?"

"She didn't say nothing," Bilal said interfering. "I'ma take care of what you need me to later." He stepped up closer to AJ. "Call me if you want me to know something before then."

"Slow your roll, little man," AJ held his hand out and walked around Bilal to Rozay. "I think this little girlfriend of yours got something she wants to get off her chest. So what you got on them small ass titties of yours you want to get off?"

"Boy, bye!" She said throwing her hand up in his face.

AJ looked at Dirk and Dirk just dropped his head. He knew something was getting ready to pop off, the only question was what. Irritated by the girl's outbreak, AJ grabbed her by the hand and broke all four of her fingers.

"Awwwwwww!" She screamed dropping to the floor. "HELLLLLP, MEEEE!!!!"

When she was at his feet AJ looked over top of her and spit in her hair. "In the future when you see a real nigga present, you'll know how to talk to him."

Bilal knew he should be defending his girl, but was also smart enough to know that he couldn't take both AJ and Dirk by himself. Still, seeing the fire in Bilal's eyes, Dirk conveniently raised his shirt so that Bilal could see his weapon.

"Bilal, be expecting my call." AJ said walking toward the door. Before he left out he said, "And I'm sure you'll be able to handle her now. She's been tamed."

"Put some ice on that shit," Dirk laughed walking behind him.

When they were gone, Bilal ran over to her, dropped to his knees and said, "I'm so sorry."

She was crying hysterically holding her hand and when he touched her she scooted backwards and looked at him evilly. Then using the wall, she slid upwards to stand on her feet.

"You let him do this to me," she cried holding her hand. "You let him break my fucking fingers!"

No...if you would've shut the fuck up, this would have never happened. He thought.

"I'm sorry. I...I didn't know what to do."

Using her good hand she wiped the tears and snot off her face and said, "Well I hope you know how to run, 'cause when my brothers find out about this shit, you as good as gone, dead boy!" She left the apartment in a hurry leaving Bilal to his thoughts.

Mah Jong Dynasty

Yao sat on the sofa with his men surrounding him. He was looking at a fight that took place back in the day. Although many years had passed, he still blamed the man fighting his cousin, Genghis Kong, for his death.

He didn't care what he had to do, but he knew no matter what, that the man responsible for his death would pay with his life that weekend. In Vegas. And if anybody stood in the way, or fucked shit up for him, he wouldn't hesitate to kill them either.

Shyt List IV

Sin City

Yvonna

Yvonna and Ming walked into their suite and Yvonna hit a switch by the door. The moment she did, all the lights went out, and because the blinds were drawn, she couldn't see anything. It was totally dark.

"Turn light back on, bitch!"

"Ming, shut the fuck up! You been working my nerves from the gate." Yvonna turned the lights back on and they both removed the hoodies from over their heads. "It shouldn't even turn off like that. That's dumb."

"Well it does. And Ming doesn't understand why we must wear these when we walk up the halls." She said holding the hoodie in her hand.

"Because I don't want anybody knowing it's us. We gotta be incognito at all times while we're here."

"But they saw us in the lobby!"

"Ming, wear the fucking hoodie when you walking the hall! It ain't like it's not Gucci!"

They both took the hoodies off and settled into their beautiful suite. Like Bricks, Yvonna also rented two suites and both had two bedrooms inside. Terrell had his own suite and seven-year old Delilah and Boy shared it with him. Yvonna and Ming shared the other suite.

"So what you going to do?" Ming asked, looking into Terrell's room from the connecting door.

Silence.

"Bitch, are you hearing me?!" Ming yelled.

Yvonna was still thinking about Carmen. Sure she told Bricks she didn't want the relationship, but she felt after their daily long conversations, and their nights out on the town alone, that he knew her heart. The more she thought about her the angrier she got. Never once did she flaunt any relationship in Bricks' face. It emptied her mind how she lived with Terrell, fucked him on a regular and that Bricks had a feeling all along despite her lies.

"So, what is the plan? Ming wants to take up with this bitch at once." Ming lit one match after the other as she sat at the table with her legs crossed. Over the past year, fire had become entrancing to her and she was comfortable with the fact that she was a pyromaniac.

"I have to wait for Terrell." Yvonna said looking out at the sexy lit Vegas landscape.

"What are you talking about? Ming wants to know why you won't step to Bricks about bitch NOW."

"Because he's not my man! That's why?"

"Child, please! Ya'll can play them games with each other if you want to. But everybody knows you're together." Ming said putting her words together more hood like. The more she hung out with Yvonna, the more pieced together her language became.

"Ming, I'm not trying to get in a lot of shit this weekend. All I want to do is what I came to do, and go home. That's it."

"My uncle has you locked."

"Look, just because you can't stand him don't mean I can't stand him either. I just wish ya'll get over the bullshit and leave me out of it."

"You tell him that! For whatever reason, he wants Ming not to have a relationship with her mother. And Ming can't do that!" Yvonna ignored her having had this conversation many times before. "So you're going to let him have her?" She said skipping the subject. "If you do, Ming thinks you're crazy."

Yvonna walked up to her and said, "What did you just call me?"

"Nothing."

"I didn't think so." She said thinking about Carmen again. "Okay," she sighed. "I'm gonna ask Bricks if she's here for him or not. But we can't leave until we see Terrell. Since he's coming with Boy and Delilah any minute. Plus I miss my baby, I haven't seen her since we left the house. "

She sighed. "Let's go now, Ming wants to have fun." Ming used all of the matches and now resorted to flicking her silver lighter over and over again. Yvonna was so use to this, that she said nothing.

"Ming, we waiting." Yvonna's stomach hurt at the idea of losing Bricks' attention and affection. "Let's just get dressed first. You wanna nigga to catch federal charges and go to jail for life on account of some stupid shit. Relax!"

After getting dressed, Yvonna tried her hardest to keep her feelings at bay. She had a lot to lose if she allowed herself to get emotionally out of control. For starters, she could have a serious setback and see the *Gabriella* personality on a more frequent basis. And since the real Gabriella was a big part of her life now, that could cause problems in and of itself.

When Terrell finally got there an hour later, Yvonna and Ming were amped up and ready to confront Bricks about the Georgia bush. Terrell's six foot four inch frame covered the doorway like an NBA player. His black and white heritage gave him a steady bronze tone at all times. To say Terrell was handsome was an understatement.

The moment he walked in with Delilah and Boy, as usual the kids were going at each other's throats. The funny thing about it was, although they fought constantly, if one was without the other, they'd miss each other terribly. At the end of the day they were brother and sister and cared about one another even though most times you'd never know it.

"You have to have your own mind, Boy. You can't get what I want all the time." Delilah said walking in slinging her pink Juicy Couture purse to the floor which she carried everywhere. "I want juice, you want juice. I want candy, you want candy!"

"Whatever! I have my own mind." Boy said following behind her.

Delilah put her hands on her hips, walked over to him and pointed in his face. "Well use it and stop trying to use mine." Her small neck rolled. "Like my mama said, there can only be one Delilah and it definitely ain't you!"

"Bitch, please!" Boy said walking around her. He had a Jade bracelet and necklace on, which Yvonna hated. She felt any boy of African American descent should not be wearing Jade anything. Ming told her that in the Chinese culture Jade represented purity, beauty and grace. To which Yvonna responded, *'Exactly. What you trying to do, make him gay?'*

"Boy! What I tell you about that language?" Terrell said looking at Yvonna and Ming for parental reinforcements. He didn't get shit because although Yvonna and Ming loved their kids, they handled their behavior in their own way. In Yvonna's mind people had silenced her all her life, so she had no intentions of raising Delilah like that.

"Uncle Terrell, she makes me sick. She always trying to start fights and stuff. And my mama says I'm a man, and man always rule over women."

"You told him that shit?" Yvonna asked.

"Yes. In Ming's country, men do rule over women."

"Since when have you let any nigga rule over you? Name one?"

"I said in my country. I'm not in my country though am I?"

They both laughed. "Where is Quita?" Terrell said ignoring them both. "I need to drop them off so I can get a break."

"She downstairs."

"Alright, maybe I can freshen up and you and I can grab something to eat, Yvonna. It would be nice to enjoy your company for a few hours away from home." He said.

"I can't do that. I'm kinda busy."

He frowned. "Well, I guess I'll hang out with one of my female friends who's in Vegas for the weekend," he said trying to make her jealous. Let me take a shower and change my clothes."

"You have a date?" Yvonna laughed not really caring. Terrell had dated many women and in the end they all wanted him to break things off with her. And since he never did, his relationships all ended in vain.

"Yeah. I guess so." He paused. "Why? You're jealous?"

"Ming is!" She pouted.

"Terrell, please," Yvonna said ignoring Ming. "You belong to me and any bitch you fuck with knows it." She walked up to him and kissed him on the lips and his dick got hard. Ming watched in lust.

"Yeah but you don't belong to me." He frowned. "I'm tired of being in a one-sided relationship with you, Yvonna."

"Do I fuck you like we're in a one sided relationship?"

Silence.

"Exactly." She smiled. "So what we not a couple. What we have works for us." She winked. "Well, I'm gonna see if Quita is in Brick's room. I'll be back later."

"Ming goes with you." Ming said grabbing her purse as they both approached the door.

"Hold up, nobody's gonna give me a break with them?" Terrell pointed down at Delilah and Boy as if the kids were too naive to know he was talking about them. "After all of their yelling and fighting on the plane, I really do need a drink."

"So go get one. They'll be fine here by themselves. " Ming said showing her bad mother side.

"I can't leave them by themselves. They're too young and bad."

"Okay...I'll take care of it," Ming said, turning toward the kids. "Boy! Delilah! Front and center!" They walked up to her. "What did Ming tell you two?"

"I can't remember, Aunt Ming." Delilah said.

"Ming told you two that no matter what, to always look out for each other and stick together. You're brother and sister and you must stop fighting!" Then she stood up straight. "Now, Boy, you take game player and go in room over there," she paused pointing at her room within the suite, "and Dee, you take your game player and go in room over there." She continued pointing at Yvonna's room. "Now, no more fighting. Understood? You've made Uncle Terrell mad enough as is."

"I never want to see that bitch again!" Boy said storming into the room slamming the door behind him.

"Fine with me, 'cause I never wanna see you either!" Delilah replied going into the other room.

When they disappeared Terrell looked at the women. "Ya'll have to talk to them about their language." He said. "They can't go into the real world like that."

"They'll be fine. Now we're gonna find Quita. I'll be right back." Yvonna said.

"Before you go," Terrell interrupted, "Yvonna…Delilah is talking about the two scary lines again. She really thinks somebody is out to get her."

"I know. I keep telling her that it's in her mind. She'll be fine."

"She seemed really nervous about it, Yvonna. Maybe you should get her some help or allow me to try and help her."

"I SAID SHE'LL BE FINE! MY DAUGHTER IS NOT CRAZY!"

Ming and Terrell looked at each other and he said, "Okay, well, I just wanted you to know."

"Good, and I'll see you later."

Yvonna and Ming grabbed their hoodies by the door and before they turned the corner, they ran smack dab into the men of the Mah Jong Dynasty.

"Stay." Yvonna said to the statuesque Chinese men. "We'll be right back."

"We can't do that. Yao would kill us if something happened to you." One of them said.

Yvonna sighed not feeling the bullshit. "Well just one of you need to follow me. I definitely don't need all of you. You're making us hot enough as is."

"I'll go." Said Onik Yu.

Onik Yu, who the other bodyguards joked about had a crush on Yvonna, chose to follow them to Bricks' suite. In their native language, they laughed behind his back saying that his hopes of ever hitting that pussy were futile and would never happen. Onik was definitely a looker and although the yellow man was not usually Yvonna's flavor, if she was to give one of them some pussy he would definitely be it. Onik Yu, was extremely handsome with his tall slender frame, dark hair and deep brown eyes. Although he was born and raised in China, everyone was sure he had either Indian or African American in his blood.

After calling Quita on her cell and finding out which room Bricks was in, Yvonna took a deep breath and knocked on his door. She wasn't shocked, just irritated that Kelsi who she knew couldn't stand her, answered.

"Wait right here." He said blocking her entrance.

"I can't stand his ass!" Yvonna said beating her feet outside the door. "He act like I did something to him. Bitch type ass nigga!"

"Aw, shut up! You hate him because he's just like you. From the same cloth you came." Ming suggested.

"Whatever. Seems to me you're the problem."

"How is Ming the problem?" She said pointing to herself.

"Seems like every time we try to go somewhere together they look at you and keep me waiting on the outside of the door. I'm starting to think you're bad luck."

Ming laughed and said, "Ming has made you a millionaire, just by her affiliation alone. If anything you're bad luck."

When Bricks came to the door he seemed shocked to see her there. He partially stepped into the hallway and used his foot to hold the door open. "What up, Yvonna? I thought we were meeting at my party tomorrow. Is Yao here or something?" He asked looking down the hall only to see Onik who was grilling him with evil stares.

"No. Yao's not here, Bricks. I came to talk to you. Can I come in?" She moved toward the door.

"It's not a good time, Squeeze." He said calling her by the nickname he'd given her years earlier. He blocked her entry. "I got company."

Yvonna swallowed hard and said, "But you told me nobody before me. That whenever I needed you, you'd be there? Now I'm at your hotel door, miles away from home and you turn me away? Is what you told me a lie?"

Bricks looked down at his feet, opened the door wide and said, "Alright...come in."

When Yvonna walked in with Ming closely behind her, she had a smile on her face having gotten her way until she saw Carmen and her two friends sitting on the sofa with Tina, Melvin and now Kelsi. None of which cared for her very much.

"I got my eyes on you, Yvonna! I'm watching your every move!" Melvin said.

"Kick rocks, Melvin!" Yvonna replied. Then she turned her attention to Carmen, who looked better now than she did the last time she saw her in the hospital, on the day Swoopes shot Bricks. "I see you've flown your Georgia branch ass all the way here from Atlanta. What, there wasn't any more cotton to pick, bitch?"

"Georgia peach, baby." Carmen corrected her. Her voice was seductive and sensual, even when she was mad. "And I was flown out here by *special* request."

That hurt. "Why aren't you somewhere fucking Urban Greggs? I seen your groupie like behavior in the lobby earlier today."

Carmen smiled. "Just a fan meeting the champ. Ain't nothing wrong with that now is it?"

"Yeah, whatever," she said tiring of her already. "Bricks what the fuck is she doing here? I thought I told you I ain't want you banging with this whore no more! Anybody but her, baby!"

"Bitch, you can't tell him who to be with."

Yvonna felt heat creep up her body. And then she saw *Gabriella*. "I don't know why you just don't kill this chick right where she stands." *Gabriella* whispered closely in her ear. "Gank this bitch and get it over with. And Bricks too for that matter."

Trying to do what Yao asked, by staying out of trouble she said, "Bricks, can I please talk to you in private? Please. Before I hurt this bitch."

"Yeah, come to my room."

"Don't keep me waiting out here long," Carmen said. "I came all this way to see you, and I'm not going to let her take that from me again."

Fed up, Yvonna walked toward her and said, "Bitch, you'll get him back when I release my leash off his neck!" Carmen and her friends stood on guard, while Ming watched to see which bitch she could cut first.

"Hold up, the fuck you just say?" Bricks asked. "What type shit you talking about? Leash on my neck."

"I'm sorry, baby," she said realizing she'd gone too far.

"Girl, this bitch is trying it! When Me-Me come we rolling out of here before we hurt somebody." One of her friends interrupted.

Ming flicked a knife Yvonna didn't even know she had. "Ming wishes one of you bitches would make a move." They all looked at the short but feisty girl. "Ming has access to twenty Chinese men in that hallway who could bury all of you with a wave of her thumb. Who's first?"

"Who is Ming?" one of Carmen's friends asked, not use to someone referring to themselves in third person.

"ME BITCH!" They all sat down.

"Yvonna," Bricks said grabbing her by the arm, "come into my room. So we can talk. Alone."

"I'm sick of her shit." Yvonna looked at Carmen ready to dig a grave and bury her. "She don't even know who the fuck I..."

"You came to see me," he whispered putting his hand softly on her lower back, "now let's talk. Come with me."

"Okay," she said calming at his touch. Ming followed behind them until Yvonna said, "Girl, stay out here! You following me closer than a bloody pad."

"You leave me out here with all of them?" She pointed.

"You'll be fine, girl. They won't eat you. And even if they do don't act like you won't like it." Ming smiled momentarily relishing the horny thought.

Yvonna disappeared into the room with Bricks and the smell of his cologne made her weak. Not to mention he was so fucking handsome it was ridiculous.

When the door closed Bricks said, "Don't ever tell somebody you got some shit around my neck."

"Sorry." She said under her breath. "I went too far."

"Fuck all that," he paused, "You got me alone now what's up, Squeeze?"

She sat on the bed and he sat next to her. *I can't believe after all these years, we still haven't fucked.* She thought. Trying to maintain some control she decided to talk business. "Yao is coming tomorrow around six. We can meet with him before your party if that's okay with you."

"It's fine, now is there anything else? I got company."

"Uh…how was your flight over?"

"Cool."

"Really?" She asked with raised eyebrows. "Because we had a lot of turbulence and Ming was terrified. She had to rub my titties most of the way over here. She said it was the only way she could calm down…"

"Yvonna?" He interrupted her, touching her softly on the shoulder.

"Yes, *baby?*" She inhaled, breathing him in. Realizing the way she said '*baby*' expressed too much emotion, she tried to toughen up and said, "I mean...what's up?"

"Do you wanna tell me something else?"

"Something like what?" She said staring into his eyes.

"You tell me. You say you had something to talk to me about. Now that we alone you ain't saying nothing."

Feeling backed in a corner she decided to keep it one hundred. "Why...I mean...what is that girl doing here? You know she's just a user, Bricks. You don't need nobody like that around you. I mean, long distance relationships don't work anyway...you know that. Why don't you get rid of her?" She paused. "You want me to kill her for you?"

"What?" He asked shocked at her question.

"I'm just playing," she lied.

Still getting over her question he said, "Me and Carmen not together, Yvonna. So don't worry about that."

Slightly relieved she grew arrogant. "I'm not worried about shit. You can do whatever you want."

He laughed having seen her true feelings and said, "I know you not worried, but since you asked, my brother hooked that up and she came through. You know everybody was going to be in Vegas for the fight anyway."

"Is she staying here? With you?"

"Squeeze, you haven't grilled me this much in years." And then he was silent. "Or maybe before Carmen, you didn't have anything to grill me about."

"Boy, please, half the bitches in DC wanna fuck you. Including Quita, and don't think I don't know."

"You right. But we both know loving and fucking is two totally different things. Yeah, I found my way through a pussy or two back home, but I'm a nigga. Shit, I got needs and you not fucking me." Then he looked at her as if he could eat her alive. "I want nothing more than to be with you, shawty. But I'm sick of the fuckin' games you play. I mean…you want a nigga or what?"

"What games?"

"The ones you playing now," He paused. "I know what it really is, you scared of losing me."

"What? You sound crazy! I don't care what you do or who you do it with. My reason for seeing you today is for business purposes only."

Her words hurt him and the air could be seen leaving his body. "Aight, then" he said shaking his head, "well if that's the case, I guess I'll see you tomorrow."

Yvonna stood up and tried to relieve herself of the sinking feeling she had in the pit of her stomach. She said the wrong thing and had accomplished nothing by coming to the man's room. Truth be told, she loved Bricks…more than she loved any man before, including Bilal.

Yvonna walked to the door and said, "I guess I'll see you tomorrow." And then in an effort to pick a fight she said, "You never loved me anyway."

He threw her up against the door and raised his shirt. Five bullet holes covered his chest. "I took these for you, and never, not once brought it up until now. Now tell me again I don't wanna be with you, and I bet I fuck you up."

She shook him off and said, "That don't mean shit. Just that you can't dodge a bullet."

He laughed a little. "I'ma eat that." She turned for the door again, "Squeeze." Facing the door she smiled. "I mean, Yvonna." The smile was gone. "If you keep it real with me, about how you feel, I'll keep it real with you."

She still didn't face him. "What does that mean?"

"It means I'm ready to be your man, baby. But you gotta stop running from me, because I ain't chasing you no more."

She examined the ridges in the door, unable to keep it real with him. "Bricks, please stop acting like..."

"Do you hear me, I'm not chasing you no more, Yvonna." She swallowed the lump forming in her throat. "But I'm telling you right now, that I still love you even after all these years. But you gotta let me take care of you like I told you I would back at my house. And you gotta start trusting me. I waited five years for you. Never gave you no shit 'bout nothing you did, including living with the nigga Terrell. But now, baby," he said massaging her shoulders, "I want a woman in my life, I'm almost forty years old. But you gotta ask yourself if you're ready for me to be your man. Are you?"

Yvonna turned around and said, "It's obvious you don't know me like I thought you did, Bricks. 'Cause love don't live here. I'll see you tomorrow." With that she turned around and walked out the door. Bricks stayed in the room for a second, needing a minute to get himself together. She succeeded at fucking his mind up again.

When she walked into the living room part of the suite, she saw Ming flicking her silver lighter, sitting behind the couch in a dining room chair.

"That was quick," Carmen said as her friends laughed.

"Fuck you!"

Carmen laughed as everyone focused their attention back on the TV. And in that moment, Yvonna's eyes roamed to Carmen's long jet-black hair, which was hanging off the back of the couch. Being next to her hair when Ming saw Yvonna's gaze she grinned. Without saying words, Ming knew what she wanted her to do. So on the way out the door, Ming flicked the lighter again and put the flame on the bottom of Carmen's hair, setting her long black mane on fire.

Shyt List IV

They were all the way in the hallway when she heard Carmen's scream followed by, "I'MA GET YOU, BITCH! I'MA GET BOTH OF YOU!!!!!"

Yvonna

The casino was busy with every walk of life imaginable. The Cha-Ching sound of the slot machines resonated in the background and Yvonna tried to clear her mind. Finally she was alone but getting the "Me Time" she so desperately desired wasn't easy because at first Ming was having none of it. Afraid Yvonna was going to meet some men with friends and she'd miss out. That was until she said her ass looked flat in the jeans she was wearing and that if she wanted some dick, she had better go change her clothes.

Anger over Carmen being in town had rubbed her all sorts of raw. She hated that bitch more than anything and would've murdered her there if it hadn't been for the witnesses who would've loved to sit in a court of law and point narrow fingers in her direction.

Yvonna's mind was heavy. Because after taking a heavy dose of what she considered to be rejection from Bricks, she didn't want to talk to anybody, not even her best friend. She was so use to niggas fighting crazily for her, that when a man actually said the words *'I want to be your man'*, she brushed it off as weak and meaningless.

On the way to a slot machine, some girl talking on the phone bumped into her knocking her to the drab carpet. Yvonna's diamond earring fell from her ear and her MCM purse was knocked from her arm.

"I'm so sorry," the girl said.

The girl helped Yvonna up and handed her back the MCM bag off the floor along with her earring. Yvonna saw the girl, but for some reason, her eyes focused on a man in the corner, off to the side. He seemed to be intently watching her and the scene.

"Bitch, next time watch where the fuck you walking." Yvonna said putting her earring back on. "Stupid ass huzzy!"

The woman frowned. "Whatever, bitch. I was trying to help you out." She stomped away.

Yvonna still angry at the world, sat down at a quarter slot machine and put her card into the entry hole, which had ten thousand dollars worth of gambling money on it. She was on her fifteenth pull and was winning some but losing most. In the end all she really wanted to do was fuck Bricks and tell him how much she loved him, but her pride wouldn't allow her to.

When her phone buzzed she looked at the text. It was Terrell. *'I really hope we can spend some time together, like you promised. Otherwise I came out of here for nothing.'* She frowned and threw the phone back in her purse.

On her second drink, it dawned on her that Onik was not following her. In fact, Onik was not outside of Brick's room when she and Ming left in a hurry after burning Carmen's hair. *Where had he gone?*

Looking around the casino, she wondered if anybody else had a life as fucked up as hers. And when she looked to her left, she saw a man and a woman, butt ass naked on the casino floor fucking. When she closed her eyes and opened them again, they were fucking doggie style and the woman was drinking a martini from a shoestring.

"Fuck! Fuck! Fuck!" She said rubbing her temples. "This is not happening!"

Again the psychiatrist's voice played in her mind. *"But always, always, take your medicine. If you don't your mind will convince you of the most absurd things and you'll find yourself in the craziest situations."*

"You winning much?" A pretty chocolate colored girl said sitting next to her waking her out of the freak fest before her eyes. When she looked at the place where the couple was fucking, this time they were gone. Still tripping off of the scene, when she focused on the girl next to her she wondered if she was real.

In one second Yvonna peeped her black Giuseppe heels and new Gucci purse, which came out two weeks ago. "I was down here earlier and ain't win shit." The girl continued. "Please tell me you doing better than me."

"I just got here, too," Yvonna said, not up for company. "But I'm a sure shot so I'm sure I'll win something."

The girl laughed. "The name's Satori." She extended her pink colored minx nails. "Your name?"

"Yvonna." She said turning her rude neck to focus back on the slot machine.

"Well, Yvonna," the girl dropped her hand, "you look like you just lost your best friend. I wouldn't happen to be right now would I?"

"No, unfortunately for me my best friend is upstairs trying to find some jeans to make her ass look phatter than it already is," she laughed.

"I heard that. So…what brings you here? Business or pleasure?" Satori bet back the small winnings she had just earned on her slot machine.

"Well, let's see, I was here to exterminate someone for my boss, and mediate a drug deal between him and the man I love. But as time passes, I think the only reason I came was to lose the man I love and be humiliated in the process."

Yvonna thought the information she gave her would be too heavy, but Satori didn't seem phased. "Well, did you tell the man you love that you love him?"

"So nothing I just said shocked you?"

"Look, I've learned to never ask a question I wasn't willing to hear the answer to."

"I like you," Yvonna said opening up more, "But no, I couldn't tell him. I had my chance but my pride forced me to let the opportunity slide by."

"Why didn't you take it?"

"I don't know." She shrugged. "It's like this," she paused, "I'm bad luck."

"Bad luck?"

"*Very* bad luck...every man who has ever loved me has died or been murdered. I know for a fact, that if I give him the time of the day, and take the relationship seriously, that he'd be next. In my mind I'm keeping him safe." A single tear fell from her eyes. "I just...I just I love him sooo much." Yvonna was shocked at her heart-felt confession; she didn't realize that it was always easier to admit your feelings to a complete stranger.

"I know what you need to do."

"What?"

"You need to change your train of thought. You have to work on being a good person and loving those around you. Love conquers all. If you don't, and this is a promise," she paused, "things in your life will get worse before they get any better. It's law."

"Law?"

"Yes...the law of attraction. Basically it says that which is likened to itself is drawn. In your mind you know bad things will happen, so by law it has to happen."

"What are you, some ghetto self proclaimed profit?"

"No. I'm just someone who finally gets life." She says pulling the lever on the machine again. "I know now that I can be rich, happy and treat people well all at once without sacrificing a thing. I'm kinda living my dream."

"So you get everything you want in life, by living like this?"

"Pretty much. And if I don't get it, it's not for me and I usually end up getting something better." She said looking at Yvonna intently.

Silence.

Always jumping to the wrong conclusion Yvonna said, "Hold up, let me get something straight, I ain't no dyke. Yeah I might've licked my best friend's pussy a few times under the influence of alcohol, but that was then. I have no intentions on fucking you."

"What?" She said with raised brows. Satori couldn't believe she called her a dyke after she just admitted *she* licked a pussy.

"You came over here talking about getting what you want and shit, yet you looking at me sideways. I'm just saying."

Satori stood up and the bells of the slot machine rang out indicating she had hit big. The lights on the machine flashed brightly with different colors and she collected her card and said, "I gave it to you how you needed to have it. It's up to you to take my advice. Good luck in life. I really mean that."

Managers and other employees of the casino rushed to Satori so she could claim her fifty thousand dollar prize. It took five minutes before all of the pictures were taken and all of the celebrations were over. And when she finally walked away, Yvonna rolled her eyes, ordered another drink and forgot everything Satori said. Her mind was still on the facts of her wicked life, when all of a sudden she saw three security guards rushing in her direction with Carmen leading the pack.

Now Carmen's hair was cut in a cute black bob and Yvonna was mad that it actually looked better on her than the long hairstyle before she sported an hour earlier.

"There she is right there!" Carmen pointed.

Yvonna stood up and said, "What is this about?"

The security guards wasted no time rushing Yvonna to the floor. She fought desperately trying to get away from their grasp but they held on to her tightly.

"She stole my wallet!" Carmen yelled. "She's a fucking thief. I saw her put it in her purse."

"Wallet?" Yvonna said confused at her statement. She may have given the order to burn her shit, but she certainly didn't steal shit from her purse.

"Mam, let me see your purse."

"Go 'head. I ain't got shit!" Yvonna said confident that with one swoosh of the zipper, all the proof they needed would be given.

The guard took her purse and when he opened it, he saw a gold Gucci wallet inside. The moment he removed it, Carmen smiled slyly. Yvonna played the mental tapes back of her mind, and realized the girl who bumped into her earlier, must've put it there. It was a set up, and a smooth move.

"You sure you don't want to tell these people the truth." Yvonna said coldly. "That you framed me?" She paused again. "You don't wanna fuck with me, Carmen."

"Bitch, I told them the truth already!" Carmen was angry and hateful and it was showing in her eyes. "You stole my shit. Now lock this bitch up! I want her prosecuted to the fullest extent of the law!"

"You picked the wrong person, Carmen. Are you..."

Before she could finish her statement Carmen with wild jealous eyes spit on her shoes. Then she leaned in and whispered in her ear as the guards held Yvonna tightly. "You're not going to come in between me and him, bitch. He's mine and he belongs to me."

"We'll see about that."

Carmen pulling this shit now was fucked up on many levels. With her in custody, it was impossible to carry out Yao's orders. Yvonna had been in Vegas for less than twenty-four hours and already she was in trouble. Her head started throbbing when she realized again she still hadn't taken her medicine when she first got to the hotel. *Calm down. Calm down. You're getting too upset.* She thought. She tried to close her eyes and rationalize that she could get out of the situation okay, but anger consumed her and wasn't trying to let go. With penetrating eyes, she stared down at the floor and then back up at Carmen. *Sorry, Uncle Yao, but there's been a change of plans.*

Shyt List IV

Sin City

Penny

The Diamond Motel stank something fierce when Penny and Thaddeus walked their asses into the lobby. Penny didn't bother hiding the anger on her face when she checked into the nasty, dirty, funky, dingy Vegas spot with her boyfriend, Thaddeus.

"What's ya name?" The Check in Agent asked.

"Penny. I checked in under Penny."

"Oh yeah, here you go." She handed her a plastic key. "Your room is number 1011 and it's in the back of the motel."

They dragged their luggage out of the lobby and outside. It wasn't anywhere near as luxurious and fly as other hotels on the strip but it could have been a hole in the wall as far as Penny was concerned. She was there for one reason, and that was to get her hands on Yvonna.

When they finally got to the room it was evident that Thaddeus had never been anywhere classy. Because although it was filthy, he acted as if he were at the Bellagio. "This is nice," He said. "Damn, baby, if I knew you were gonna splurge like this, I'da licked that pussy just a little bit longer last night."

They walked fully into the room and placed their bags down. "Now yous do know you can still do that don't yous? Old Penny ain't got no problem laying down to let ya handle ya business if that's how ya feel. In fact, I welcomes it."

"Did your herpes break out go away?"

She sighed a little. "I think so."

Thaddeus had given Penny a case of herpes due to his obsession with prostitutes. She wasn't the only one he'd given his nastiness too. He'd also transferred the disease to his forever-faithful wife.

"It don't matter none to me, baby. I'll still lick that coochie. Puss bumps and all!"

Thaddeus laid on the bed and grabbed her large body pulling her to his even larger one. His three time grungy white t-shirt rubbing against the black hot sweater she wore. Not only were they dressed for a different season, but also a different decade.

"You know, ever since you came into my life, I been in heaven. My wife never treated me like you. I love you, old ass Penny."

"If yous really love me then how come yous won't just leave her?" she crawled on top of him and it looked as if two hump back whales were fighting on the beach. If the entire scene was on TV, folks would have changed the station for fear of throwing up their meals. "She ain't neva gonna treat ya as good as me, Thaddeus."

"Baby, come on now, you know I told you I can't do that right now." He pushed her off and she thumped to the floor. "Oh, shit, I'm sorry, baby."

"No problem." She said crawling back on top of the bed, this time in a seated position. Her knees cracking with every move she made. "But I don't know how long I can be your Tender Roni. I need you full time."

What the fuck? He thought hearing her analogy. *She ain't hardly a tender anything.*

"If I leave her now, she gonna try and stick me for my pension. I needs my pension. How else we gonna get that beach house you want in Miami?"

"I understand. Well...let's forget 'bout her. We gonna take care of what we came ta take care of, and have a good time." Penny said.

"That sounds like a plan." Then a dumb look took over his face. "But baby," he said holding her head, "I ain't bring no money with me. I forgot to go to the cash machine."

"We can still go ya know. If you got ya card."

"That's just it, I ain't got my card. I forgot it." He said. "You got me don't you?"

He never had any money and Penny knew it. But she wasn't with him for his money; she was with him because no matter what, he was the one person who never went anywhere or left her alone. She turned to her left, he was eating all of her food, she turned to the right and he was digging in her pocket book. No doubt about it, they were in ghetto love, as far as old ass Penny was concerned anyway.

"I got us. Yous know I do."

"Great! So what we gonna do first, baby? I was thinking you could give me a few bucks, and let daddy win us a few thousand. That way I can earn my keep like a real man instead of depending on you."

"We can do whatever ya want, but I gotta find the whereabouts of Ms. Yvonna Harris first."

Yvonna

Yvonna was heated as she sat in the plain holding room in the hotel waiting on her fate. "It could be worse," she thought out loud. "At least nobody I did wrong knows I'm in Vegas. I can get out of this, I just have to play it smart."

The bland cream clothed walls were a far cry from the luxury she experienced in her suite before she decided to burn a bitch's hair. She couldn't believe she had allowed herself to get caught on some stupid shit on day one in Vegas. However, she rested easy when she thought of different ways to seek revenge on Carmen. She was scratching the wood paneled table with her pink nails when the locked door opened. A man and a woman entered.

"How much longer do you think I'll let you keep me here?"

Both of them seemed to be uneasy. "Yvonna Harris," she cleared her throat, "this is detective Phillip Sanders. The other detective who arrested you is gone for the day."

"I bet."

Phillip Sanders was twenty-eight years old and out of his league. He knew it the moment he walked into the room and looked into her piercing eyes. His cocoa brown skin and chinky eyes made him a favorite with the ladies but Yvonna was not impressed.

"Detective Sanders will be asking you some questions from here." It was clear that the woman wanted no part of matter.

When she closed the door she said, "Why am I still here?"

"Because you weren't willing to cooperate."

"I told these mothafuckas in here that I didn't take that bitch's wallet."

"And they heard you but don't believe you."

"I need to make a phone call." She said sternly. She had enough experience with officers to know that they all had buttons. Press the right one and they didn't have a chance.

"We want to ask you some more questions first."

"You ain't gonna ask me shit first." She paused. "What you gonna do is bring me my purse so I can make a phone call, Phillip. This ain't even no real jail."

"I don't think you understand the severity of this issue, Ms. Harris. Someone has accused you of stealing."

"Let me put it this way. You and I both know I didn't steal that girl's wallet. In fact you've already reviewed the tapes of me on the casino floor when her friend bumped into me. And the tapes revealed that you couldn't pin this shit on me right?" Silence. "If the plan would have worked, you would have transported me to a police station by now." She laughed. "The only reason I'm still here is because somebody fucked up and ya'll are trying to cover your asses." Then she got confident and as sexy as she could and said, "Now, if I don't get out of here within the next fifteen minutes, I'll sue this hotel for enough money to close one of its wings. And when I do, what do you think will happen to you and your job?"

Silence.

"I think you got this all wrong. This is…"

"She paid you." His expression went from worry to horror. After all, how could she know? "I know she paid you." Yvonna said leaning back into her chair. "She paid you to set me up."

"No, it's not true."

She leaned in. "NIGGA, I FUCKING SAW YOU WHEN I FIRST WALKED INTO THE CASINO! YOU WERE STARING AT ME IN THE CORNER! WATCHING EVERYTHING I DID! I GOT PEOPLE TRYING TO KILL ME, NIGGA!" She threw a balled fist on the table. "I KNOW EVERYTHING ABOUT MY SURROUNDINGS! NOW DON'T FUCK WITH ME!!!"

Silence.

She calmed down, leaned back and said, "Now it's okay...you probably don't get a lot of money for what you do here. I get that, I was once in your shoes. But unlike you, I'm rich now, and if you don't let me out of here, I have enough money to ruin your life. And most importantly, I have enough money to take your life."

He started crying. "I didn't want no parts of this! I was just trying to do what my girlfriend asked me to do. Her cousin Carmen said your friend burned her hair, and since she couldn't pin it on you, she wanted to set you up like this. I'm sorry."

He was a snitch, and she didn't like him. "Phillip..."

"I really am sorry." He interrupted. "I just want to..."

"PHILLIP!" Yvonna yelled disgusted at his display of emotion. "Just bring me my shit and let me out of here!"

"I'll be right back." He ran out of the room quickly.

As Yvonna waited by herself, she thought about all the things she was going to do to Carmen. Her anger was boiling over when she thought about all the time she wasted because of being locked up for three hours. And what if she got into serious trouble and lost custody of her daughter? She needed her to live. Yvonna hated her on many levels now. It didn't help that Carmen wanted Bricks.

They probably fucking and everything by now. She thought. *She probably sucked his dick and all kinds of freaky shit. I'ma kill this bitch!*

Pain was rushing up the sides of her temples and covering the front of her forehead, when she blinked, and rubbed her head. She was trying to prevent the darker side from taking over. She was losing control and her sanity was slowly slipping away.

"Calm, down Yvonna," she said to herself rubbing her temples so hard they itched. "You good. You can do this."

More throbbing pain in her head followed by a vision of what it would feel like to stomp on Carmen's throat with a pair of steel toe boots danced in her mind. When the anger was so blinding she couldn't take it anymore, she opened her eyes to a familiar face sitting at the table across from her.

"Bitch, what the fuck are you doing now?" *Gabriella* said crossing her legs as she leaned back in a chair to file her nails.

"You're not there...you're not there...you're not there." She chanted.

"Giiiiirrrrlllll! This game is as dead as this spiky hairdo you insist on wearing. I mean damn, can we put a little hang time on that bald ass head of yours or something? Please!"

"I don't need you!"

"Yes you do because before now you were faking about who you really are. You finally realized that you are a killer and you finally realized that you enjoy doing it. The reason I'm here now is because Uncle Yao has placed unreasonable conditions on you that you can't meet. You like to kill for fun, Yvonna, but Uncle Yao wants to tame a bitch. He wants you to follow his rules and you hate fucking rules. And when you feel restricted, you produce me."

"You don't know what you're talking about!"

"Precious," she paused, "and you are starting to look a little like her too," she pointed looking at her thighs, "you may wanna push back from the table, honey." She paused. "I come as a gift to you whenever you hold yourself back. Consider me your reward for being different."

"I'm not holding myself back. I just told you I'm fine."

"Let's see, Bricks gives you a chance to admit that you are in love with him, and instead of grabbing both ends of his balls you run away. Then you force him into the woman's arms who's in town for the weekend by burning her hair." She massages her shoulders, "Which by the way looks better with the changes don't you agree?" Yvonna shakes her off and *Gabriella* laughs. "Bitch, look at you. You are getting old and you're about to let a younger bitch take your man."

"Ms. Harris, here are your things," the detective said reentering the room. When she turned her head *Gabriella* was gone. And although she knew no one else could see her, she could never really understand why. In her mind she was as real as the people in front of her. "Can we keep this between us?"

Yvonna grabbed her purse and suddenly had a great idea. "I'll let bygones be bygones on one condition."

"Just say the word. I'd do anything within my power."

"Oh no, honey, I'm gonna need you to go outside of the scope of your power for this one."

◀••▶

When Yvonna stomped back toward her hotel room, Onik, her bodyguard, was on her heels.

"Where were you?" She said, with an attitude as she continued to walk.

"I went to the bathroom, and when I came back to the room, I thought you both were still inside." Then he paused and said, "But I tore this hotel up to find you. Are you okay?"

"Yeah, but when did you realize we weren't in Bricks' room?" Her steps were quick and he kept up. "A lot of shit happened to me and I needed your help."

"I realized it when the girl who's hair you burned came out screaming."

Yvonna laughed out loud. "Where is Yao, Onik? Is he here yet?"

"Yes. He's actually in your room waiting on you."

Yvonna stopped walking and said, "How long has he been there?"

"About twenty minutes."

"Fuck! Fuck! Fuck!" She said pacing the floor in a circle. Then she put her hands on her face and leaned up against the wall. "Does he know where I was? Or what happened?"

"Yvonna, I don't fully understand what happened." He walked up to her placed his hand on her shoulder and said, "But is everything okay? I mean, can I do anything for you?"

"I said I'm fine." She regained her composure. "Let me get this over with."

When they got to her room uncle Yao was inside looking like a million bucks in his black suit with fine grey pinstripes throughout. His skin looked as if he'd been somewhere soaking up the sun. When he saw her face he examined the time on his Presidential Rolex watch. Seven men covered him, including the man with the missing ear who usually chauffeured him everywhere. But she didn't see Ming or Terrell so she wondered how did he get in?

"Yvonna, come." He said extending his hands toward her. She walked toward him and he kissed her softly on the forehead. "Where were you? Are you okay?" He said massaging her shoulders.

"I'm fine. But how did you get in?"

"Doors can't hold me out or in." He grinned. "Now are you okay? Onik said you were missing, and that stupid niece of mine didn't know where you were either."

"Uh...yes." She was still taken by his response. "I'm fine. Everything's fine."

"Are you sure?" he gripped her tighter forcing her eyes wide open. "Because we can't have any problems this weekend. Now I need him taken care of. And I don't need any trails leading back to me."

"You can count on me."

"Great, because I don't want you getting caught up in frivolous matters while you're here. There are other more important things to care for."

"I understand."

"Good...now when are you meeting him?"

"Tomorrow. Although he hasn't called yet."

"Don't worry, he'll call." Then he paused. "But remember, our plan has two parts. First you get him to drink the poison the night of the fight and then you wait until after the fight to kill him." Then he handed her the vial of poison. "Put this in his water right before the fight. It'll take hold slowly. You understand?"

"I understand, but is it possible to call the men off? If Urban sees me with a band of Chinese men he'll be suspicious. I'm trying to stay low-key."

"And I'm trying to save you. How many attempts have been made on your life?"

"Many, but no one knows I'm here. I'm safe. But the more attention I bring by having them follow me, the harder it will be to complete your mission."

"I understand. It's done." He said looking at them all. "I'll just keep Onik on you." He eyed Onik who nodded. "But don't worry, he'll stay in the background. And if you need any of my men for any reason, they are yours."

"Thank you."

"Don't thank me yet. Because I think the biggest distraction of all is that niece of mine."

"She isn't a distraction."

"Don't let her twist your mind. She's a disgrace to me and had it not been for your affiliation with her, and the fact that I'm using her name for the salons, I would've had her murdered."

"Uncle Yao..." He put a finger over her lips.

"I will stop at nothing to see this mission through, even if it means killing a person whose bloodline resembles my own. Am I understood?"

"Yes. You are."

Swoopes & Crystal

Heavy laughter filled the MGM Grand hotel in Vegas. People were buzzed from the steady flow of alcohol and excited about the fight between Greggs and Santiago. Amongst them sat a couple whose only mission was to take what didn't belong to them, at any cost.

Crystal laid eyes on the perfect couple to rob while she and Swoopes were in Vegas. Funds were severely low and they needed a come up and he figured his gun skills coupled with her charms would do the trick. A pretty girl was better bait than a man missing his fingers and an eye so he sent her along to make a friendly connection.

Ever since she met Swoopes on the prison pal site, she'd dedicated her life to him. Whether it was to sleep with Chavis, one of his gang members that he killed the moment he left her pussy, or giving up her kids because he didn't like them, she proved over and over that she was down for him, every step of the way.

"Please tell me ya'll didn't lose as much money as we did," Crystal said approaching a young couple that looked solemn at the casino bar. She sat in one of the four available seats next to them. "I need to know somebody came out on top."

"Giiiirrrl, we did alright," the pretty girl said, twirling the straw in her cup, "but damn, them tables cold right now."

Swoopes sat behind her and watched her work. For a brief second the couples observed each other and gave their silent approval. Both were in their late twenties to early thirties and both were stylish. The only thing off putting was Swoopes' eye patch and the three fingers missing off his right hand. But even with the patch Swoopes wasn't hard on the eyes and had amazing swag and confidence about him that made him appealing to strangers.

"What were ya'll playing?" Swoopes asked the dude.

"Black Jack. Nothing serious." He responded. "I told my baby to get the fuck up when she was winning but she didn't. Before I knew it she lost almost everything."

"*Almost* everything?" Swoopes repeated.

"Yep. I stopped her before she got too far."

"Why you put me out there, honey." The girl said. "You was the main one handing me chips and shit."

"This girl crazy," he said, "she thinks just because chips are on the table you're supposed to use 'em all. I told her you gotta quit while you're ahead."

Swoopes and Crystal laughed. "Well we have some vouchers for a nice restaurant at Bellagio's. If ya'll up for it we'd love the company." Crystal said.

"I don't know," the girl said looking at her man. "We don't want to intrude."

"Come on," Crystal insisted. "Drinks on us. You can't beat them odds."

The girl looked at her boyfriend and he said, "Fuck it. We ain't got nothing else to lose."

◀ •• ▶

When they made it to the restaurant the couples drank liquor and had a good time. Crystal and Swoopes found out the young couples names were Gerron and Ginger and they were from Atlanta. He liked that they seemed naive and trusting, and they were just the type of people they wanted to meet and deceive.

Although plotting was in full mode, Swoopes and Crystal were surprised at how much they had in common but knew they had to push forward with the plan. They needed enough money to get as close to Yvonna as possible while she was in Vegas, otherwise they'd lose her again. But if their current plan didn't work, he had Plan B formulated in his mind and ready to go. Through the grapevine, he learned that the only regret Yvonna had in life was poisoning Bilal Jr., almost killing him, and if things didn't work, he had plans to capitalize on that weakness.

If Swoopes wasn't fucking around with drugs, and if he went back to work with the YBM he wouldn't be in this situation. But he vowed not to hit the streets again until Yvonna's heart stopped beating. It wasn't easy because Yao's people were gunning for him as much as he was gunning for her and it made it difficult to move.

After they finished their meals Swoopes and Crystal were trying to formulate in their minds how to get the couple alone. But then Gerron said, "We got some drinks in our room. Ya'll wanna go back there and play cards or something?"

"We don't want to put you guys out," Crystal said.

"It's not a problem," Gina replied, "It would be our pleasure."

This was better than Swoopes and Crystal could have hoped for. In their room they could take them for all they had. "Sounds like a plan to me," Swoopes said giving him dap.

Within twenty minutes they were back in the hotel, and Swoopes' entire demeanor had changed. On Beast-Goon mode, he thought about how much a nigga like him must've had on him, and better yet, how much he had access to from the ATM.

"We're going to freshen up. But we have some Berry and Coconut Ciroc on the table. Make yourselves at home." Gina said.

"Thank you." Crystal said as they took their seat on the couch.

When they disappeared into the bedroom portion of the suite Swoopes whispered, "This plan could not have gone any better."

"Did I make you proud, God? Did I do what you wanted?"

He pulled her closely. "If this shit works out you did better than make me proud. And I'ma show you how much I appreciate your loyalty, too." Swoopes checked for the gun under his shirt and was waiting for the best time to pull it out. "Now in a minute, babes, it's gonna be time to push. I'ma put the heat to the nigga's head and you drop his bitch. I need you to hit her hard like we talked about."

"I got you, God." She said with wide eyes. "I won't let you down." After he killed Newbie she promised to always refer to him by the name he loved, even if he was nowhere near deserving.

"Good." He said planting a kiss sloppily on her lips. She wrapped her arms around him tightly not wanting to let him go. "After we rob these mothafucka's I'ma take you out and show you a good time, and then we can get at that bitch."

You would've thought he asked her to marry him the way she was acting. Days of sleeping in airports, and abandoned cars had taken its toll on her body.

They were involved heavily in another kiss when they felt a barrel on the back of their heads. The pressure of the guns gave them temporary headaches as they realized they'd fucked up majorly.

Swoopes was about to reach for his whistle when Gina walked around them and said, "Don't move, baby boy. Get your mothafuckin' hands in the air." Then with her free hand, she relieved them of their weapons.

With the guns in her possession she stepped back to Gerron who planted a kiss on her lips.

"That's my bitch, nigga!" He laughed. "That's how we do it!" She winked at him and looked back at Swoopes and Crystal. "You know what time it is, nigga!" Gerron said with his gun planted on the back of his skull. "Give it up, 'fore I blow your other eye out from the back."

Shyt List IV

Sin City

Quita

Quita was taking Chomps back to Bricks and she had Delilah and Boy with her for the walk. As usual the two were fighting about anything and everything under the sun. She tried not to let them blow her, but that was becoming next to impossible. Fixing herself up before she knocked on Bricks' suite door, she adjusted her earrings and her itty-bitty jacket. When the work was done she knocked two times before Kelsi appeared.

"Is Bricks here?" Quita found herself adjusting again, she hadn't expected to see Kelsi's fine ass.

"You must be Quita," he said staring at her.

"You got it, cutie." She smiled.

Quita wasn't the only one who was taken by Kelsi. Delilah had never seen a man more handsome in her life.

He smiled at Quita's comment and said, "Come on in."

While Boy, and Chomps moved into the suite, Delilah was stuck in her steps. She couldn't move. Kelsi picking up on the little girl's crush said, "Why you out there pretty? You ain't coming in?"

"You think I'm pretty?" Delilah asked stuck on stupid.

"Yeah. If I were your age you'd be my girlfriend."

Delilah's heart beat rapidly as she moved into the suite. *If only it could be true.* She thought, having developed her first big boy crush. When she was inside Kelsi closed the door and swaggered to the couch to finish his beer. Delilah didn't take her eyes off of him the entire time.

When Bricks came out Quita said, "I'm bringing Chomps back. I told you he coulda stayed if you wanted to have some fun. I mean, you are in Vegas, boy."

"Naw, I gotta make sure my lil man straight."

"Whatever," she sighed. "Let me know what time you want me to pick him back up tomorrow."

Bricks gave Chomps a pound and said, "Aight, I'ma holla at you."

Quita was just about to move for the door when she saw the handle of Kelsi's weapon imprinting his shirt.

"You police?" She asked.

Kelsi frowned. "Naw, why you say that?"

"I thought I saw a gun." Kelsi pulled his shirt all the way down and shook his head at the stupid bitch standing before him.

Bricks irritated said, "Fuck is you talking like that around them kids for? Matta fact, get your ass out of here before I fire you." He pushed her toward the door and said goodbye to Delilah and Boy before slamming it in her face.

Shyt List IV

Sin City

Yvonna

The TV was playing in the background in the suite as Yvonna was playing with Delilah on top of the bed. This was their nightly routine and Yvonna tried her best to never miss a night when she wasn't out of town on business.

She wasn't the kindest human being, but when it came to loving her daughter, as best she could, she came through. Her mind was on the events of the day and she hated how as it stood, Carmen had gotten the last laugh. *For now, bitch.* She thought. *For now.*

"Mama," Delilah was playing with the rings on Yvonna's fingers, "I saw the two scary black lines again, when I went to Quita's room. They were right outside the door."

Yvonna held on to her hand and said, "Delilah, I told you to stop making things like that up."

"But it's true, mommy. I saw them at the daycare and now in front of Quita's room."

"Delilah! Stop it!" She looked at her seriously. "Now let's talk about something else. Anything good happen to you today?"

She frowned and said, "Kinda."

"Okay. What happened?"

"I think I have a boyfriend." She smiled. "I think his name is Kelsi."

Yvonna rolled her eyes and said, "Delilah, Kelsi is a piece of shit with legs and arms and you are not allowed to like him. Plus he's too old for you."

"Okay," she paused, "even though I still like him anyway." Delilah looked out ahead at the TV and said, "How do you kill somebody?" She played with the contents of her pink Juicy purse.

"What?" Yvonna asked shocked at her daughter's question. It was like she was hitting her with blow after blow.

"If I wanted to kill somebody, how would I do it?" she threw the purse on the table next to the bed. "The question is very simple, mama. You should really go ahead and answer it."

"Delilah, I don't like that question and I'm your mother so I don't have to answer. You on the other hand don't have that option. Now why did you ask me something like that?" Delilah furiously pulled the covers over her head and clapped her eyes closed in frustration. "Okay, if you want to be that way." Yvonna got out of the bed and walked to the door. She didn't want her thinking she could always have her way. "Good night, Delilah."

She sighed and pouted. "Night, mother."

Feeling bad, she was unable to walk out of the door. "Is someone bothering you?"

"Yes, mama. Why else would I ask you how to kill? Think, mama."

"Delilah, don't get smart or I'ma smack you in the mouth, okay?" She lied, never wanting to beat her child. "You cute and all, but not cute enough to be rude."

"Sorry, mama. It's Little Davie. He says you're crazy and that his mother read about you in the newspaper. Said you were claiming to have different personalities so you could kill as many people as you wanted. Said you got away with it and everything. And you know what I decided mama?"

"What?"

"I decided after listening to Little Davie, that I understood why some people need to die. And I want to kill Little Davie. I want him to be my first. Ra Ra told me he would be a good person."

"I told you Ra Ra is not real!!!!! Don't say that again!"

"But I hate him! And he must go!"

Yvonna heard that the sins of a mother always found their way to her children. She had killed, betrayed and hurt many people in her lifetime. And she wondered, could all of her sins come home to roost on her child.

"Delilah, killing is…killing is…"

"Go ahead and lie to her," *Gabriella* said appearing to her left. "Go ahead and tell her that killing is wrong when you know that it's right. How many bodies you have on you now? One hundred? Two hundred?"

"Shut up, *Gabriella*!" She hated when she appeared around Delilah.

"Mama," she frowned, "Aunt Gabriella isn't here."

"I know, baby."

"Killing is a way of life, Yvonna. Stop lying to your daughter. Tell the mini you that she will continue the legacy. I've seen the future and in it she carries a gun."

"I said shut up!" She screamed and rubbed her temples vigorously. "Stop it!"

"Mama, is that your imaginary friend?"

"What?"

"I said, is that your imaginary friend?" A hopeful smile spread on her face.

"There's no such thing as imaginary friends. Hearing voices from other people means you are crazy and your mama isn't crazy."

Delilah looked sad but Yvonna, wanting to prevent the aura that was *Gabriella* from being around her said, "I love you, baby. Goodnight."

She was out of the room and on to the next thing the moment the door closed. When she went into the living room, Terrell was sitting down watching TV and she sat next to him.

"Where's Ming?" Yvonna asked, expecting to see her in the living room.

"She said she went to get some dick," he laughed. "Boy is in her room sleep." He paused, "And Onik is standing outside of the suite door. Baby, what do you really do for Yao?"

"Nothing. I just run for him sometimes." She appeared uneasy.

"He sure goes through a lot to make sure you're safe. With the bodyguards and all, and moving you from place to place." She was silent not wanting to tell him that she was a paid assassin. Terrell fell back into the sofa, "So what's up with you? Something on your mind?"

"Baby, I'm...I'm starting to see *Gabriella* more."

Terrell cut the TV off and looked at her with great concern. "What? How often?" He paused. "And did you take your medicine?"

"No. I've been too busy."

He dropped his head and shook it. "Then what set you off?"

I burned a bitch's hair. She thought. "Nothing, I don't think I was upset." He didn't believe her. "Terrell, is this illness hereditary?"

"It can be. Although I don't think you have anything to worry about." Terrell got up from the couch and got her medicine along with a cup of water. "But, Yvonna, why are you forgetting to take your meds all of a sudden? This is why I could never leave you if I wanted to, you're not ready."

She took the pills. "I don't know." She shrugged. "So much is going on," She crawled up under him. His heart rate increased having felt her touch. He was head over hills for the crazy bitch. He wrapped his strong arms around her and she immediately felt calmed. Around Terrell, she could show her softer side because she didn't care what he thought. She knew no matter what, he'd always be there.

"Yvonna, you're not cured, you'll never be. Remember that." He paused. "Now you sure nothing happened?"

She couldn't tell him about her jealousy towards Carmen, because she wasn't supposed to care about anybody. Not even the man of her dreams...Bricks. "Ming, burned Bricks' girlfriend hair." Saying *girlfriend* made her stomach rumble.

"What the fuck is up with you and Ming? That's some young ass shit."

"That's my best friend. If she in some shit, I'm in some shit." She said. "And after she burned her hair instead of going after Ming, she framed me for stealing her wallet."

"Yvonna I wish you settle down and let me take care of you." He paused. "I texted you two times today trying to hook up. All I wanna do is love you."

When her cell phone rang she got up and answered without responding. It was Phillip. She walked toward the kitchen and said, "What?"

"I have her." He paused, sounding scared. "But how long you want me to hold her?"

"Until I say when." She hung up.

She and Terrell were just about to continue their conversation when someone knocked at the door. It was an unexpected visitor.

Shyt List IV

Washington, DC

Bilal Jr.

Bilal heard his best friend Jukes talking to him as he hung outside, but he wasn't listening. He was still brewing over the nigga Marx who posted a comment on Facebook that he thought Bilal was a bitch for letting some niggas whip on his girlfriend Rozay.

"Bilal, I know you hear me, nigga! You coming with us to Kristina's tonight or what?" Kristina's Diner was a hangout spot for teenagers in the daytime, and a layback spot for adults at night. "That girl who wanna meet you gonna be there."

"Did you see the shit that Marx put on Facebook? Fuck is he talking about, son? He don't even know me like that."

"Kill! Why are you tripping off of that shit? Drop it."

Bilal and Jukes were sitting on a car in the parking lot of a Washington DC project they lived in together. After Yvonna murdered Bilal's grandmother, he moved from foster home to foster home. It wasn't until he opened up to Jukes about his home life that he told his mother about his friend's situation. Seeing how much her son cared for his friend, she did what was necessary to bring him into their home.

Life had given him a tough break and Bilal often had to fight at school. Not just because of how he looked, which often put younger insecure boys on the defensive, but also because he was angry. Everything was taken from him, and he didn't know why. Why was his mother killed? Who murdered his father? Where was his family, his grandparents? Wherever he turned for answers, he'd find nothing but lies. He wanted nothing more than to belong to a family and in the end he always felt worthless and rejected.

"The nigga wasn't even there, Jukes. What he know about what happened to her hand?"

"Son, stop worrying about that shit." Jukes jumped off the car and said, "Now let's go to Kristina's. Moms gave me fifty bucks yesterday."

Bilal's eyes widened in confusion. "Why she ain't give me nothing?"

"She told me to give you half." Bilal knew he was lying.

No matter how much Katherine said she treated the boys equal, he knew that at the end of the day, she always favored her son more. Bilal didn't buck about it too much because he didn't have plans to hang around after he was eighteen. For now he had a good friend who looked out and a bed to go to sleep in at night. And for now, that would have to do.

◀ •• ▶

"Bilal, why you sitting over there all quiet and shit?" Shawnda said pushing up on Bilal on the bench style seat. "I know you don't be this quiet in school."

"I mean, what you want me to say? I don't talk a lot." Bilal responded, his mind still with Rozay and what she was doing.

He pulled out his cell phone and logged on to his Facebook page. A few people had commented about the situation, and it fucked him up because he wished they just minded their own fucking business.

'I knew that nigga was a bitch', Ustayouttamyshit, responded.

'Ya'll some haters. Bilal still my peeps,' DC Cutie replied.

'Ain't nobody, hatin'. He just a sucka' Southeast Tony, added.

As if it couldn't get any worse, Rozay commented about two minutes earlier and his stomach flipped.

'Awww, thank ya'll. My hand is a little better but I doubt Bilal's will be too much longer. He gonna have to see my brothers soon. Real soon.'

"B, we 'bout to go to the movies or something. You rolling right?" Jukes asked tapping him on his shoulder.

Bilal put his phone in his pocket. "Jukes, let me holla at you on the side."

They excused themselves from the table. "What up?"

"I got some work I gotta move for AJ. I forgot to tell you about it." Bilal said. "I ain't gonna be able to hang out tonight."

"Why? I know you still not tripping over that dumb shit."

"It's worse than that. Rozay talking about getting her brothers. I gotta think about what I'm gonna do, and I ain't feeling the movies right now. Plus the girl Shawnda not my type."

Jukes couldn't believe his ears. "Are you serious? She a cutie."

"You ain't hearing me. I'm 'bout to bounce." They gave each other dap and went their separate ways.

◀ • ▶

Bilal worked off half of AJ's dope and was about to go into the house when a black Lincoln Continental pulled up in front of him. Everything in Bilal's spirit told him to run, but just like some people do when intuition calls, he ignored it.

"What up, son? You holding?" A tall black man with a mean grill asked.

"Naw. I ain't got shit."

Another man got out the car that looked just as intimidating. "I know you got something on you, homie. It's still early." They closed their car doors, looked around for witnesses and approached Bilal.

"Naw, like I said, I'm out." Bilal said attempting to walk away.

One of them grabbed him by his shirt and pushed him against the car. "You might not be holding but I know you got a problem knowing how to treat women."

Bilal was scared. "I think ya'll got me mixed up with somebody else."

"Fuck that," he laughed, "we wanna see if you know who we are after we do what we came to do to you."

Shyt List IV

Sin City

Young Black Millionairz

The members of the YBM swaggered to their room at the MGM Grand hotel. They were irritated and pissed the fuck off that they didn't make any progress when it came to finding Yvonna. Members of the YBM were throwing a party and they brought the best freak whores in the game from DC and ordered a few more from Vegas.

When Growl, Rook and Mike stepped into the room, it was loud and overcrowded. But what really fucked their heads up was the bitch that was butt ass naked, and bent over on all fours in front of the door. When you came in, it was the first thing you saw. The back of her ass cheeks had the words WELCOME written in a black sharpie and the room smelled of smoke, pussy, and alcohol.

"Ya'll niggas finally came back!" Ross said as he dapped up each of the men. Mike didn't bother to dap him up because his eyes were glued on the girl's ass.

"Fuck it look like, nigga?" Growl said stepping past the girl with the stanky pussy on the floor. "And we still ain't find this bitch."

"Aye, Ross, we can hit that?" Mike pointed to the girl on the floor.

"Yeah...niggas been in and out of that thang all night though, so fuck her at your own risk.

Hearing this the woman popped her left ass cheek and then her right. Loving the scene Mike smiled, dropped to his knees, kissed both of her ass cheeks and whipped out his dick. No condom covering his rod, he plowed all nine inches into her pussy. Rook looked at Growl and the both of them shook their heads at Mike.

"That niggas dick gonna fall all the way off," Rook said.

"Ross, let me holla at you for a minute," Growl replied as Rook followed.

"No doubt. Let's rap in the kitchen."

Growl and Rook dapped up several members of their crew and went into the kitchen to discuss business. Once there Growl got right to the point. "You talk to Swoopes?"

"Naw, I been calling this nigga for the past week. He ain't answering his phone. All he cares about is finding this bitch."

Growl shook his head and said, "What's that chick's name again? The one who told you Yvonna was here."

"Who? Quita?"

"Yeah. Can you get a hold of her?"

"I can do better than that," Ross said. "I can take you to her room."

Quita was in her suite eating vanilla cake batter from a bowl and farting. She had on an ear-set as she ran off all of the day's business to her best friend. She was just about to tell her how fine Kelsi was when someone knocked at the door.

"Girl, I'ma holla at you later." She rose up off the couch and moved for the door.

"Bitch, make sure you call me back, too."

When she got off the phone she opened the door without looking out of the peephole and Growl, Rook and

Ross pushed their way inside. To keep their privacy, they put the *Do Not Disturb* sign on the door and locked it. Seeing this she got seriously nervous.

"Sit the fuck down," Growl said. She obeyed.

"What's going on, Ross?" She looked up at them. "Did I do something wrong?"

"Shut the fuck up, bitch! I'm asking the questions!" Growl said. "Now, where is Yvonna?"

She frowned. Why were they questioning her about Yvonna. They weren't even friends. "I don't know, why?"

"Stop lying, bitch! You told me you watch her daughter back home."

"I do, but I don't know where she is now."

"Look, we got beef with this bitch and we want you to help us get our hands on her." Ross said. "If not, we gonna put our hands on you."

"Me? Why?"

"Don't worry about all that. Just know that if you don't help it's gonna be consequences on your life. Are we clear?" Growl asked.

As she listened to them she knew she had to protect herself. But how? And then she remembered Kelsi's gun. But getting it would be next to impossible; they barely let her in the room to use their bathroom. For now she would have to comply, until she could think of a better plan.

"Okay, what I gotta do?"

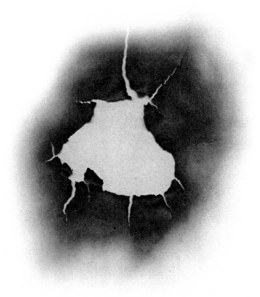

Shyt List IV

Sin City

Yvonna

It was in the mid afternoon and Yvonna decided to shake Onik off so she could grab a drink alone. She was stressing about Delilah and she prayed that her only child didn't suffer from her ailment. The moment she walked to the bar, a man she'd seen before stopped her. He was wearing a pair of blue Polo swim trunks and a red towel hung over his right shoulder.

"I knew I was gonna see your ass again," he paused. "I swear I should drop your mothafuckin' ass right here!" He said as he stepped closer.

"Who are you?" She stepped back.

"You don't remember me? After what you did to my ride you don't know who I am."

Yvonna suddenly remembered the day, when she was rushing to handle business that she ran into a BMW. And if that wasn't enough, she cried rape and hit him in the head with her car door, minutes before leaving the crime scene.

"I remember you. But the real question is, do you remember me?" She was cold as ice. "Don't fuck with me, nigga. I'm not the one. Oh, and how's the head?"

He stepped back, smiled and smacked her down. A few people pointed but no one bothered to help her. Yvonna immediately considered Yao, and how important it was to finish his mission. *Stay out of trouble, stay out of trouble, stay out of trouble.* She chanted. *Let him walk now, and get that ass later.*

Yvonna stood up, smiled and said, "You just signed your own death certificate, nigga. Remember I said that shit, too."

The man laughed thinking she wasn't as big and bad as she was the day he first met her. She'd soon prove him wrong.

After dealing with Mr. BMW, she walked to the bathroom in her suite to take her medicine, only to find out the bottle was empty. Had she used them all? *I can't worry about that right now.* She thought throwing the bottle in her purse. She couldn't get over what happened with Mr. BMW and seeing him made her realize that more people she knew was probably in Vegas than she realized.

When she opened the door to Delilah and Boy's room, she thought she was talking to him. But once the door was fully open, she saw Delilah sitting on the bed with her back faced her. She was swinging her legs and talking to herself.

"No. I'm not going to do that, Ra Ra." She frowned. "I don't want to hurt him. You can't make me. My mommy said it's not nice."

Silence.

"Please, don't make me do that." She pointed at the space. "I want to play nice. I want to be a nice person."

Yvonna was so devastated by what she had seen that she covered her mouth, slowly closed the door and tried her best to prevent the tears from flowing down her face. She was so distraught that she didn't see the real Gabriella standing behind her.

"Yvonna, are you okay?"

Yvonna released the doorknob, turned around, and said, "Oh, my God! She...she has my curse." Vulnerable, she wrapped her arms around Gabriella and hugged her tightly. "I can't believe she has my curse!"

"Come here, Yvonna. Please, sit down."

Yvonna and Gabriella walked to the table and sat down. Although she didn't see Gabriella regularly, she missed her. It seemed as if every time Gabriella wanted to be alone with her, Yao would send her on a mission or his people would be around. For that moment Yvonna was grateful she decided to pop up in Vegas to spend some quality time with her. It was a surprise that Terrell and she had put together and she was glad they did.

Gabriella waited patiently for Yvonna to relax before she said a word. It was just like it was when they were kids. Gabriella was the protector, and Yvonna needed to be saved. Onik stood by the door staring. He learned a long time ago to avoid jumping into every emotional issue Yvonna had. He only made a move when she called on him.

When Yvonna calmed down, she said, "Onik, wait outside the rom." He did. "I'm sorry. I know I'm a mess right now."

"Don't worry about it, just tell me what's wrong, sweetie. You have to talk to me slowly."

"I...I hate my life. I thought by having money, and being able to afford suites like this, and cars like the ones at home, that all my problems would go away. And now that I have everything, I realize all I really want is for my baby to be safe and happy."

"Yvonna, you have to slow down...."

"I am slowed down." Yvonna snapped, not being able to take anymore of the slow down shit. "But are you listening? I said my baby is messed up and it's all because of me."

"Listen," she said softly, "by slow down, I mean for you to slow your life down. You have to focus on what's important." She softly put her hand on her knee. "Yvonna, you are not well. Neither one of us is for that matter. We experienced a lot and we never had a chance to deal and heal. One minute we were eating rats and living beneath a church and the next minute we're adults." Gabriella paused. "I been running all my life, hoping they wouldn't get me," she paused looking out into the distance, "and in a sense you were, too. We have never really felt safe."

"I hate that life dealt us this hand."

"We gotta move on." Gabriella smiled, hugging her again. She paused and said, "When are we going to take that vacation we wanted? Away from everybody? I just want to get you alone to talk about things we can't tell others."

"Whenever I can get a break." Yvonna shrugged. "I really would love some girl time, plus I have so many questions I need answers to."

"I know. But some of the questions I can't answer, because I'm not ready."

Her hesitation about speaking about their time as kids angered Yvonna but she let her be. But soon, whether she wanted to or not, she was going to give Yvonna the answers she wanted. Yvonna was plagued with so many questions about that period in her life. Like why didn't she take her with her, when she escaped?

Changing the subject slightly Yvonna asked, "Do you think...I mean...do you think they are still looking for us? It's been like five years since Terrell found you. Is it possible that they may still want us dead?"

"Like I told you then, Yvonna, a lot of established people have children who were raised in that church. And they paid a lot of money for them, too. If they even think there is a possibility that we may know who they are, they won't hesitate to kill." Gabriella said with seriousness in her eyes. "I had to move thirty times since I left that church. Thirty times, and there ain't a day that goes by, that I don't think that today might be my last day to live."

Yvonna felt bad, she was so busy worrying about her own problems that she didn't stop to think that Gabriella was hurting too. "You were always good at hiding. And running," she laughed, "I'm still surprised Terrell was able to find you."

"He got in contact with the right people." Gabriella said. "So what, you're not happy I came back in your life?"

"You know that ain't hardly it." She playfully hit her. "How can we move on with our lives?"

"I don't know, but I wish I did."

"I never asked you this before, Gabriella. But…do you know who any of the children are now? The ones who have famous families?"

"Yes. I wrote down the names of all of the children that were sold. And I have the information in a safe deposit box in a small town called St. Augustine in Florida. I've had something to do with ten of the locations closing, and before I die, I want to see all of them closed for life."

Yvonna sat back in her chair. "How could you put your life in danger like that? You're messing with people's livelihoods."

"How can I not risk my life? Look at everything they took from me. Look at everything they took from you." Gabriella said softly. "A lot of children in that place committed suicide, Yvonna. They couldn't function. And until I see the person responsible for this madness fall, I won't stop doing what I have to do."

"Do you know who is at the top of all of this shit?"

"No." She said softly. "I don't. We just gotta be careful."

"I want to move. When everything is all said and done, I want to move to a small island in the Philippines."

"Why?"

"No extradition treaty with the US."

"Why would you need that?"

"Gabriella, there is a lot going on that you don't know about me. I mean, yeah you know I suffer from Schizophrenia. But I think I dealt with my issues as a child in a different way. By taking care of people's dirty work. It helps me relieve stress."

"What does that mean?"

"I won't go into detail, but when I finally leave, I would have caused so much havoc in the US, that I need to move to a country with no extradition to the States. The Philippines is one country."

"Are you telling me that you...I mean...that you kill people for a living?"

"Let's just say if we were fictional characters you'd be the hero, and I'd be the villain."

"That Uncle Yao doesn't have anything to do with this now does he?"

"Why don't you like him? You wouldn't believe what he has done for me. I mean, yes he can be a little creepy because of all of his power, but he keeps me safe. I had so many attempts on my life that if it wasn't for Yao, I doubt me and Delilah would be alive today."

"I don't care what you think he does for you." Gabriella persisted. "I don't like him and never will. He gives me the..."

"MING SUCKED MORE DICKS LAST NIGHT THAN TEN HOES ON 14th STREET PUT TOGETHER!" Ming yelled, entering the suite. Yvonna and Gabriella looked at her in silence. When the door closed she said, "What? Did Ming interrupt something?

◄ • ►

Shyt List IV

Yvonna, Gabriella and Ming were waiting on room service when something dawned on Yvonna. Why was Gabriella in her suite when she ran into her after leaving Delilah? Her room was on another floor.

"Morning," Terrell said exiting his bedroom out of the suite. "How are you ladies doing?"

"Fine. About to eat breakfast." Yvonna said. "You hungry?"

"Yeah. Did you order me three pieces of toast and black coffee?"

"I didn't but Ming did," Yvonna said.

Ming smiled when Yvonna told him of her consideration. She had a crush on Terrell for the longest and although he never gave her the time of day, it was not for lack of trying. Having been use to her flirts he winked and said, "Thank you, Ming."

"Fuck thank you," Ming replied. "How 'bout you put something in Ming that will prove your gratitude."

Everyone laughed. "I'll pass for now." He joked entering the kitchen.

"For now?" Ming repeated with hopefulness.

"Forever. I'll pass forever." He continued trying to hide his embarrassment.

"Ming, what's going on with your mother? Are you guys still hooking up next week?" Yvonna asked, saving Terrell from more of Ming's wrath. Plus she really wanted the relationship with her mother to go the way Ming wanted.

"Yes." She exhaled. "Ming is looking forward to visiting again in China next week."

"I'm happy ya'll were able to move past the bullshit. I would kill to have a mother in my life."

"Me, too." Gabriella said touching her hand.

"So, what time is the party tonight? Ming wants to shake her new fat ass."

Yvonna's mind was so wrecked that she forgot all about the party. More importantly, she forgot about what she did to Carmen last night. If things worked out in her favor, before the night was over, Carmen would continue to be held up in a room within the hotel, and unable to attend Brick's party.

Serves that bitch right. Shoulda never been dumb enough to fuck with me.

"The food is here!" Ming said opening the door for the waiter.

The waiter wheeled the cart in and left after Yvonna gave him a fifty-dollar tip. She wasn't being nice; she just didn't have anything smaller.

"Let me go get, Boy. He's probably up now."

When Ming walked through the connecting door to her suite, Yvonna pulled the silver tray off the first plate and saw a note that said, *'Yvonna, read me alone.'*

She snatched the note off the plate thinking the message would be from Yao. And since neither Terrell nor Gabriella knew what she did for a living, she tried her hardest to keep it a secret.

Terrell and Gabriella were laughing it up over breakfast when she stepped outside on the balcony to read the note in private. The sound of the city was heavy as Nevada's heat slapped her in the face. Turning around to make sure no one was coming on the balcony she opened the letter and the message gave her chills.

'I've never forgotten you. I lied patiently in the darkness waiting for the right moment to strike and this weekend you will die.'

Was it Mr. BMW? Was it Swoopes?

"Whoever you are, I hope you know who you fucking with."

Shyt List IV

Sin City

Penny

Penny and Thaddeus sat in a Vegas diner eating extra greasy fried chicken and fries. Although Thaddeus was totally engrossed in his meal, she was nervous about the call she was expecting. The cell phone sat in the middle of the table and she hoped it would never ring.

RING!

With no such luck Penny picked up the phone and Thaddeus seeing the nervousness on her face said, "You want me to answer it?" Food rolled around in his open mouth. "Cause I ain't hardly scared of them people." He sounded ignorant and was clueless about the magnitude of her situation.

"No...no, sweetheart. Eat ya food. I got it." She answered the phone hand shaking the entire time. "Hello."

"Do you have her yet? And before you answer, I'm asking you do you have her in your custody now?"

"N...no."

"Why not?"

"Because we haven't been able ta get next ta her. But I'm in Vegas, waitin' for my chance. It shouldn't be too much longer now."

"If you're in Vegas, and she is too, it should be easy. Between the two of you it should be done already."

"I knows, but I don't too much like that girl. She seems ta think she can handle things on her own. We work best a part."

"I don't care, Estelle!!" He yelled calling her by her government name. Tears filled up in the wells of her eyes. "I told you to take care of this problem when you use to care for her back in the day. But you were so sure she didn't know anything."

"She didn't." The phone shook in her hand. "I'm sure of it."

"You're sure of nothing!"

"I just figured the chile couldn't a known much. 'Cause of the condition of her mind and all."

"That may have been the case then, but that's not the case now. Besides, we all knew you were really trying to get your hands on her child."

"I can't lie, I care for the child but…"

"Estelle Hightower, between the both of you, if Yvonna is not brought to me by the end of this week, you might as well stay where you are. Otherwise I will see to it that I stand over your dead body! And that goes for your boyfriend, too."

When he hung up she saw a woman walking quickly in their direction holding a gun. "Baby, is that woman holdin' a gun?" She asked Thaddeus.

He turned around slowly to see his wife approaching. Without saying a word she fired three shots in their direction. One bullet crashed into a customer's coffee cup, one hit the counter and the last slammed into the cash register.

"Baby, what are you doin'?! He yelled running away from her at the same time. He and Penny caught wheels as they ran out of the diner.

"I'm tired of you cheating on me, nigga! I'ma about to put a stop to this shit permanently." She was trying her best to keep up.

Shyt List IV

Thaddeus and Penny ran into the street missing a cab by inches. His left shoe fell off and flopped behind him. He didn't bother going back to get it, his life was in danger and getting as far away from her as possible was all that mattered.

As they continued to run Penny knew one thing, if they made it out of this alive, whether she liked it or not, she was stuck with this nigga for the long haul. And the quicker she got her hands on Yvonna and got the fuck out of Vegas the better for them both.

Yvonna

Ming, Gabriella and Terrell went downstairs to enjoy themselves before night fell on the city. Although they invited Yvonna, she declined their request knowing that she had other matters to tend to.

Besides, she was in her room preparing to meet with Urban Greggs at his request and figured a little bit of warming him up before she killed him couldn't hurt her mission one bit. Urban was attractive, easy on the eyes and a pleasure to hang out with and since Bricks had been acting up, what did she have to lose? She didn't even know if she was going to his party since she was responsible for Carmen's absence.

She was in Terrell's suite when her cell phone rang. "Hello."

"Yvonna, its Quita."

"Is Delilah okay?" She asked with a concerned tone.

"Yeah, but I wanted to know if you wanted to come over. I'm thinking about making some drinks and stuff."

Yvonna took the phone from her ear, looked at it and frowned. "How you gonna make drinks when you babysitting my daughter tonight, bitch?"

"Uh…I…uh…"

"Quita, do your fucking job and don't call me unless something is wrong with my child."

When she ended the call, it rung again. "Hello." She was irritated.

"Yvonna, I gotta rap to you. You got a few seconds?"

Her heart sped up at the sound of Bricks' voice. There was no doubt about it, she was hopelessly in love with him. "What's up? I'm kind of busy right now," she said, hoping he'd push more.

"I'm coming anyway."

When he hung up she walked into the living room portion of her suite. Onik was standing inside, watching her as usual.

"Onik," she smiled.

"Yvonna," he smiled back.

"You know you don't have to watch me everywhere I go don't you? It's not that serious."

"When it comes to Yao, everything is serious."

Arguing with him was useless so Yvonna went to the bedroom to spray a little perfume behind her ears and on her wrists. But when she searched for her favorite fragrance, she found it wasn't there.

Figuring Ming's bitch ass had taken her shit again without asking, she went into her bathroom to look. But when she opened the door, Gabriella was standing inside facing the bathroom mirror on the phone. Her beige shirt rested over the edge of the sink and droplets of water from the faucet left small stains on the sleeve. Gabriella was so engrossed in her phone that she didn't know Yvonna was looking at her.

"I'm doing the best I can. You gotta give me more time. Please."

When she put the phone down and turned around, Yvonna saw strange scars all over her stomach. It was the first time she'd seen Gabriella's nakedness and she definitely didn't expect it would look like shit.

"Yvonna, what are you doing here?" She asked covering her scars with her shirt.

"What are you doing in Ming's room?"

"Oh…I got a little sweaty after losing some money, and needed to freshen up. So I used Ming's bathroom. She walked me up here and then left."

"That's how you got past Onik?"

"Yeah."

"Why not go to your own room?"

"I don't have perfume in my room and Ming said I could borrow her Beyonce' Heat." Then she lifted the perfume off the counter.

Yvonna looked at the orange bottle in her hand and said, "That's my shit."

She laughed and handed her the perfume. "You know how your friend is." Then she turned around to put her shirt on so that Yvonna could no longer observe her scars.

"Where is Ming anyway?"

Once dressed, Gabriella turned back around. "Still downstairs trying to convince Terrell to sleep with her. I don't know how you deal with her sometimes."

"What you mean?"

"To me it would be hard trying to deal with a friend I know is trying to fuck my man."

"Terrell isn't my man."

"You know what I mean…your ex."

"Ming is going to be Ming and as much as I can't stand her sometimes, I love her even more. You always know where she's coming from because she tells you straight out. I can't ask for more than that."

Gabriella smiled and walked toward the bathroom's doorway and Yvonna let her past. She followed her into the living room. "I get that," she paused, "I just think you need to be careful that's all. I don't trust Yao or his niece." Hearing this Onik frowned. "But look, let me go."

She was acting different and Yvonna was uncomfortable. "Going back to the casino?"

"Yeah. You coming? I'm having a nice time even if I'm losing."

"No. I'm waiting on Bricks." Yvonna sprayed the perfume on her arms and neck and placed it on the table.

"Oh...well, let me go." Gabriella said walking to the door. "Later, babes."

"Later." Something about her felt strange. Real strange.

Yvonna ignored it and five minutes later, Bricks came over and she asked Onik to let him inside. Bricks smelled so good and even though he was only wearing a pair of grey Gucci sweats and a white t-shirt, her knees grew weak at the sight of him. His beard was neatly shaped up, leaving a hint of five o'clock shadow.

"Yvonna, I wanted to talk to you about Yao." His gray eyes looked deeply into her. "But before I talk about all that, did you fuck with that girl?"

"What girl?"

"Carmen, her peoples can't find her."

"Don't fucking ask me about no Carmen!"

"I'm sick of you talking to me sideways. Answer my fucking question before I fuck you up."

Onik adjusted and was about to go for his weapon. "Onik, please wait out in the hall." His eyes said are you sure. "I'll be fine." When he left she said, "Bricks I'm sorry about coming at you like that, but I don't know where she is."

He sat back into the chair and said, "Why you have Ming burn that chick's hair?"

"I know you not still asking me about no bitch I can't stand. You can't be serious. Plus, I ain't have nothing to do with that shit."

He knew she was lying but left it alone. "You know what, fuck all that, I wanna rap about Yao."

"Why don't you wait for the meeting with Yao if you want to talk about him. I got somewhere to be right now anyway."

"Where you going?"

"None of your business." She was about to walk to her room.

"Sit the fuck down, Yvonna."

"Bricks, please stop tripping."

"I swear you gonna make me choke your ass out. Now sit the fuck down!"

Yvonna plopped down on the sofa like a kid not having her way and said, "What could you possibly want to hear from me that Yao can't tell you himself?"

"I just wanna know if you sure about him. I wanna make sure he's on the up and up. You feel me?"

"Bricks, I've been working for Yao for years now, and I wouldn't hook you two up if I didn't think it would work."

"Yeah, but running packages for him ain't the same as dealing with him." Bricks thought she was a runner because that's what she told him.

"I think you should wait to meet him. I want to stay out of this. I mean, this meeting has been in the works for a minute."

"It's like this, remember Cameo, who you met at my party five years ago?"

"You mean the one we got into a fight about? The same nigga you wanted to throw me and my baby out on the streets for, just because I mistakenly brought someone I didn't even know was affiliated with him, to his party? Yeah I remember that nigga."

"Well he came by yesterday to speak to me about dropping his prices slightly more, not as low as Yao's but low. And I'm not trying to get into a situation with Yao that might not work out. Especially if I can move forward with Cameo."

Yvonna was angry with him for putting her in that position. She had given Yao her word that Bricks was good peoples because she wanted to help him out. And now he was about to pull out on the deal? *Doesn't he know what kind of man Yao is?* Yvonna thought.

"Bricks, you a grown ass man. You gotta decide on your own what the fuck you want to do."

"Who the fuck is you talking to?"

"You, because I know you smart enough not to play games with Yao. This is not the kind of man you say you want to deal with and then later change your mind. I mean you do read the papers right?"

"Yvonna, don't threaten me. I respect Yao for the businessman that he is but he breathes just like me."

"I wouldn't put you at risk and I wouldn't waste Yao's time. So if I thought for one minute he couldn't be the connection you needed to make the moves you wanted, I would not have said anything to you."

Bricks smiled. "Is that right?"

"I wouldn't say it if it wasn't so," she paused.

With that he took his cell phone from his pocket and called Cameo. When he answered he said, "What's up?" Silence. "I'ma roll with my current situation." Silence. "Yeah, I'm sure."

When he ended the call Yvonna smiled. "Now, is there anything else you want to talk about?"

"Naw, I'm good."

She saw something in his expression. "Are you sure?"

"It's small shit." He paused. "Last night somebody lifted Kelsi's gun."

"What the fuck?"

"Yeah. I think it's Quita." He said. "Me and Kelsi stepped to this bitch and halfway choked her out and everything. Then we went through her room and her purse. She ain't have shit."

"That bitch called me earlier trying to hang out. What's up with her?"

"She's good with kids but she be on some other shit sometimes." He paused. "I'ma keep you posted though. I don't know what she would need a gun for."

Then her mind went on the letter she received at breakfast again. Outside of the people who were there with her, and Mr. BMW who she ran into, she was pretty sure that nobody else knew she was in Vegas. Still, she decided to ask Bricks if he mentioned she was coming in town to anyone.

"Bricks, you ain't tell nobody I was here right? In Vegas I mean."

"What you talking about? *Everybody* in Vegas this weekend. So if you trying to be secretive you in the wrong fucking city."

"No, I mean you didn't tell anybody I was going to be here directly did you?"

"If you asking me if I held a conversation with somebody else about you, then I have to say no. Outside of Quita, and Melvin didn't nobody *I know* know you was here. My fam know now because they saw you yesterday. But I would never give your position knowing the nigga Swoopes could be anywhere at any time."

Swoopes. She thought to herself. *Did that little message come from you?*

Shyt List IV

Sin City

Quita

U nlike her friends who were living it up in Vegas, Quita had to watch kids during her stay and although Bricks paid her to watch just Chomps, Delilah and Boy, she decided to come up on some more cash by watching the kids of a few drug dealers she knew. It wasn't the fathers who brought their kids all the way from DC to Vegas, but their gold digging ass baby mothers' who were sneaking up on them.

When it came to money she could be greedy and was expensive. She knew you could get your baby watched at any daycare center, but if your kid was bad, spoiled, rich or if you required a sitter at any time of the day or night, Quita's Day Care center was the only center you could trust.

Sitting in the living room portion of her suite, Quita sat on the couch and watched Delilah, Boy, Chomps, Little Davie, Joshua and Miranda play on the floor. Normally she'd be making a drink but the YBM had her brains wrecked with the Yvonna shit.

"So Delilah, what your mom gonna get into this weekend?" Quita asked.

"What you mean?" Delilah asked, looking up from her pink Juicy purse she was busying herself with.

"I know she going to the fight, but where else is she going? I mean, do your mother and your Uncle Bricks got plans together?"

"Dang, Ms. Quita," Boy said, "you awfully nosy today."

"Yeah, Ms. Quita, you doing the most." Miranda said.

"She can do the most all she wants, if my mama ain't tell her her business, she must not want her to know."

Frustrated, Quita threw her body back into the sofa. "There's no reason to get smart, Delilah. Don't forget you still a child. And I'm only asking because I wanted to know how long I gotta watch y'all for."

"My daddy said he paying you right?" Chomps asked.

"Yeah."

"Alright then, you watching us until the money run out."

The kids all laughed at his statement knowing they were too grown for their ages. Still, Quita often acted like a child herself, and because of it, the kids had minimal respect for her.

"Miss Quita, did you know Delilah's mother is crazy? And that she was in a insane asylum." Little Davie said.

Delilah spun toward him and said, "You better stop telling lies on my mamma. If you know what's good for you!"

"She's crazy, she's crazy, she's crazy," Little Davie chanted like a little bitch.

Delilah stood up and stood over top of him. "I'm gonna kill you. If you don't stop it, I'm gonna kill you, Davie."

"Delilah, sit down!" Quita yelled. When she didn't budge she said, "Delilah, sit down now! Or I'ma call your mother." She rarely said she'd call their mothers but when she said it she meant it.

"You gonna stop fucking with me sooner or later," Delilah said, pointing her finger in his face.

"And Little Davie you better stop talking like that." Quita added. "It's not nice."

Having gotten Delilah upset he smirked and said, "Yeah…whatever."

Quita grabbed the remote and channel surfed. After thinking about the YBM she thought about Bricks and the fact that she hadn't been given an invitation for his party tonight. She didn't understand that she would always be the whore, never the girlfriend. Plus who was going to do her fucking job and watch the kids? Bricks had fucked her back in the day and although she remembered it clearly, he didn't.

Whenever she'd come on to him he'd say, *'You want this money or what? Because you watch my son and the money gonna keep flowing. But I don't pay a bitch I fuck.'* Bricks would say.

'The money, Bricks.' She'd respond, mad he wasn't taking her seriously.

When Little Davie went to the bathroom Delilah took this opportunity to step to Quita. "Miss Quita, when Little Davie's mother gonna come pick him up?" Delilah asked breaking her out of her thoughts.

She turned the TV off. "Not sure. Why?"

"Because I'm tired of him picking on me and my brother. If he don't leave me alone, we might have to have a conversation." As grown as the kids were, every time they opened their mouths she was always amazed.

"Well when your mother brings you back tonight so she can go to that party, you can converse with him then."

Delilah frowned. "My mom says conversate isn't a word."

"Well, tell your mother she doesn't have to conversate with me when I use it. Because in my vocabulary it is a word."

"Now, Miss Quita, do you really want me to tell my mother that?"

Grateful for the chance to take shit back she said, "Naw. Don't tell her that."

Delilah smiled and continued on with playtime with the kids. She allowed kids to do and say more around her than most parents would in a year. Figuring the kids were settled, she left them to play with the high tech toys she brought with her from home. Then she walked to the kitchen to prepare a martini. When she drank it all she made another one before someone knocked at the door. Flinging it open she was surprised to see Mike and some girl with a skimpy skirt.

"You got her to meet you yet?" He asked, as the girl hung on to him like a jacket. It was the same slut he fucked on the floor at the party.

"No, she's not really a friend of mine so it's kinda hard."

"Bitch, I don't give a fuck! I want you to hook that up or you gonna have problems." Then he looked into the room. "Wait...one of them kids hers?"

Quita felt the blood drain from her body. Blocking his view with her body she said, "No!"

"Oh, because I was gonna say I know a sure way to get her attention."

"No, none of the kids are hers." She waited for an indication that he believed her and when she saw something fall on the floor, underneath the girl's body, her stomach churned. It was a piece of bloody toilet paper that was used as a pad. "What the fuck is that?"

The girl looked down, saw it and said, "Oh, I ain't have no more pads so I used some tissue." Quita was disgusted.

"You don't have on draws?"

She shook her head no.

"Hook that meeting up!" Mike said ignoring everything. "I'm not going to tell you again." They walked off leaving the makeshift pad on the floor.

Quita closed the door only to see Little Davie drinking the martini holding the stem of her glass. "Boy what is wrong with you?!" He dropped the glass and it crashed to the floor.

"I was stressing so I needed a drink."

"Your father let you drink?!" She screamed.

"Yeah. Sometimes."

"Little Davie go sit down somewhere!"

She needed a break and decided to walk away from the kids to go into her room for some alone time. She had gotten herself into shit she couldn't get out of. It was all her fault the YBM was there because she had an extreme case of diarrhea of the mouth. And it was the exact same reason people who Yvonna didn't want to know she was in Vegas, knew anyway.

◀ • ▶

Some Days Back

"Girl, I knew he liked you!" Quita's hairdresser Coins said as she curled the kitchen part of her hair. "I'm so happy ya'll going together to Vegas. You deserve that nigga, honey. As hard as you worked for him."

"I'm glad too, girl." Quita said. "It's about time he give me a chance." On top of many other things, Quita was a big liar.

"So he ain't messing with that crazy bitch Yvonna no more?" She said holding the iron away from her hair. She didn't want to be so heavy in her concentration that she'd missed what she had to say and burn her ass.

"Naw, but I heard she going to be in Vegas, too. Wait 'til she sees me show up with him." She laughed. "I can't wait to see the look on her face."

The entire shop was on pause because as far as they knew Yvonna didn't take time out to go to fights, clubs or anything else for that matter. To those who heard of her but never got a chance to meet her, Yvonna was something like an urban legend.

"So who running your center while you in Vegas?"

"My cousin got it for me."

"Well have fun girl," Coin said. "Like I said, you do deserve that shit."

The moment Quita's rolled up ass lifted off of the cushion of her salon chair, Coin got on the phone and told everybody who would listen that Yvonna was going to be in Vegas for the fight. One person in particular worked with Penny at the hospital. And another person she told kept in contact with Crystal who would later tell Swoopes. In the end, Quita was responsible for the two people Yvonna didn't want to know, knowing she was in Vegas.

Because of it Sin City was in for a shakeup of biblical proportions.

Shyt List IV

Sin City

The fight was tomorrow and Yvonna had decided to meet Urban in his room like he requested. Although he wouldn't fuck her, because his coach said sex would mess with his energy before the fight, he wanted company.

When she knocked on his door she was surprised to see that his bodyguards weren't around. Normally, Urban didn't go anywhere without them.

"Come in," Urban said opening the door. He gave her a strong hug. "You smell good." Then he paused. "But why you got that hoodie on and shit? It looks like a disguise."

"No reason," she lied.

"You ain't trying to kill me are you?" He joked.

"Boy, please!" She laughed. "And thanks for the compliment on my perfume." She walked further into the suite and he closed the door.

Looking around she said, "Where are your bodyguards?" The TV played softly in the room.

"This is my secret room. They don't know about this one. My coach be on my shit sometimes and I got to get away. It's under a fake name and everything."

She smiled. "So where did you tell them you were going?"

"To catch some air."

Urban was clad in a pair of black slacks, and a black button down shirt. His large muscular arms and wide neck was a little too big for her liking but for the sake of Yao, she'd stare at the wall-necked man all day.

"Come over here, talk to me." Urban said inviting her to the couch in his suite.

Yvonna swaggered over to the couch and they both sat down. She could feel him eyeing the curves of her body and the motions of her hips. A seductress from birth, no man could resist her if he tried.

"You know I ain't think you were gonna see me tonight."

"Why wouldn't I see your fine ass?" Urban said.

She smiled. "Well, I thought you were too busy and you've been acting a little different lately. And plus I texted you yesterday when I saw you giving a girl your number but you didn't answer."

"I'm a boxer, baby. Bitches approach me all the time, but how am I acting different?"

"You told me we would get up before you got to Vegas, and I waited for you but you never called. And just so you know, honey, I hate to be played."

"Well I'm here now, so what you wanted to say to me?"

"I didn't have anything I wanted to say, Urban. Was just expecting you to keep your promise that's all."

"Are you sure that's it?" He said tugging softly at her ear.

She smiled. "That, and the fact that I wanted to see you."

People told her that Urban was nothing more than a moody, fighter but whenever he was around her; he was always so laid back and calm. It was a shame that Yao wanted him killed before the weekend was out. His reason? Three years ago Urban fought Yao's cousin Genghis Kong in an International Boxing match that ended with Genghis being killed. Although everyone said that he died due to a blood clot in his brain that had gone undetected during his many doctor visits, Yao blamed Urban and wanted him to pay. For years Yao tried getting close to him by using people in Urban's camp, to no avail, they were all too loyal. Each employee, from his trainer to his massage therapist, all let Urban know what Yao had been trying to do.

Eventually he told the authorities in an effort to cease the threats against his life but it was hard proving Yao's involvement, and there was no one ballsy enough to bring him up on charges. Yao's sadistic reputation preceded him wherever he went. Through it all, he could never get his hands on Urban.

It wasn't until Yvonna was in a restaurant she'd knew he'd be in cussing a waiter out, that she caught his eye. The fight with the waiter wasn't a part of the plan. As always when Yao sent her on a simple mission, she managed to find a way to make a covert operation open and public.

The moment she stood up and threw the ice-cold water into the waiter's face, Urban knew he had to have her. He could tell by the partially wet Birken bag on the table and Rolex watch on her arm, that she was well kept. Now whether the money belonged to her or someone else remained to be seen.

If he was going to meet her he first had to diffuse the situation. So he spoke to the waiter and they came to a monetary arrangement. Basically he was paid handsomely for her disrespect. Then he sent one of his men to catch the security guard right before he tossed her out the front door.

"I'm sorry, sir, I have direct orders to get her out of here." The guard said to one of Urban's men.

"Get the fuck off of me!" Yvonna yelled at the guard who had not released his hold of both her underarms.

Urban's employee looked at the feisty girl with apprehension. "I understand that you have orders, but I'm with Urban Greggs."

"The heavyweight champion of the world?"

"Yes, sir." He smiled. Then he reached in his pocket and handed him a few bills. "And he's requesting her company tonight."

The man stared at the bills and said, "Uh...I don't know. I think they really want her out of here."

"Had that stupid waiter not told me to shut up just because I asked where my food was, none of this shit would've happened!" Yvonna yelled.

"Young lady, please," Urban's employee said, "relax." She settled down a little, briefly remembering her original purpose, to get at Urban. "Like I said, I'm with Urban Greggs and he would like her company. Now, I can take the money back into the restaurant and have whoever's in charge bring her back inside. But wouldn't you want to make a few bucks and let bygones be bygones?" The guard looked at the money again. "My offer is not going to last always."

With that he immediately released her pits and she shook him off. "Stupid ass, nigga!"

"Come with me," Urban's employee said leading her back into the restaurant.

The moment Urban saw her up close he was happy he'd given the order to bring her back inside. She was more attractive than he thought and he loved the way she wore her clothes. After some light conversation, he invited her out and when she said, "*No, I don't date boxers.*" His dick got hard.

She left shortly after their meeting but not before they exchanged numbers. After a few calls and a lot of persistence on Urban's part, he finally got his date and Yao was excited that he would eventually get his man.

After many years, Yao finally found the woman who could get Urban's attention and take his life. But not before he earned millions after the bet he'd placed that Urban Greggs, the heavyweight champion of the world, would lose. That's why it was important that he be drugged on the day of the fight. He needed him to fight but not at his best and the next day he wanted him killed.

Sitting on the couch with Urban in his suite, she could feel the heat he was throwing her way. With his arm wrapped behind her, he looked over at her. "Give me a kiss." He ordered.

"No." She frowned.

"No?" He said looking at her suspiciously. "What you mean no?"

"You told me that coach said no sex before the fight," she smiled, "so I'm honoring his request by giving you no sex before the fight."

"I said kiss me."

"And I said no."

He softly hit her face with his fist. "Kiss me."

"I said no, Urban. I don't know why you think I'm playing with your ass. You don't always get what you want when it comes to me. I'm surprised you don't know that already."

He then turned to her and said, "I'm serious, I want you to kiss me."

"I'm not about to kiss you, Urban."

He softly hit her in the face again. "You not gonna say yes? Even after I've asked you more times than I've ever asked a bitch before."

His use of the word *bitch* angered her. "All I can say again is, no."

This time he hit her hard enough in the face to force her jaw to shiver. Yvonna was stunned. For a minute she didn't even know what happened. "Urban, what...what happened..."

Before her words could fully leave her lips she was on the floor and he was hovering over top of her. "Kiss me," he said stooping down.

"Urban...why are you doing this?"

He stole her in the face so hard this time that the side of her mouth cracked. Almost as crazy as she was, he smiled at his work, bent down and licked the blood off her face. Then he hit her in the stomach forcing food out of her mouth. She could take a lot of pain, but the pain felt from a gut punch was something else. It was clearly her weakness.

"You know you're so fucking pretty. You got them soft lips like a pussy." He ran his rough finger over her lips. "I love women with soft lips like yours. Tell me something, Yvonna, why are your lips so fucking soft?"

"I don't know." Yvonna said. Her body was trembling and she could not stop crying. Hot tears rolled down her face and she allowed them to wet the carpet beneath her. All she thought about was Delilah and not being able to see her again. Is this how my life will end? Having Delilah made her more sensitive, but if she were to die, she was happy to have experienced real love.

"Tell me something, Yvonna, how long have you been working with Yao?"

Silence.

He knew.

But for how long?

"I don't know what you talking about." She tried to move away a little but he stayed over top of her as she moved a few feet. "Who is Yao?"

He helped Yvonna to her feet by her throat and pushed her up against the wall. Standing in front of her he asked, "How long have you been working for Yao?"

"If I knew who Yao was I would tell you." She sobbed. This was the first time she had been truly scared in a long time. It's one thing to stare evil in the face and prepare, but if you didn't know it was coming you were no match. "I really think this is a mistake, Urban" she smiled lightly, "maybe we can just continue with the rest of our evening. I'm okay, really."

"So you really gonna continue with this bullshit? Even after I told you I know who you are and what you came to do to me? You supposed to kill me right?" He paused. "My men saw Yao walking into your room last night, bitch! We put one and one together and got you!"

He was about to hit her again, when she blocked it with her wrist. Her wrist stung so badly from his crashing blow and she was about to scream out.

He smiled and said, "I see you pretty quick."

"Please...I just wanna go back to my room. I won't tell nobody about none of this. But if you don't leave me alone, I'm gonna have to defend myself. And I don't want to hurt you, Urban. I don't want to hurt you right now."

He stepped away from her so that she could see his large muscular build. He figured the first blow had caused her to go delusional if she thought she could beat the heavyweight champion of the world. Little did he know she was a trained assassin. When she was in China she learned Wushu, a martial art that taught her how to control her pain levels and how to defend herself. What she hadn't worked on however was how to control her anger, despite Yao telling her that handling her emotions was the greatest asset unknown to man.

"You could never hurt me, bitch."

"On the contrary," she smiled. "I can hurt you, and I can hurt you very badly."

"I'm going to ask you again." He laughed, "How long have you..."

Urban was surprised that the wind was knock out of his body so suddenly. She had kicked him in his gut forcing him backwards. Although he was a trained boxer his skills were based primarily on tightening his stomach muscles, expecting solid punches as they came. But now he was caught off guard just as much as Yvonna had been moments earlier from his first blow.

Mad and embarrassed, he grabbed her by the throat and she kneed him in the groin. When he released his hold, she kicked him several more times in his face. She was smart enough to know that although she had gotten a few good blows, she had to land several more and get out of there quick if she wanted to survive.

Running for the door, she wasn't surprised when Urban caught her from behind and knocked her to the floor. Trying to keep her eyes on him she flipped over.

Grabbing her by her feet he drug her on her back and she fought hard to survive. "Get the fuck off of me!" She yelled hitting him everywhere blows would land.

"You stupid, bitch!" He smacked her. "You going to pay for putting your hands on me."

With his words she knew there was no way that both of them could leave that room alive. One of them had to die if the other was to survive. Yvonna thought about Yao and how mad he would be if Urban didn't fight Santiago, but she reasoned that he would understand eventually, with time and a lot of care. It was him or her. It was do or die and it was kill or be killed. So she hit him again, this time in his eyes, temporarily blinding him. Since he didn't have the use of his eyes she decided to finish him off.

"You crazy, bitch!"

She stopped where she was and said, "What did you just say to me?"

"Fuck you, bitch!"

As he spat evil obscenities she tried to figure out the best way to crawl back on top of the huge beast. The fact that they both were covered in blood didn't make matters easy. Everything was slick, bloody and wet. She moved toward the kitchen, and got a little help. For a moment her thoughts went back to the initial plan and Yao's message to her before she got to Vegas. *"Complete the mission I've assigned, get out and get paid, Yvonna. Don't let that temper of yours get you into trouble with me."* Oh yes, Yao would be enraged. But what's a bitch to do? In the end Yvonna fought him tooth and nail, and just as she predicted, only one was able to survive. And it damn sure wasn't Urban.

Yvonna

Yvonna's mind was racked with fear and nervousness as she paced the floor. Not only had she killed a man who stood to make her boss a lot of money, she also killed the heavyweight champion of the world. If she was caught what would happen to her dearest daughter? She loved her and in her heart of hearts, only wanted to see her grow into the woman she could never be.

"Oh, my God! What did I just do?" She paced around his large body leaving bloody footprints everywhere. "Why did you make me do that, huh? What did I just do?"

"You killed his ass," *Gabriella* appeared sitting on the sofa. "Now all you gotta do is get out of here *without* leaving traces."

"But I can't leave. They'll know I was here."

Gabriella laughed. "You were always so indecisive."

"Shut up! Shut up!" Yvonna screamed to herself with the bloody knife used to kill Urban still in her hand. "I gotta think. I gotta think things through."

Gabriella laughed at her. "If you're *thinking* anything, this is about to be a long ass night."

She needed help. But who could she call to help her out of this bind and who would not judge her while simultaneously keeping her secret? Ming? No, she couldn't call Ming because she'd fuck around and say some dumb shit to get herself smacked, killed and put on the floor right next to Urban. The real Gabriella? No, she couldn't tell Gabriella because she didn't know about her lifestyle as a hired killer. Could she call Terrell? No, because once Terrell saw the man lying in his own blood he'd think she went back to her old ways.

No…she needed somebody who could handle death and calm her down at the same time. She needed Bricks. Placing the knife down and taking her cell phone out of her pocket she started dialing. The blood on her hands was drying and becoming sticky.

"Bricks. I…I need your help." Yvonna said. She could hear the music in his background and figured people were already having a good time at his party.

"Yvonna, you know I'm having my joint tonight. I can't help you with nothing right now."

"Bricks, please. I really need you. Can you come to room 2020?" He was hesitant. "Please, baby, I can't do this alone. Come now and wear a hoodie."

Bricks heard the fear in her voice and said, "Give me five minutes."

As she waited on Bricks she looked at the death before her again. If it got out that she killed Urban Greggs not only would people be mad at her, they'd also be mad that she killed the heavyweight champion of the world. She needed to clean up her mess and she needed to do it quick if things were going to work out in her favor.

"Why did you have to hit me?" She asked the dead body pacing the floor again. "And why couldn't you just let me go?"

"He can't answer stupid." *Gabriella* said. "You killed him remember?"

"Fuck you!"

Gabriella laughed.

As promised Bricks arrived in four minutes and 34 seconds in disguise. Yvonna knew this because she'd been watching the clock on the wall ever since she placed the call. When he walked into the room, he fell up against the wall when he saw the champ on the floor.

"Yvonna, please tell me Urban Greggs is not dead than a mothafucka on the floor." He said as sweat formed on his head. "Please tell me you ain't kill the champ."

Silence.

"Why you not saying nothing?" He asked. "You hear me fuckin' talking to you? Answer me!"

"You said not to tell you that the champ was dead on the floor, so I ain't say shit."

"You playing with me?!"

"I'm not playing with you, Bricks." She said anxiously. "But you can see with your own eyes that he's dead. And I need your help." He paused and stared at the TV for a moment trying to get his thoughts together. "But if you gonna come in here and judge me then just walk back out the fucking door. And don't worry, nobody will know you were ever here. That's why I told you to wear that hoodie."

He thought about leaving her crazy ass the moment he walked through the door but she was his baby, and there was no turning back now. "What happened to your face?"

"He tried to kill me." She cried. "And I defended myself."

As if he remembered something he said, "Hold up, what the fuck is you even doing in here with this nigga?"

"Bricks, please! If you don't want to help just leave!"

Silence.

"I'm in too deep to leave you, plus since I seen this shit, I gotta make sure both of our tracks are covered." He paused looking at the champion once again, "Okay, who knew you were coming here tonight?"

"Nobody."

"So Terrell doesn't know you came here tonight? Ming? Gabriella? None of them bitches?"

"No, none of them knew I was meeting him here tonight."

"Good. That's good." He said moving around so that he could think straight. "Okay what did you touch while you were here?"

"Outside of the knife and the doorknob, I don't think I've touched anything. When I came in I went straight to the couch and the next thing you know he's hitting me in my face."

"This nigga actually put his hands on you?" He asked as if he could kill him again. "I can't believe this shit."

"It's true, baby and that's how it all started." He stared at her bloody face and softly touched her.

"You did what the fuck you had to do, babes." Then he started walking around. "Okay this is what we gonna do, we gonna wipe down everything anyway. Then we gonna walk out of this room as if nothing happened."

Silence.

"I'm with you, baby, but that's not gonna be enough."

"What you mean?"

"Somebody is going to have to be framed for the shit. If not, it's gonna fall back on me."

"Yvonna, there's one fucking problem with your plan. We ain't got nobody to frame." He paused. "So let's just get the fuck out while we still can."

"No," Yvonna said shaking her head, "I don't want this shit floating over my head. I need someone to take the fall for this shit. If I don't Yao is going to kill me."

"What?"

"I gotta be honest with you, I was supposed to drug him before the fight and kill him afterwards. He killed

Yao's cousin and he's been after him for some time now. But since he's dead, baby, if I don't frame somebody else, he's going to know I was involved. I can't have this over my head."

"You stay getting into shit!"

Just when he said that Yvonna's head whipped in the direction of the TV. There was a commercial on that held her undivided attention.

"Please don't hurt me! I'm sorry." A well-known actress said while standing over a less popular one with a knife.

"You should have thought about that before you crossed me. Now you must die."

After the dialogue a black screen covered the TV and red words floated in slowly. The name of the movie was 'Be Careful Who You Cross', based on the Yvonna Harris story. It was premiering on the Lifetime channel in a few days.

Yvonna was beyond angry. She remembered the day Mora Flasher and Tim Spicer came to the house she shared briefly with Dave to get her story. Now it appeared as if they started the project without her.

"Babe, what the fuck was that?" Bricks asked upon hearing her name. "They making a movie after you?"

"I don't want to talk about that!" She snapped. "I gotta stay focused." She turned the TV off.

"Are you sure you okay with that shit?"

Ignoring him she said, "I got a plan." Yvonna got on the phone and called Phillip who was holding Carmen in the hotel. "Hey, I need you to bring Carmen upstairs, Urban Greggs wants her." She told the man. Bricks looked at her suspiciously having heard the name.

"Urban Greggs? Why wouldn't he ask her to come himself?"

"Because you've been holding her for a while that's why."

"I don't know about this."

"Nigga, do what the fuck I asked and bring the bitch upstairs to room 2020. And if I were you, I wouldn't say shit about this. You feel me? You don't know nothing and you ain't hear nothing." She slammed the phone down and tried to avoid Brick's knowing eyes. "Stop looking at me like that."

"Shit just keeps getting worse with you."

There was a knock at the door and she looked at Bricks seriously. "I need you to follow up on whatever I do okay?"

"Yvonna..."

"Are you gonna fucking help me or not?!" She yelled interrupting his sentence.

"What the fuck I tell you 'bout yelling at me?"

"I'm sorry, I just want you to know it's too late. We gotta push forward." She paused. "Now let me get the door."

When Yvonna opened the door Phillip was on the other side with Carmen and she snatched her inside of the room. Once she was inside Yvonna hit her in the stomach and followed it up with a few rough blows to her head using her feet. But Carmen wasn't giving up easily. She fought for all she was worth until Yvonna with all of her special training finally got the best of her. Carmen was lying on the carpet before the wig that rested on her head flew off causing Yvonna to laugh hysterically.

"What is going on?" She cried. "Why are you doing this to me? Bricks?" She looked into his eyes for help yet he turned away. "All I did was spit on your shoes."

"No, whore, you did more than that. You set me up and had me detained for hours. Payback's a sexy bitch ain't it?" She paused. "Now, put her in the chair, Bricks."

He looked at her like she'd lost her mind, which she had. "Please." She said nicely, "Can you please put her in the chair."

"I thought you ain't know where this chick was? When I asked you about her earlier."

"I lied."

"Bricks, why are you letting her hurt me like this?" Carmen interrupted. "I thought you liked me? Please, baby. You gotta stop her before she takes things too far." He ignored her; it was tough enough as it was having to clean up Yvonna's shit. "Bricks, please don't do this to me. I...I don't know what's going on. But whatever I did, I'm sorry." Carmen sobbed.

Bricks couldn't lie, she was tugging at his DC heartstrings but there was nothing he could do. He had to trust that Yvonna had a plan that would work.

"Hold her down." She told Bricks.

Carmen fought a little but all her attempts ended in vain. When Bricks had her secure in the chair, Yvonna slit her wrists and watched the blood drain from her body until she was unconscious.

Standing back to look at her work Bricks said, "Who are you? Really?"

"I'm a paid assassin, baby." Then she smiled. "You still love me?"

He shook his head and avoided her humor. "A whole lot of shit gonna come back after this. You ready?"

"But it ain't gonna come back to us. Now let's wipe the room down like you said and get the fuck outta dodge."

They made sure all their prints were off every place in the room, and then they took the knife used to slit Carmen's wrists, and used to kill Urban and placed Carmen's prints all over it. If they'd done their job right it would look like a murder-suicide.

"I can't believe we doing all this shit." Bricks said looking over at Yvonna who seemed distraught.

"I went too far didn't I?" She asked, as if she hadn't past the point of *far* a long ass time ago.

"You did," he said breathing heavily. When it appeared that she was on the verge of breaking down he said, "But shit gonna be alright."

"He's gonna kill me. Yao's gonna fucking kill me if he finds out about this."

"He won't find out."

They were just about to leave when the door opened slowly. Thinking quickly, Yvonna grabbed the wig off the floor and made sure to put the bang over her eyes while Bricks hid behind the door. Yvonna prevented it from opening wide only to see the maid.

"Can I turn down your bed for you, mam?" The maid asked.

"No! Get the fuck! We want our privacy."

"Oh…okay, I'm very…"

Yvonna almost slammed the woman's lips in the door she shut it so fast.

"Now can we get the fuck out of here?" Bricks asked. "Before somebody else come up in this bitch."

Yvonna

Yvonna was nervous as she rushed down the hallway toward her room. Things had gotten out of hand and although she knew the world would be rocked after learning of his death, she hoped it wouldn't happen until tomorrow.

She and Bricks had decided that in order to create an alibi, it would be best if they both went to his party and tried to act normal, but first she had to clean up. Deciding to go to her room to get dressed for his party; she searched nervously in the pocket for her key. *Oh shit. Where is it?* She thought searching her pocket again. *Please say I didn't leave it in Urban's room.* Yvonna was famous for losing her room key; she exhaled when she dug deeper into her pocket and found it.

When she walked into the room she almost fell out when she saw Gabriella riding Terrell's dick on the couch. Not believing her eyes, Yvonna walked further into the suite in total disbelief. It wasn't until the door closed behind her that they stopped the motion of their oceans and saw her standing there. Was this really happening? Or another figment of her imagination.

"Oh my God!" Gabriella said jumping up covering her body with one of the couch pillows. "We…I…I mean, I thought you were at Bricks' party."

"So you decide to fuck my man in my room?"

"Your ex," she reminded her kindly. "Remember you told me ya'll weren't together no more earlier today. And that you didn't care if Ming fucked him or not."

"That was Ming. This is you." Yvonna said approaching her, wondering what she would do next.

"Yvonna," she put her pants on, "if I had known you still cared about him," she put her shirt on, "I would not have slept with him," she put her shoes on.

"You still care about me?" Terrell asked. "And what happened to your face? Why are you covered in blood?" They had already seen too much and taken up too much of her time.

"I bust myself in the face." She lied. "And no, I don't care about you."

She would not give him what he needed to sleep better that night. Plus she was too angry to decide how she felt about anything at the moment. Although Terrell and she were not together, he was her ex-boyfriend and as far as she knew, ex-boyfriends were off limits to friends. The last bitch (Sabrina) was killed for fucking her man (Bilal) when they were supposedly not together anymore. She took any dick she hopped on or off seriously.

Deciding to wrap her hands around Gabriella's throat, she remembered she'd just killed earlier that night. Certainly she couldn't kill so quickly and get away with it.

Biting her tongue, literally, she said, "If ya'll were gonna disrespect, the least you could've done was gone into your suite." She walked past them and they couldn't believe she didn't go off.

Once in her room in her peripheral vision she saw them scrambling to get themselves together but she was on to the next thing in her mind. She closed her door hoping they wouldn't bother her with the, *'I'm sorry, we didn't mean to hurt your feelings'* bullshit. Just when she threw the wish up in the air, it came back with Gabriella knocking on the door. She entered without asking.

"What?" Yvonna asked locating a change of clothes.

"What happened to you?"

"Mind your fucking business."

Gabriella dropped her head. "Can we talk?"

"Well I know why you don't like Ming. You both have a crush on Terrell."

"Please...can we talk?"

"Do I have a choice?" Yvonna removed the clothes with the bloodstains on them and balled them up. Then she went into the bathroom and ran a tub of water. The thing was, Gabriella didn't move a bit.

"Are you going to say something?" Yvonna asked bending over to adjust the temperature of the water. "Or just stare at me?"

"I want to know if you're mad."

Yvonna laughed, and slid in the warm water before the tub was full. Blood from her hands and face ran into the tub turning it a slight pink. For some reason whenever she was mad she got a kick out of people seeing her naked.

"Look, Gabriella, you fucked Terrell and that's that. But on the real, I don't feel like a whole lotta shit tonight. I got a lot I'm dealing with."

"I know, but Yvonna, it's not what you think between me and Terrell."

"Let's see, I think you were fucking my ex-boyfriend raw, on the couch in my suite. Now I know I have a mental condition, so please forgive me if I'm a little confused. If that's not what I thought I saw than what really happened?"

"You did see that but that's not what I meant. Me and Terrell are in love." Silence. "We are in love, Yvonna. And it's been that way for some time now. We wanted to tell you but we didn't know when would be the best time."

Taking the rag out of the tub she threw it at her. It landed on her face and dampened her shirt.

"Get the fuck out of the bathroom!" She pointed to the door.

"I deserved that," Gabriella said throwing the wet, bloodied rag to the floor. "And I'm sorry you're not happy for us. But acting this way won't change things."

She was about to leave when Yvonna said, "How long have you been with him?"

She turned back around and faced her. "For about six months now."

Since she wasn't really in love with Terrell and she wanted Gabriella in her life, with time she was willing to overlook a little fucking, but she needed Terrell on a daily basis. If he ran off into the sunset with Gabriella, who was going to help keep her illness at bay?

"So here it is, after all this time I thought you were back in my life to be with me. When for real you were here all along to fuck Terrell?"

"What sense does that make, Yvonna? When he came looking for me I didn't even know things would progress between us."

"So that's why you really in Vegas? To fuck Terrell."

Silence.

Yvonna bathed, threw on a fresh pair of True Religion jeans and a Gucci t-shirt. Then she did her make-up to conceal the bruises. When she was done dressing she combed her hair and grabbed her oversize black Gucci purse.

"I don't want to lose you as a friend, Yvonna."

Yvonna laughed. "You and Terrell can fuck ya'll selves into prime time TV for all I give a fuck. Just stay out of my way."

When she left the room *Gabriella* appeared. "I don't trust her. You betta watch our backs."

◀ •• ▶

Bricks' Suite, Bricks' Party

Bricks party was fully crowded when she walked into the suite and Melvin was staring at her with daggers in his eyes.

"Damn, who bust you in the face, bitch." He mouthed.

She waved at him and closed the door behind her. Seeing her troublemaking ass caused all of Bricks' family members to stop what they were doing to momentarily stare.

"What are you doing here?" Kelsi asked stepping up to her. "And who fucked you up?"

"I fucked myself up." Yvonna moved further into the suite, giving him her ass to kiss. "Where is Bricks? And before I forget I don't want you talking to my daughter no more."

He smiled. "As cute as that little girl is, I can't believe she popped out of that pussy of yours."

"Nigga, you don't know shit about this pussy. Now where is Bricks?"

"He went to check on Chomps and the kids."

Happy he went to check on the kids, she sat down on the sofa. It wasn't long before the flowing liquor caused his family members to forget she was even there. Soft chatter about who was going to win the fight between Greggs and Santiago made her stomach churn, as she thought about the two dead bodies she left on the suite floor. Little did they know, their money would go to waste if anybody were to bet on Greggs and the person responsible for their loss was sitting on the sofa.

"Hey, Yvonna," Tina said walking up to her. "When did you get here?"

"I been here." She lied working on building her alibi. Tina sat next to her.

"How you been here when you just walked in?" Kelsi asked jumping into a conversation he wasn't invited in to. He held a drink in his hand.

"It don't matter anyway because I'm not talking to you." Tina responded looking at him. "And since you so busy breaking off relationships because somebody told you to, I'm not trying see your fucking face."

Yvonna looked at Kelsi and broke out in laughter, "Bwwwaaaahhhhhhh!"

"I can't believe you mad at me. You got a fucking nigga!"

"What I'm really mad about is that you not your own man, Kelsi. I was fucking feeling you and you act like that ain't mean nothing to you." With that she walked away and he didn't follow.

"Seems like you got a way with the ladies," Yvonna laughed.

"Whatever." Taking the only available seat on the sofa Yvonna stole looks at him. Although she couldn't stand him, she couldn't deny that he was very attractive. His hair cut was neat and it would appear that not a hair on his head was out of place. He was clad in the finest fashions and appeared very confident when he did the simplest of actions like folding his arms.

"Why don't you like me?" She asked turning toward him.

He frowned and turned toward her. "Are you serious?"

"Yeah. What did I ever *really* do to you?"

"You want me to answer that shit for real? 'Cause what I got to say won't be nice. I ain't 'bout to sugar coat shit for you. I'm not fucking you...my man is."

"Nigga, is you gonna answer the question or not?!"

He nodded and said, "From the moment I heard your name you been a problem. I remember when Bricks called me some years back, when I lived in New York. We was on some business shit and I could hear you in the background acting like a bitch."

Yvonna was confused because she couldn't recall the place or time. "You sure that was me?"

"Yeah, it was you. I don't forget a face or name." He paused. "As a matter of fact, he had to tell you to sit the fuck down or somethin' like that. Called you crazy and some more shit."

She would let the crazy shit pass because he didn't know any better. Not to mention she'd reached her dead nigga limit for the day. But if he talked sideways in the future she'd have to deal with him too. "So you made an assumption about the kind of person I was, without even getting to know me."

"I made an assumption off of how my mans was talking to you. He don't usually get too hype so I figured you had to be bad news. Then there was the drama at the hospital when he was shot because of some nigga you know."

Yvonna thought about how Swoopes had shot him in his own home and shook her head. Even to this day she hated having come so close to losing him.

"I think your reasons are so fucking stupid. You need to draw your own conclusions instead of basing your opinions off of shit you don't know. You such a fucking jerk."

"What did you just say to me?"

"I called you a jerk."

"Fuck you, bitch!"

"No, fuck you!" She yelled pointing at him.

Immediately there was a sexual tension between them. It was so strong that she stood up, got a drink and looked back at the couch. When she turned around he was gone. Maybe he felt it too and needed to splash some water on his face.

When Ming finally got to the party Yvonna was relieved. Finally she'd have someone with her to keep her mind off of everything. "Bitch, look at all these fine ass niggas in here!"

Yvonna yoked her up. "Look, winch, you might be able to get away with a few nigga calls around me, but you can't do that shit in public. Because contrary to what you may believe that fake ass you bought don't make you black."

"Alright, alright. Ming sorry." She snatched away from her. "But what's wrong with you?"

Not being able to give her all of the troubles of the day she decided to drop the less important one. "I caught Gabriella fucking Terrell." Disappointment washed over Ming's face. "What's wrong with you?"

"Why does he fuck Gabriella and not Ming?"

"Bitch, I don't know. But it's fucking me up that she would do me like that."

"Why? I thought you said you were through with him."

"Well I lied."

Ming saw the seriousness on her face and said, "Gabriella is a good friend. And shit happens. You shouldn't let this break up bond."

Yvonna couldn't get over how helpful she got when she needed her the most and decided that in the future, she'd trust her with more life changing matters. "Well, I don't know about all that. Right now I gotta keep my head straight on some other shit."

When Bricks came into the party he didn't look himself. Yvonna walked up to him and said, "The kids okay?"

"Yeah."

He walked past her and into his room. "Ming, I'ma be right back."

She knocked on the door but he wouldn't open it. "I'ma be out in a second."

"Can I talk to you?" She spoke at a closed door.

"Not right now, Yvonna. Give me a minute."

It was obvious that Bricks was taking the champ's death harder than she thought. She just hoped he'd get over shit quickly.

She walked away from the door to see Ming mingling with Melvin. *I guess he don't have a problem with her even though he can't stand my ass.* She thought. Grabbing another drink, she couldn't wait for the affect to take hold of her body. Yao was going to kill her when he found out about Urban. To make matters worse, Kelsi and Melvin ice mugged her everywhere she went. And when she couldn't take their stares anymore she put her drink down and raised her shirt revealing her titties. That got them to stop staring real quickly.

She laughed and when her phone rang she answered. It was Yao. "I'll be meeting your friend soon. Is everything okay?"

"Yes, Yao. Things are in order."

"I'm on my way up."

When she hung up she told Ming that unless she wanted to run into her uncle that she had to get out of dodge. The moment she mentioned his name Ming flew out the front door. Alone with her thoughts she knew she had to take it easy, after all, she was playing hostess for Yao and Bricks. She hoped no evidence of the fact that she killed the champ showed on her face.

She was about to alert Bricks that Yao was on his way when he came out of the room. "Yao is on the way up."

"I know." He said walking past Yvonna and into the living room. "One of his people just called me."

Yvonna stopped him and grabbed his hand. "Are you okay, Bricks? I mean, we still cool right?"

"Yeah." He took his hand from hers. "Never better."

She snatched him again. "What the fuck is wrong with you?!"

"You lied to me!" He yelled not caring who heard because he was in the presence of his family. "I asked you did you know about that bitch and you lied." He paused. "If you ever do some shit like that again, we through!" He walked away leaving her stunned.

Melvin opened the door for Yao. The moment he entered, his presence seemed to fill up the suite as he and five members of the Mah Jong Dynasty followed.

Once he was inside, the music was immediately turned down and Yvonna went to greet him. He hugged her and then massaged her shoulders as always. "What happened to your face?" Yao asked looking at Bricks. Bricks shifted a little.

"I fell, Yao. He would never do something like that."

"He better not," he said touching her softly. "Oddly, with the bruises you are even more striking. How is that possible?"

"I don't know Yao, but they say beauty is in the eyes of the beholder."

"I guess I'm beholding your beauty then." Bricks wasn't feeling his advances on Yvonna but there was nothing he could do about it. She didn't belong to him.

"Uncle Yao, I would like you to meet Bricks." She softly took his hand and walked him over to him. Bricks' men, including Kelsi walked behind him. "He's been waiting to meet you."

Uncle Yao extended his hand and Bricks shook it firmly. "And I've been wanting to meet him, too." Yao said. Then he clapped his hands together. "Now that we're all here, let's get down to business."

Shyt List IV

Washington, DC

Bilal Jr

AJ's building smelled of fried chicken, old trash and pine sol as Bilal crept slowly up the stairs. But he finally made a decision after hiding for hours and the time had come. He had to tell AJ that someone had stolen his work and that he'd do what he could to make it up. He was confident that the proof was in his bruised and battered face. Rozay's brothers had smashed his fingers, blackened his eyes and bloodied his lips. And when they were done with the lashings, they stole his work before taking him into his house and stealing the money he'd saved up for his car. Which they knew was under his bed, courtesy of Rozay.

Creeping up the stairs, he knocked on AJ's door using his elbows. His fingers hurt so badly he was sure they were broken. When the door opened he wasn't surprised, just scared, when Dirk appeared on the other side of the door. Together they seemed to do more harm than good. "It's Bilal." Dirk yelled within the apartment. "And it looks like somebody got to him."

Laughter filled the apartment. "Let his young ass in."

Bilal limped into the apartment and the door slammed behind him. He turned to look at it wondering if he desired, would he be able to leave back out of it. Walking deeper inside he slowly approached AJ.

"I know you ain't got my money yet." AJ was sitting at a computer station as his back faced Bilal. He was smoking a blunt and playing a computer game. His keystrokes were steady as he approached his highest score yet. "I mean, I know you fast, but I ain't never known you to turn over work that quick."

"No...I ain't got your money, but I got something to tell you."

The keystrokes stopped and AJ turned around in the chair and said, "Nigga, this bet not be about my money."

"I was robbed. And I'm coming to tell you that I'ma do what I got to, to get your money back."

"I know that. My only question is, why are you here now? Seems to me you should've settled the problem first and begged for forgiveness later."

"I was just letting you know. My girl's brothers robbed me because of what you did to her."

AJ stood up and walked over to him. "So you saying this shit is my fault?"

Bilal backed up a little and when he did, Dirk's body stopped any further movements. Bilal looked back at Dirk and then at AJ. "No, I'm just telling you what happened."

"Oh, because I was about to say, accusing me for shit in my own house costs extra. So if you here to say this shit *is* my fault, I'ma have to add fifteen percent to what you already owe me. Are you prepared to pay that, boy?"

"No...no! I'm not saying..."

Loving his fear he said, "Get the fuck out of my face."

Bilal was on the way out the door until AJ said, "Dirk, give him that other package too." Right before Bilal reached the door, Dirk hit him in the stomach causing the food he ate at the diner to come flying out of his mouth.

Both of them laughed as he crawled on his elbows and knees to the door. When his hand touched the doorknob he screamed out in pain from the condition his fingers were in. However he eventually pulled himself up and leaned on it for support. The punch was harder than he anticipated.

That's when AJ said, "Bilal, if you come back here without my money. I'ma kill you. You understand, boy?"

"Yeah. I do."

Penny

Thaddeus was looking at the TV and had been farting every five minutes. "Can you believe they made a movie about that crazy, bitch!" he said having seen the commercial.

"I's sure can. They paid me some money ta get my point of view. It's been a while but I can't wait to sees how theys do's it."

The room smelled of rotten eggs and fifty day old beef as Penny sat in the only chair in the motel room. Both of them were still on edge after the attempt on their lives. And since his wife was still not found, they weren't sure if she'd make an attempt in the very near future.

"I'm gonna be right back, baby," Penny said to him holding the doorknob.

He removed is gaze from the TV. "What? My gas got you leaving me already?"

"Nawl, you know old Penny love everything 'bout ya. But I gotta handle what we's came ta do. I'ma be right back." She grabbed a few tissues with the motel's name on it to pat the sweat off her face.

"Well be careful, I don't want that crazy wife of mines to find you again."

She briefly considered what he said and responded. "I'm sure I'lls be fine."

Once outside of the room she leaned up against the cold brick wall. Traffic rushed past her as she thought about the ultimate goal. It didn't help that he was working her nerves and that his wife had tried to kill them. The sooner she could get Yvonna the better.

Pulling out her cell phone, she called her coworker who told her that Yvonna was going to be there. The phone rang a few times before she got an answer. "Hello!"

"Gracie, ya got a few minutes, hun?"

"Miss Penny?"

"Yes," Penny said standing up straight pacing back and forth. " I forgot to look at my schedule before I left the hospital. Ya mind checkin' on it for me? I wanna know which days I'm due back in."

"I got you Miss Penny. One second." She waited for her to frivolously check a schedule she already memorized. It didn't take long for Gracie to return. "You off for the next week, Penny. But you gotta come back on Tuesday of the following week."

"Thanks, hun."

"No problem. You having fun?"

"Yeah...but you know I leave all the partying and other foolery ta you kids. But, I am lookin' forward ta the fight."

"Oooohhh, I shoulda let you put some money on Urban for me. I know he's gonna kick Santiago's ass!"

"Ya may be right. But look, didn't you say that chile was gonna be here."

"Who?" Gracie asked slightly confused.

"Yvonna."

"Oh yeah...I hear she staying at the Aria hotel. She may be..."

CLICK.

After Penny got the information she wanted she didn't waste any more time on her ass. Besides, she was sure the other culprit working for the organization was there already. She wanted to be the one who brought Yvonna to them. She immediately caught a cab from her motel to the Aria and once there she went straight to the front desk.

"How ya doing, sweetheart." She asked the Agent whom Yvonna had irritated upon first sight. She patted her face with the napkin again. "My niece is here and I really need to find her. She has me watchin' her kids, and I'm gonna have ta leave ta go back home to DC. My father died and I need ta be there for him."

"I understand, mam," she said liking her instantly, "What's her name?"

"Yvonna. Yvonna Harris."

The Agent smiled slyly. "Mam, I'm not supposed to give out room numbers for our guests here. I can really get into a lot of trouble."

"I know. And I don't want ya ta get into any trouble." Then Penny looked sad and vulnerable. Preparing to turn around she said, "Well, you have a nice day."

Penny was about to leave when the girl said, "Mam, I'll help you." Penny's face produced a devilish smile before she turned back around.

Finally facing the girl she said, "Thank you, hun. I sure do 'ppreciate ya."

As the woman typed the information she needed, Penny spotted a girl with a group of kids. But it was one child, one very pretty child who held her attention. After all, she knew this little girl because she'd raised her for most of her life. "Delilah." She said to herself as tears formed in her eyes. "Is that my dear Delilah?"

Chocolate City

Bilal Jr.

Bilal limped out of AJ's building bruised beaten and battered. He walked a few blocks to his apartment when a car pulled up right before he entered his building. When a strange man wearing an eye patch and a woman walked up to him he wondered how much worse his life could get at this point. He was robbed, had lost his girlfriend and was into his boss for a few thousand. At the end of the day, he needed a plan and more than anything he needed help.

"Hello, Plan B." Swoopes said to Bilal as he leaned against a fence.

"Do I know you?"

"No, and we ain't got a lot of time." He paused looking him over. "But first we gotta get you fixed up."

◀ • ▶

Crystal's Cousin Sarah's House

Swoopes and Crystal had been robbed of everything they owned from the young couple they met in Vegas. And to make enough money to catch a flight back to DC, Crystal had to sell her pussy to three different strangers.

Now back in town, they took Bilal back to Crystal's cousin Sarah's house. It was a quiet house with not a lot of activity since Sarah was out of town in Vegas. Even she had sucked a few dicks and licked a few balls to be able to go.

Being her favorite cousin, she allowed Crystal and her boyfriend to come anytime they needed a place to get away. She didn't ask a lot of questions and they didn't provide a lot of answers. For the most part all Sarah knew was that they were on the run. She was unaware about Newbie, the preacher's daughter that Swoopes killed after she advised Yvonna that he was after her. She was unaware about Kendal, whose body was left dead in an abandoned car in a DC project. She also didn't know that Yao had an open hit on his head because he was trying to kill Yvonna. For sure, she was clueless about everything, and they loved her for it.

Crystal opened the door and said, "Sit down on the couch, Bilal." He did. She cut on the radio. "Hungry?"

Caressing the different parts of his body that were riddled in pain he said, "No, but you got Tylenol?" They had taken him to the hospital to get stitched and bandaged up. He was in extraordinary pain.

"Yeah...I'll get you something."

She went into the bathroom and Swoopes walked into the living room from the kitchen and looked at Bilal. "You know what, you look just like your father. I mean, so much like him its crazy."

Trying to maintain conversation since he had no control over anything else he said, "Nobody I know ever met my father. So it's nice knowing we look alike."

"Fuck alike you look JUST LIKE that nigga." Bilal's outburst startled him. "And I knew your pops for most of my life before he was killed. I been trying to find you for awhile, young B."

Bilal frowned and sat back into the couch. "Why?"

"Because of the bond I had with your father. We were like brothers."

Bilal grew angry thinking about his life. Why out of all of the kids around him, did he have to be parentless? "Well how come I don't have him in my life? How come I don't have no family?"

Crystal walked into the living room and handed Bilal two Tylenol and a glass of tap water. Sitting next to him she said, "You don't have family because of one person."

Looking at her inquisitively he said, "Who?" He took the pills and downed the water before sitting the glass on the floor.

"You see that's what I want to talk to you about. Because Bilal, you are in a bind, and we are too. We need your help and you need ours." Swoopes said.

"You need me?"

"Yes, and in turn I'll help you."

"Help me with what?"

"Anything." Swoopes said pulling up a chair to sit in front of him. "Because just by looking at your face, and hands, I'd say you pretty bad off."

Remembering AJ's threat and his lack of money he decided not to write them off just yet. But first, he had a few questions. "You said you and my father were like brothers. Can you explain?" Swoopes took this time to give Bilal a whole lot of information in a little bit of time. In the end Bilal had a throbbing headache.

"So, my father and mother were killed by this person named Yvonna?" He was confused having never heard of her before.

"Yes. I believe she also had something to do with your grandmother being murdered. And she's the reason why you don't know your brothers."

Bilal's eyes widened. "I got brothers?"

"Yeah, they twins. They live in DC, in the projects. They a little older than you, about twenty something." Swoopes didn't tell him that the twins, who were actually Treyana's sons, once had a relationship with him until he stole their money to buy booze and drugs.

"You got their number?"

Thinking the more they could get him to trust them the better, Swoopes looked at Crystal and said, "Write the number down."

"You sure?" She asked knowing the boys would talk badly about them both.

"Yeah. Go 'head."

She wrote the number down and handed it to him. He observed it closely realizing that finally he'd have some answers to the questions he always wanted to know, and more than anything he'd meet his family. When he tucked the number in his pocket, Swoopes handed him an old article from the Washington Post. It was about the case where Yvonna was charged with Bilal's murder, only to get off a few years later because of her illness. After Bilal Jr. finished reading that article, Swoopes handed him more of how his mother Sabrina and his grandmother Bernice were also murdered. Then another article of how Treyana, his brothers' mother, was killed.

Bilal held the grey papers in his hand, gripping them tightly he said, "I remember my mother a little, but I remember my grandmother more."

"Let me get those up off of you." Swoopes said taking the articles. He handed him a picture in its place. "Now this right here, is Yvonna Harris."

Bilal accepted the picture and suddenly, his mind blasted back to the day when he was at the doctor's office and accepted a soda from a stranger that would later make him violently sick. He later learned that the coke was laced with lead paint and almost cost him his life. "I remember her. She came to me one day when I was at the doctor's office. She said her daughter Paradise liked me and that she thought I was cute." A confused look covered his face. "She had an extra soda in her hand…said she wasn't going to drink it, and I took it from her. That soda made me real sick."

Swoopes grinned. "See what I'm saying? She's an evil bitch."

"Why does she hate me so much?"

"The bitch is crazy!" Crystal chimed in.

Bilal looked at her and said, "If she's responsible for my family's murders, why did she hate them? I mean, did they do something to her?"

"She hates them because she was mad that your parents had you. Your mother and father were married when Yvonna ruined their lives." He lied.

Trying to trust him more he said, "Can you tell me more about you and my father?"

Swoopes looked at Crystal and then at Bilal. He was trying to determine how much to say without digging too much into his personal wounds. There were a lot of things he didn't talk about and even more that he hadn't told Crystal. But for some reason, he wanted to reveal more than he ever had.

"We were step brothers. My father, Poris Mitchell, tried to…," he swallowed the dryness in his throat, "he tried to rape him. Like he raped me. But Bilal fought back and after that, so did I."

Swoopes went on to give him more information about their lives as kids. And when he was done, Crystal and Bilal Jr. sat with their mouths agape. Swoopes hadn't expected to be so honest in his plight to capture Bilal's young mind, but the fact was, he didn't care anymore what any-body thought. In a lot of ways, he was free.

"So what do you want with me? I'm confused." Bilal said.

"We are going to capture Yvonna and pay her back for everything she's done to you. And you're going to lead me to her."

"What? Why me? I never killed nobody before."

"I'm not asking you to kill her. Just lead me to her."

"I don't even know her." Bilal suddenly believed he was in over his head. "I think I wanna go home."

"Fuck home. Where is home for you? If we let you go whoever did this shit to your face and hands is liable to do worse the next time they see you."

He was right. "I...need to think about this. Give me some time."

"You ain't got no more fucking time. We know where she is but we can't reach her unless you help us. She moves frequently so if we don't move in on her now, it may be years before we catch her again."

"I can't do this."

"You don't care that this bitch took your mother, fa-ther and grandmother away from you? You don't care that it was because of her, you have moved from foster home to foster home? Come on Bilal, be a fuckin' man. You would still have a family if it wasn't for her." He paused. "I mean, look at yourself. You fucked up and it's all this bitch's fault." He looked down at himself and grew silent. "Bilal, you owe somebody money and if you don't pay them, them niggas gonna kill you." Swoopes paused. "Now we all the fuck you got! Do you really wanna go back out there on the streets alone?"

"Think before you answer, baby." Crystal said.

"What I got to do again?"

"I'll tell you all that later. First we got to catch a plane tonight."

"Where we going?"

"To Vegas. We already got a room there."

After convincing him to finally come, Crystal's cousin's phone rang and she answered. The caller surprised her. "Crystal, its Growl, is Swoopes there?"

"It's Growl," Crystal said covering the handset.

Swoopes knew they were going to ask him to come back to the YBM so they could use him for the connect information. After all, the connect made it clear that he wasn't fucking with anybody but Swoopes. But since they weren't willing to help him find Yvonna, and constantly mocked him for the hold she had on his life he said, "Tell him I ain't here."

"He ain't here."

"I know the nigga there." He paused. "I heard his voice. Now tell him I'm in Vegas, and we gonna help him get this bitch."

Crystal held the phone and said, "He said he's in Vegas, and they gonna help you get Yvonna."

An evil smile spread across Swoopes' face. "'Bout mothafuckin' time!"

Yvonna

Bricks' suite wasn't jumping like it had before Yao had stepped up in the place. So to put everyone at ease, and since the meeting was supposed to be brief, Bricks took Yao and the other members of the Mah Jong Dynasty to the suite he had reserved especially for the meeting. They had been discussing business for fifteen minutes and it was brief and to the point. After all, Yao had been trying to get a steady pipeline into the area for his drugs and with Bricks and his soldiers, he had just that.

Sitting at the table on Bricks' side was the heavy hitters in the family who lived off of 65th avenue, in Maryland. They were Melvin, Kelsi and Forty, Bricks' oldest cousin. Along with his cousin Jace, whose baby mother Pam, was murdered by Yvonna, without his knowledge. Tracy who saw her mother being murdered by Yvonna was doing well, and kept her secret to this day. On Yao's side were several members of the Mah Jong Dynasty including Onik. And then there was Yvonna.

"I think we're going to do good business together," Yao said closing out the meeting. "I'm impressed with you."

Yvonna smiled feeling relieved the meeting went well. "We appreciate the opportunity. And don't worry, we gonna make a lot of paper together." Bricks said.

"I'm not worried." Yao said confidently. "But if you fuck up," he looked intently in his eyes, "you should be worried."

Bricks looked at his brother Melvin and then Kelsi. "Enough said. But I doubt we'll have any problems on our end."

"Great, then how do you niggas say it, "Let's get this money!"

The room was filled with uncomfortable silence. "Not for nothing Yao, but only niggas can call each other niggas." Bricks clarified. Melvin and Kelsi adjusted a little where they sat and Yvonna squeezed her ass cheeks tightly to avoid shit from popping out.

Everyone was on pins and needles as they waited for Yao's comeback. After several more seconds of silence and rapid eye play between he and Bricks Yao laughed and said, "You are right!" Then he stood up. "I'll leave that name play to you." Then he paused. "So, are you a betting man, Bricks?"

Not knowing where the question was coming from he said, "Sometimes."

"Well who do you have to win the fight tomorrow night?"

Now it was Bricks whose stomach swirled while Yvonna felt as if she would pass out. "I'm not sure."

"Come on, tell me who you think will win."

"Uh...Urban."

Yao looked at Yvonna and smiled, "Good choice, Bricks. Now if you don't mind, I'd like a few moments alone with Yvonna."

Yvonna knew then that Yao was testing her. He wanted to see if she had given him a heads up on who would win the fight, since she was helping him fix it. Yao had no idea that somewhere in that very hotel, Urban was deader than a roach out in the open.

While everyone else cleared the room Bricks didn't move. He wasn't sure if Yao knew what happened to Urban and would hurt her. "You okay?" Bricks asked, bypassing Yao's curious eyes.

"Yeah...I'll be fine." Yvonna said.

Bricks looked at Yao again and slowly walked out the door. The Mah Jong Dynasty stayed outside the room just in case Yao called them. "Yvonna, I see you didn't tell your friend everything." He rubbed her shoulders again. For whatever reason, the massaging of the shoulder blades was his thing. "So you can be trusted."

"What do you mean?"

"Because he couldn't possibly bet against Santiago if he knew my plans for him."

"I told you, I'm loyal to you, Yao. Very loyal."

"Good, because there's something else I want to talk to you about." He paused. "Something very serious."

"Like what?"

He looked deeply into her eyes. "Yvonna, I want you to be my wife."

Fear washed over her and she was afraid that if she didn't have the right answer, he would kill her. After all, how many different ways could one say, 'Fuck no!'

"This mothafucka is crazy!" *Gabriella* said appearing from her right.

"SHUT UP!"

Yao frowned. "What did you say to me?"

He wasn't aware of her mental condition or else he would never have demanded her hand in marriage. "Uncle Yao, I wasn't talking to you. I was..."

"Yao. Call me Yao, Yvonna."

"Okay, Yao, where is all this coming from?" she said trying not to focus on *Gabriella* circling them. "I mean I'm not good enough to be your wife. I have too much going on in my life right now."

"I know you're not good enough for me, so consider it an honor."

"But..."

"I also know," he said cutting her off, "that you know, that I always get what I want. And what I want is you."

"But, I don't think I'm ready for marriage. I mean...it's not for me. There are some things about me you don't know. I..."

Growing irritated with her rebuttals he said, "You have one month to get whatever out of your system you need to get out." Then he squeezed her shoulders again...just tighter this time. "Including that young man out there, because I'm sure you don't want me to hurt him now do you?"

This was exactly what Yvonna feared. Whoever she loved, ended up getting killed or hurt. "I don't know what you mean, Yao."

"Yvonna, don't be coy. I can always tell when a man is in a standoff with me over a woman. It was obvious." He said. "Like I said get him out of your system because after a month, I'm coming for what I want, and what I want is you."

"What about my daughter? I can't up and move her again. She loves our home in Virginia."

"We'll find the best boarding school for her." Yvonna felt heat rush over her body. "To live the life we desire, we can't have her with us everywhere."

Everything he was saying after this point didn't matter, there was no way on earth she was leaving her daughter anywhere.

He released her shoulders and kissed her softly on the forehead. "Don't worry, our time together will be memorable. There are a lot of perks that come along with being my wife."

She was so shocked she didn't hear the next words leave her mouth, "Like what?"

"Like what?" he repeated with a smirk. "For starters no one, and I do mean no one, in the world would be able to harm you without dealing with me and my dynasty. And you'll have more riches than you could ever imagine."

"Oh...," she said not interested in anything he said.

"Now have I made myself clear enough for you, Yvonna? Because I have to say, this is the first time I've had to go into so much detail when I've made a request. That should show you right there how much I care about you."

"Yes. I understand."

"Good, now I know you want to celebrate with your friends, but I don't need you out too late tonight. You have a big job ahead of you tomorrow night. And you will not let me down."

With that he left her alone, with her own thoughts.

Shyt List IV

Sin City

Penny

One person after the other crossed Penny's path in the hotel lobby. Yet her eyes remained focused on Delilah. She couldn't believe how big she'd gotten.

"Delilah," she said softly out of earshot from the little girl, "I miss you."

After getting the information she needed from the Agent, she followed behind Delilah until they walked toward a room. She was sure to maintain her distance. Tears filled Penny's eyes when she thought about how much she missed her, and she decided then, that no matter what, she was not leaving Vegas without her after she killed her mother.

When Penny's phone rang it startled her. "Hello," she whispered backing up against a wall, so that Delilah and the lady she was with would not see.

"Where are you, baby? That woman of mine ain't get ya did she?"

"Nawl...I's still breathin', but I ain't got time to worry about her right now, noway."

"I understand, but look, I'm hungry."

"Thaddeus, I told ya I had somethin' to do. Ya just gonna have to wait now."

"But you didn't leave me no money."

Irritated she went off on his ass. "You know I'm gettin' kind of tired of this now!" She was angry because he had taken her away from the last few moments she had to watch Delilah with his foolishness.

"So you saying you tired of me, huh?"

"Yes!" she said watching Delilah play with Boy. "You too fuckin' needy and greedy!"

"Well maybe I should go home. You know what, I think that's what I'm going to do, since it's obvious you don't want me here. Bye, Penny."

Her heart thumped around wildly in her chest. "Thaddeus, wait! I'm sorry."

Silence.

"Thaddeus, are ya there?"

"Yeah, but I don't know about staying. I mean, maybe I should just go back to my wife."

"Don't leave me," she said softly. "Rememba...who's gonna love you like me?" She paused. "Look, just give me a few minutes and I'll bring you somethin'. What you in the mood for?"

"Fried chicken. And rice. And French fries from that restaurant we went to earlier." He paused. "Oh, and bring me some booze, too. I wanna be right for when we make love again tonight."

She sighed. "Okay, Thaddeus. I'll be there shortly with ya stuff. Now can I call you back? I really gotta do somethin' before I come ta you."

"Sure, honey."

Penny was just about to hang up when he said, "And, Penny."

"Yes, Thaddeus."

"I love you."

"I'm sure ya do, Thaddeus. I'm sure ya do."

Shyt List IV

Sin City

Yvonna

Yvonna drank so much liquor, that she was wobbling with every step. After being forced into a possible marriage with Yao, she was trying to ease her mind but every time she saw Ming and her chinky eyes she was reminded of Yao again.

"Where the fuck is Tina?!" A man asked bolting through the door.

Melvin stood in front of him. "Greek, don't do this shit here."

Spotting her next to the door he said, "You think I don't know you been talking to the nigga Kelsi on the phone? You gave my pussy away?!"

"Baby, it's not even like that." Tina said. "Please don't do this here. I don't want my cousins to kill you."

"Fuck all that," he said. "Now get your shit and come on!" Greek continued.

Melvin stepped to him and said, "Homie, I know she your girl, but she my cousin. And I'm asking you to remember that."

Greek calmed down a little as Tina grabbed her purse. "I will." They walked out of the door arguing all the way.

Fifteen minutes later people forgot all about Greek and Tina as the alcohol continued to pour.

"Ming, maybe you should go home." Yvonna said approaching her as she was talking to Melvin.

"Why? Ming not bothering you." She replied.

"Yeah, Ming not bothering you." Melvin said in her defense. "Just because you not having a good time doesn't mean we should let you fuck up our shit."

Telling Ming to leave because her eyes reminded her of Yao was not only stupid, but also unreasonable. "Ming, I'm gonna leave you to it but I just want to say something," she swerved a little, "If something were to ever happen to me, please take care of Delilah."

"Ming will, but why you say that?"

"Just do it," she said walking off.

Ming looked at her friend until Melvin stole back her attention. Yvonna had one thing on her mind, finding Bricks. By now the party was packed with a lot of his family members, and people she didn't recognize. But when she saw Bricks stumble in his room from the back, she decided that tonight would be the first night they fucked.

When she was sure no one was looking, she snuck into Bricks' room. The blinds were closed, the lights were off, and the room was black. She could hear his snores as he lied in the bed sleep. Since he just went in, she figured he was as drunk as she was to fall asleep so quick. Removing her clothes, she stumbled a little as she got undressed and in her butt nakedness, she climbed on top of him.

"What's going on..."

"Shhhhhh." She said removing his clothes in the pitch-blackness of the room.

Feeling her warm body, he released himself from his clothes from the waist down. When he was ready he felt for her wet spot within the dark and eased her onto his dick. She was soaked as he pounded her over and over again.

"Mmmmmmmm," she moaned, trying not to let everyone outside of the room know what they were doing inside.

The juices from her pussy dampened his entire dick as he slammed in and out of her. Loving the way he stroked, she jumped off of him and ran her tongue along the shaft of his dick. She could feel his body tense up and it was obvious that he loved what she was doing. Enjoying the way his juices tasted mixed with her icing, she didn't want to stop. That is until he pulled her up, turned her on her stomach and rammed his dick into her ass.

"Mmmmmmmm," she moaned again.

He gripped her cheeks and pushed in once, before pulling out slowly. Then he pushed in harder before pulling out slowly again. Her body shivered at the pleasure she was feeling. No one could deny that drunkenness and sex was a great combination. An hour later, they had reached the end of their fuck session and drifted off to sleep. Poor little Yvonna.

Saturday

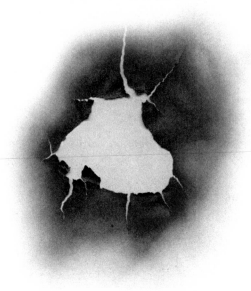

Sin City

Bricks

B ricks roamed the entire hotel before he finally made it back to his suite. Once there, he wasn't surprised when he saw it trashed. A few of his homeboys were lying on the couch sleep and he didn't see Melvin. He knew his cousin Tina was snatched out of the suite last night by Greek after he found out she was checking for Kelsi. He didn't even feel like dealing with the drama that would cause once he got back home.

Ever since Bricks had assisted in the cover up for killing the heavyweight champion of the world, he was fucked up. Murdering wasn't even an issue; he'd done it before and would do it again for her. But never in a million years would he think he'd help cover up the murder of the champ. He wasn't feeling too good about killing Carmen either, but with a little alcohol and a few blunts he was confident that even that feeling of guilt would pass, but the champ was a different story.

Since he was a public figure, he was sure they would have every lead detective in the world trying to solve Urban's case. So partying with his friends wasn't something he was trying to do. Instead, he spent a lot of time at the casino and before he knew it, it was six o'clock in the morning.

He took his shoes off deciding to catch a few hours of sleep before the world got wind that the champ was dead. But when he opened the door to his room, he couldn't believe his eyes when he saw Kelsi and Yvonna lying in the bed naked. Together. Holding each other.

"What the fuck?!" he yelled stepping closer to the bed. Both of them jumped up and it took them a moment to realize what was going on.

"OH MY GOD!!!" Yvonna jumped out of the bed like it was hot and snatched the covers to hide her body.

"Hold up," Kelsi paused looking at Bricks, "why are you over there and she's right here?"

"You tell me?!" Bricks said walking into the room with his fist balled up.

Kelsi grabbed a pillow and covered his dick with one hand. Then he got out of the bed and stuck his arm out to prevent Bricks from doing something stupid. "Man, I don't know what the fuck is going on, but it's not what you think." Then he turned his attention to Yvonna. "Fuck you doing in here?"

"No, nigga what the fuck are you doing in here?" she pointed.

"I can't believe this shit." Bricks shook his head before looking at both of them again. "You fucked my best friend."

"Bricks', I ain't know this bitch was in the room last night." Kelsi pleaded. "I came in here to get some sleep and the next thing I know I was getting fucked."

"And I thought it was you, baby." Yvonna added. "I mean, I was drunk and busted and I wasn't thinking straight. You know we had a terrible night and I needed to be with you." She said with pleading eyes. "So I came into your room to make love to you. Not your best friend."

"Man, this was a mistake that would never happen again. You know I can't stand this bitch!" Kelsi yelled. "The sex wasn't even all that."

"Picture that!" Yvonna said. "Nigga, you was moaning like a baby when I threw this shit on you."

"A baby don't moan, bitch."

"Fuck you!"

"If you ain't think it was her who the fuck did you think it was?" Bricks asked interrupting their feud. The look in his eyes told him what he thought. "You thought you was fucking my cousin Tina?"

"Man, I really did. I care about them peoples and I thought it was her. I was avoiding her all night and couldn't avoid her anymore."

"Just so you know, Greek came through last night and took her up outta here."

Kelsi seemed disappointed. "Man, this is all fucked up. This why niggas don't like to come to Vegas!"

Not trying to kill them both, Bricks left the room. Sure, he could've dropped both of them but the truth was, he believed them. There would be no way on earth, if they were both in their right minds, that they would willingly fuck each other.

"I'm sorry, man!" Kelsi called out.

"Bricks, please don't leave!"

He was gone. Besides, he didn't feel like hearing the story again. The thought of Yvonna fucking anybody but him made his ears and heart hurt. After walking a while, for some reason, he found himself at Quita's door. He knocked several times.

"Who the fuck is it?" She yelled opening the door.

"You always open the door before you know who's on the other side?"

She pulled her robe shut and said, "Sometimes."

He shook his head and said, "Where the kids?"

"They sleep."

"Look, I'm sorry about that gun shit. And going off on you. We cool?"

"Uh...yeah. I guess." She shrugged.

She looked guilty but he ignored it before grabbing her closely and kissing her passionately. It was clearly a revenge kiss and Quita loved every minute of it. He didn't want to do anything but fuck and figured a kiss would do the trick. But when their lips separated he could taste sex on her mouth. "Fuck you been doing?" He said spitting on the carpet in the hotel hallway. "Eating your own pussy?"

Just then Melvin comes from the back of her room and Quita drops her head. "The day I finally get your attention, you're too late." She sighed. "Sorry, Bricks, but I fucked your brother already."

"What up, lil bro? Everything cool?"

Bricks looked at her and then at him and said, "Yeah, man. Just checking on the kids."

Melvin walked up behind her, grabbed her ass and said, "Everything fine in here. The kids good, too."

With nothing else to say, Bricks walked away.

Shyt List IV

Sin City

Yvonna

When Yvonna walked into her suite her head was banging and her heart was breaking. How could she fuck a man she couldn't stand? The worst part about it was, the man was the one she loves best friend. To make matters worse, just hours earlier she had judged Gabriella and Terrell for sleeping together. Now she was learning that she wasn't any better. She was so distraught that she abandoned the hoodie in the hallway thing. All she wanted was some sleep. *What the fuck is it about Vegas that makes niggas go crazy?* She thought out loud.

The moment she walked into her suite she felt something was off. The hair on the back of her neck rose and she grew nervous. What was it? Her curiosity was immediately cured when she saw Ming lying on the floor with two niggas. The tattoo on Ming's back of a black leather whip was the first thing she saw. It started at the tip of her left ear and in a snake like motion extended to the crack of her ass. She shook her head in disgust when she saw the two men in her company. They were lying on their side and Ming was in the middle of them like an ice cream sandwich. Her hair was in a wild bun on top of her head and bottles of liquor were on the floor.

"Why can't people fuck in their own room?" She thought, before remembering she herself had just gotten busy with Kelsi in Bricks' room.

"Ming, get up!" Ming stirred a little before opening her eyes. "Wake up, bitch, and get these niggas out of here!"

When Ming's eyes opened she looked at the man in front of her and the man in back of her and smiled. "Wake up, fellas. It wasn't a dream. Ming has made all of your fantasies come true."

When they didn't move fast enough Yvonna yelled, "Get out, mothafuckas! You in my suite and it's time to go!"

"Damn, bitch. Calm down." The one with the dreads said. The way he looked at her scared her instantly. There was something in the back of his stare.

"Nigga! You got me fucked up if you think you can talk to Ming's friend like that! Get the fuck out." She yelled hitting him with her shoe. Looking at the other dude she said, "You, too!"

The men rose up angrily, and put their clothes on while spitting obscenities in their direction. Although Yvonna didn't say anything, she had plans to kill one if not both of them before the weekend ended if they didn't leave within two minutes. Luckily they got dressed and slammed the door on their way out before time was up.

When Ming threw on a robe, Yvonna sat down on the sofa. Ming joined her. "What's going on? You seem upset."

"Ming, how come you fucking in the living room? Why you ain't go to your room?"

"Well there are two reasons. For one, you got the liquor out here. Two, Ming brought one of them for you." She shoved her. "They said they saw you and wanted to meet.

Ming knew you were sad, and Ming wanted to cheer you up."

"Sad? What you talking about?"

"Ming, saw in your eyes something was wrong. Especially after you made me promise to take care of Delilah before going into the room with Kelsi."

Yvonna's head spun so quickly in her friend's direction it almost snapped. "Went into the room with Kelsi? You saw me?"

"Yeah."

Her eyebrows pulled together and she was livid. "Bitch, why didn't you stop me? I thought it was Bricks."

Ming burst into laughter. "Bricks? They aren't even the same build." Ming laughed slapping her knee. "Yvonna, please stop playing with Ming."

"I was that fucking drunk, girl! And then Bricks had the nerve to walk in on us this morning. Now he don't wanna have nothing to do with me. Ever."

"So Kelsi didn't throw you out?"

"No, we fucked."

Ming was stunned. "You fucked, Kelsi? The man you can't stand?"

"Yes."

"Well…how was it?"

Yvonna tried to hide the delight brewing on her face but she couldn't help it. "He was great. I never in my life had sex as raw and as nasty as that. I just wish it were Bricks." She shook her head remembering the ass sex.

"Will you fuck him again?"

"Ming, stop tripping. I can't stand the mothafucka so I definitely won't be fucking him again." She sighed. "Right now I gotta take care of something else. Then I gotta get dressed and beg Bricks back, if he'll have me." She paused. "But I gotta tell you something."

"What?"

"Your uncle," she paused, "your uncle asked me to marry him. I told him I don't want to but he's not taking no for an answer."

Ming looked at her friend with saddened eyes. "Yvonna, you don't have a choice. Yao gets what Yao wants and if he doesn't there could be problems for you."

"But I don't understand. I mean…why all of a sudden is he looking at me like this?"

"Ming knew it was going to happen. Ming just hoped it didn't."

"If you knew why didn't you tell me?"

"Uncle Yao has done this before, to another friend of mine." Yvonna was horrified. "And when she said no, he had her entire family murdered."

"Ming, you should have stopped me! I would've never gotten mixed up with him had I known all that."

"Ming did tell you not to deal with him. In fact Ming begged you but you said you had it under control. Ming couldn't give you the details because Ming needed to know you trusted Ming more than him. This is serious, Yvonna. Very serious."

"What can I do?"

"Like Ming said, you have to marry him."

Before she could say anything else, Gabriella and Terrell walked through the door. "Did you hear? The FBI is swarming the hotel. They can't find Urban Greggs!"

Shyt List IV

Sin City

Swoopes

Swoopes, Crystal and Bilal Jr. had just made it to Vegas. And to ease Bilal's mind, they gave him a few Vicodin to relax. As far as Swoopes was concerned, it was either that or kill his ass before he could help them lure Yvonna. In Swoopes' mind he was soft and nothing like his father, and that pissed him off. Every five minutes Bilal Jr. was saying how he was scared and wanted to go back home. He even resorted to saying he'd rather have AJ kill him than to participate in the crime. But now, here he was, relaxed and ready for whatever.

They checked back into the same motel room they had when they were first in Vegas, and Crystal went out to get them something to eat. Digging under the bed, Swoopes told Bilal to have a seat. With a dope bag in his hand he made a little concoction.

Swoopes turned the TV on only to see the commercial for the upcoming Lifetime movie about Yvonna Harris. "What the fuck?!" He laughed looking at the TV. "Shit just keeps getting weirder and weirder with this bitch."

When the heroin was ready he said, "Hold your arm out."

"Why?" Bilal was already high.

"Just do it."

The moment he did Swoopes tied his arm off and inserted a needle. To Swoopes' surprise Bilal didn't fight much. After injecting him he did himself and when he was done they allowed the euphoric feeling to take over as they lie face up on the bed. When he was coming down a little he stared at Bilal who was smiling from ear to ear.

"How you feel now, nigga?" Swoopes asked.

"Good," Bilal smiled, "Real good."

"You ready to put some work in now?"

"It's whatever."

Shyt List IV

Sin City

Ming

With a little time on her hand, and since Yvonna went about her business for the afternoon, Ming had chosen the opportunity to be a snoop. She had stolen Gabriella's key card and entered into her room because she wanted to know who she really was.

Going through Gabriella's drawers, under the bed and in the bathroom, she was relentless in her search. But it wasn't until she went through the pocket of her jacket that was hanging in the closet that she found some useful info. On a sheet of paper was several numbers. Including Pastor Robinson's and Penny's. There was also a third number with no name. "Pastor Robinson? And Penny?" She said looking at the piece of paper in her hand. "What do you have to do with all of this?"

From the many conversations she had with Yvonna, she knew Pastor Robinson preached at the church where Gabriella was first discovered but what about Penny?

Ming was just about to leave out when Gabriella entered the room. Trying to hide, she slid into the closet and prayed she wouldn't open the door. Gabriella not knowing anyone was in the room walked inside talking on the phone.

"Sorry it took me so long to call you, I misplaced my room key. But I swear I'm doing all I can. It's just hard to get her alone, she's surrounded by people all the time." Silence. "Please, please don't do that. I won't tell anybody anything. I promise." More Silence. "Yes." She paused, sobbing. "I understand. It's either her or me, and it won't be me."

Shyt List IV

Sin City

Yvonna

Meandering pathways and impressive colorful planting themes surrounded the outside ellipse shaped pool. The mid-afternoon sky provided an ambiance so relaxing one would mistakenly assume they were in heaven. The only thing is, in heaven the devil doesn't roam.

Rodart Holmes was getting his daily swim on in peace and quiet. He liked these times best; when people traded serenity for the ding, ding of the casino instead of the tranquility of the pool. He was alone and on his last lap when out of nowhere, a shapely woman wearing a red bathing suit eased into the water. He couldn't take his eyes off of the curves of her hips or the roundness of her breasts, although he should have. Diving into the ice blue water, she swam in his direction and her long blond hair moved with her. She was a natural. Even the intricate carving of several names embedded on her right shoulder was appealing. Her strokes were long and precise and she looked as if she were dancing.

The woman was approaching him and Rodart was preparing to go around her, to get out of her way, until the woman slivered up to him. Her head gently touched his stomach before she wrapped her arms around his waist.

"What are you doing?" He looked down at her hoping she didn't make a mistake.

The woman didn't respond, she just moved his trunks in a position where his stiff dick would show. She stroked it a few times with her hand before placing it in her mouth. Her warm tongue ran up and down the sides and the feeling overcame him. It didn't help that he had two glasses of Hennessey Black before swimming.

"This kind of shit never happens to me," he said enjoying the moment.

Not wanting anyone to ruin his fun, he looked around in the hopes that no one was watching. But when the pleasure got too much to conceal, he leaned his head backwards and focused on busting a nut. It amazed him that the sexy water creature still hadn't come up for air and he wondered what he had done to deserve such a pleasant favor. He would soon find out.

Easing out of the water, she plopped on the edge of the pool. Disguising her voice she seductively said, "My turn."

In Rodart's mind, the woman looked somewhat familiar. But the long blond weave and black swim cap on top of her head threw him for a loop. Not to mention the shaded goggles shielded her eyes. "Who are you?"

"You can call me Miss Sin City, baby. Now are we gonna have fun or what?"

She opened her legs wide, moved her bathing suit to the side to reveal the pink flesh of her pussy. Taking the back of his head she forced his eager lips to her wet mound. He sloppily licked up the last few droplets of the pool's water along with the silky oil, which the anticipation of his murder created. Then she wrapped her legs around his neck and tightened gently. Rodart didn't mind her forcefulness thinking the moment he made her cum, he'd be knee deep into some pussy.

Shyt List IV

She was on the verge of cumming when a white male pool employee walked out and saw them. "Oh, I'm sorry," he said slyly, stealing a few more looks. He'd seen this type of thing far too often. "I'll leave you two alone. But you better hurry. A new shift starts in a moment."

Yvonna waved feeling confident that no one would recognize her. How could they, she was in disguise. When he was gone she went back to her focus, Mr. BMW. Loving to get her rocks off, she allowed him to bring her to a point of ecstasy without his knowledge. And after she had cum all over his face, she removed the razor tucked from the bra lining of her bathing suit, and sliced him once on his neck. Then she sliced him twice! And then three more times! He held on to his neck and stumbled backwards with wild eyes. At first he didn't know what hit him. When she saw the pool's water turn a slight red she looked down at him and smiled.

"When I hit your car back then, I told you not to fuck with me" Then she got up in his face. "And like I told you when you slapped me, you signed your own death certificate. Good bye, nigga."

Yvonna

Vegas and the rest of the world were trying to find out where was Urban Greggs. Yvonna was a nervous wreck and felt the only thing that could put her mind at ease was her daughter Delilah. So she scooped her up from Quita's so they could have a little 'Girl' time. But picking her up proved to be an event when Quita made more attempts to get Yvonna alone for drinks. It wasn't until she saw Onik's glare that she dropped the issue.

Onik watched over Yvonna and Delilah as they sat in a restaurant within the hotel. She tried to block out the many people whispering around her about Urban and because of it, Delilah didn't have her undivided attention.

"He's a punk." One person proclaimed. "That Greggs kid."

"I told my husband he couldn't beat shit but his dick!" Yelled another.

"Mommy, what's a dick?" Delilah asked.

"Something I'ma bust you in the mouth for if you say again." Delilah shielded her lips thinking the blow would come any minute. "It's a nasty word and a nasty thing." She paused as if she didn't have a mouth full of dick a few hours earlier at the pool. "Now, how's your breakfast?" Yvonna sliced her pancakes with the knife. "Your pancakes aren't too cold are they?"

"They fine, mommy."

Thinking the dick thing was still on her baby's mind she said, "What's bothering you?"

"A few things."

"Give me the first." Yvonna stirred the coffee on her table.

"I'm saw the two scary lines again. When Quita took me to the bathroom at the bottom of the hotel. Right in front of the door."

"Delilah, stop it! You don't see scary lines because it's impossible for lines to be scary!" Yvonna paused. "Now tell me what else is bothering you."

Delilah frowned. "I've decided that I'm going to kill my co-daycare person tomorrow. I've decided that I can't deal with him anymore, and neither can my friends."

"Okay…let me ask the first question, how do you plan on killing this kid?"

"I have my ways."

"And what did I tell you about killing? Didn't I say it was wrong?"

"Ma, you didn't want to talk about it at all, but I'm tired of him bothering me. And I'm tired of him talking about you."

"Would you ladies like anything else?" The waitress interrupted.

"What?"

"Would you like anything else, honey?"

When Yvonna turned to Delilah she was busy doing something. "What were you just doing?"

"Nothing, mommy." Yvonna didn't believe her. "You want anything else, to eat?"

"No, mama."

"Okay here is the check." The waitress said tearing a piece of paper off her pad before setting it on the table.

"And did you hear about Urban Greggs? They can't find him."

"Bitch, get the fuck away from my table! I'm trying to talk to my daughter."

"With that language?" The woman frowned stomping away.

"That wasn't nice mommy. The lady was only being nice."

"Forget all that," Yvonna said. "Listen, you can't talk about killing that little boy, okay? It's not nice and it's not good."

"Well what am I supposed to do? Let him keep messing with me?"

"I'll take care of it, okay? Don't you worry about a thing."

"If you say so, mama."

"I do say so. Now who are your friends?"

"What friends?"

"The ones you were talking about. The ones who you told you were going to take care of the kid?" Delilah didn't want to say it because she knew how mad Yvonna would get. "Delilah...I asked you a question."

Delilah swallowed hard and said, "Ra Ra."

Feeling like she couldn't avoid the inevitable too long, she decided to ask the tough questions. "Baby, do you actually...can you really see..."

"Yes, mama. I can see Ra Ra and my other friends. They are so nice, mommy."

"What do they look like?"

"Different people. Why, mama?"

"Baby, I don't want you to see people. I don't want you to be like me."

"You see people, mama?" Her eyes widened in hopefulness. Here it was after all this time, she thought she was all alone, and now her mother said she too could see people that weren't there.

"Sometimes," Yvonna said wanting to cry.

"Well I even see people I've seen before."

Yvonna was trying to get her mind straight before she said anything else. Delilah suffering with her condition was enough to make her wanna go ballistic and kill everyone who ever sexually abused kids. But now she wanted to get Delilah to stop talking like that, until she could get some private help for her. Even if it meant scaring her to death.

"Delilah, I don't like when you talk about stuff like that."

"It's true, mama. I saw the lady that use to…"

"Delilah, stop it! People may think you are crazy and wanna take you away from me. Do you want that?"

"No, mama," she cried. "I wanna be with you always. I would be so sad if someone took me away from you."

"And so would I. That's why you can't tell anybody that. Or else they…" Yvonna's heart stopped along with her words, because in the hotel walked someone she hadn't seen in years. She had loved when she was a kid, yet here he was now, with the same face he had before she killed him. Sure it was a little bruised, but it was him all the same. But how could it be?

Rummaging through her purse to find her medicine she took out her makeup bag and the key to her room. She still didn't find what she was looking for until she saw the orange pill bottle. It was empty and she realized she still didn't know what happened to her pills.

"Yvonna, are you okay?" Onik asked.

Not wanting him or Yao to know she was crazy she said, "Yes, I'm fine." Then she focused her attention on Delilah. "Baby, I want you to do something for me." She paused. "Put down your fork and look over there for me." She pointed. "Behind you."

"Where, mama?"

"On your right." Delilah looked. "Do you see that boy over there, in the blue jeans and black top?"

"The one with the curly hair?" Yvonna exhaled having gotten her answer. "Yes, mama. I see him. And he's looking straight at you."

"Thank you, baby."

"But, mama, why is he so mad?"

Bilal Jr. walked slowly in her direction and stopped a few feet from the table. Onik blocked him until Yvonna said, "It's okay."

He was tired of hearing those words, either he was there to protect her or not. "Are you sure?"

"Yes."

Bilal's eyes were bloodshot red and he looked angry. "I remember you. You gave me a soda when I was a kid that made me sick. Why you do that?"

"Look, I think you got me mixed up with someone else." She turned to her daughter. "Delilah, hurry up and finish eating. We're about to go, baby." Yvonna gathered her makeup bag off the table and threw it back in her MCM purse.

"So you won't even talk to me?" He stepped closer. "And tell me why you would do something like that? You won't even give me that much."

"Bilal...look..."

"So you do know me." he interrupted.

"Yes, I knew your father."

"Mommy, who is this?"

"Nobody you need to concern yourself with. Now hurry up we're getting ready to go."

"I know you're busy, but when I saw you I couldn't believe you were really here." Bilal interrupted. "I came with my friend's parents and I left them because I needed to see you up close. Can you at least talk to me later? Alone?"

Yvonna had changed since the last time she poisoned him. She wasn't the same person. Having a child made her have slight consideration for other people's children and she never forgave herself for what she did to him. After killing both of his parents, and his grandmother, she felt she owed him at least a fifteen-minute private conversation, just as long as it was away from her own child.

"Aw, help him, mommy. He seems sad."

Yvonna sighed and said, "Not sure what I can say to you, but if my words will make you feel better, I'll talk to you later."

"When?"

"Let's say tonight. About 7:00pm."

"That's around the time of the fight."

"Do you want to meet me or not?"

"Yes." He paused. "Where?"

Taking a pen and piece of paper out of her purse she said, "Here is my room number. And here is my cell. I'll meet you there at 7:00, but don't be late. If you're even one minute late, even if I'm there, I won't talk to you."

"I won't be late. Thank you."

When Bilal walked away, her phone rang. It was Ming. "Hello."

"Please come back to the room. Uncle Yao is here, and he's very upset."

Her heart rate sped up. "Why?"

"I don't know...something about Urban Greggs."

◀ • ▶

Quita's Room

Yvonna knocked on the door once and Quita swung the door open. "Quita, I'ma need you to keep Delilah now."

"Okay, but, did you see Bricks? I been trying to reach him to find out if he's bringing Chomps by or not."

"Why wouldn't he?" She said as she ushered Delilah into the room.

"Mama, please don't push me. I can walk just fine if you let me."

When Delilah dropped her purse Yvonna picked it up, handed it to her and said, "Delilah, I don't have time for your sassiness. Now be good and I'ma be back when I can."

"Can we go see Kelsi today, Quita?" Delilah asked. "I gotta see him bad.

"Girl, what did I tell you about him? Stop being fast! That's a grown ass man!"

Delilah walked in and flopped down on the sofa without another word. "Bricks wouldn't answer the phone." Quita continued. "I mean, I know the fight is to-night so I'm just wondering."

"Is everything okay with you in general? And with Bricks? You been acting weird lately."

A half smile presented on Quita's face and she said, "Yeah...why wouldn't it be?"

Yvonna stepped to her and said, "Because the nigga belongs to me, whether he knows it or not. So if you got him in your mind, you need to get him the fuck off of it. Do I make myself clear?"

"Yeah, Yvonna."

She was about to leave when she remembered Little Davie. "Where's the kid name Little Davie?"

"Over there."

Yvonna walked up to the kid who was sitting on the couch playing a portable game player. She snatched it out of his hands, dropped it on the floor and slammed her foot on it breaking it into many pieces. Then she bent down and got into his face, the child was so scared he couldn't stop shaking. Giving him an evil look, she moved her mouth closely to his ear so no one else could hear her words.

"Everything you heard about me is true." She whispered. "And if you fuck with my daughter or mention my name again, I will kill you." Then she looked into his eyes. "You understand me, little fucker?" He nodded yes. "Cool." She walked toward the door. "Quita, I'll be back when I can."

YBM

Swoopes walked into the YBM hotel room and was greeted by his gang members. It had been months since he'd been around them and he couldn't lie, it felt good that they finally set their feelings aside about the whole matter to help him get Yvonna.

They were in the living room drinking Hennessey when Growl said, "We glad you back, nigga." He raised a glass in the air. "Shit ain't been the same since you been gone."

Crystal ran her hand up and down his arm as all of the members stood around. "Once I get this bitch, shit will be back to normal. Trust me." He paused. "So, ya'll got any information on her?"

"We think she at the Aria but it's hard to find her." Mike said.

"You know if we don't get her this weekend, we may not ever catch this bitch." He paused. "But I got a plan I'm working on now, using Bilal's kid. He downstairs talking to this bitch now."

"Why you ain't tell me?" Growl said. "We could've grabbed her."

"Naw, she always got one of Yao's guards with her."

"So you sure your plan gonna work?" Mike asked.

"Trust me. I think this may be it." Swoopes said.

Shyt List IV

"Well if it don't work, we got a plan in the works that is guaranteed to bring this bitch to us."

Yvonna

Perspiration formed on Yvonna's head as she moved toward the door. *Does Yao know I killed Urban?* She thought. Taking a deep breath she was surprised when Ming swung the door open. Onik was on guard as usual.

"Stay out here, Onik." She walked into the suite and inside was Gabriella, Terrell and Bricks.

Terrell and Gabriella immediately jumped up and said, "We have to talk."

"Actually I was waiting to talk to her first," Bricks said stepping in front of them.

"This ain't about you and the fact that you been trying to fuck her. What we got to say is serious." Terrell said.

"Nigga, who the fuck is you talking to?" Bricks said running up to him.

"WAIT!!!!!" Yvonna screamed stepping between them. "I don't have time for this shit right now!" Then she turned to Gabriella and Terrell and said, "Is this about the both of you? Being together?"

"Yes." Gabriella replied.

"Then I don't want to hear it." Then she turned to Bricks and said, "Come in my room."

"Yvonna, this is important." Gabriella demanded. "And we have to do it now. You can't be mad at me forever!"

Shyt List IV

Yvonna stopped, turned around and said, "Why are you so incessant upon involving me in your relationship? You're fucking each other, so be happy."

"Wait...they together?" Bricks asked.

"It's not that we are incessant, Yvonna, we just don't want to lose your friendship." Gabriella replied.

"It's a little too late for that isn't it?"

"Come on, Bricks."

Stopping her again Ming said, "Yvonna, before you go just give Ming five minutes of your time. It's about Yao."

Yvonna looked at Bricks and said, "Wait in my room. I'm coming."

When Bricks walked into the room and closed the door Ming grabbed Yvonna by the hand and carried her into the kitchen part of the suite. She wanted to get away from Gabriella and Terrell. "Uncle Yao wants you to meet him in his room. He says it's about Urban and it's very important." Yvonna sighed. "What happened, Yvonna?"

"I'll tell you everything. I promise." She paused. "Now let me talk to Bricks."

She was preparing to leave until Ming spoke in Chinese. "Ming, I don't know fucking Chinese. Stop being stupid."

With seriousness in her eyes that Yvonna hadn't seen in a while she said, "I snooped around Gabriella's room. And I don't trust her."

"Why you say that? Because she fucked Terrell?"

"No. Ming saw the pastor's number in her jacket pocket, along with Penny's number."

"Penny?" Yvonna was confused. "How? Why?"

"Ming doesn't know."

Yvonna felt the room spin. "Are you sure?"

"Yes. Ming is."

Rubbing her temples she said, "So what does what you said in Chinese mean in English?"

"It means, '*be careful. Because those who really do not want to be found, can not be found.*'"

"Ming, I have a long day ahead of me. Just give it to me straight."

"Ming thinks you need to watch her." Yvonna seemed uneasy. "Think, Yvonna, it doesn't seem right that all of a sudden she could be found so easily. People have been trying to find her for years, since she was a kid, yet Terrell walks into the church one day, steals a piece of paper and finds her."

What Ming said resonated with her, but too much other shit was happening at the moment. In less than forty-eight hours she had killed three people, scared the hell out of a kid and fucked Bricks' best friend. She really needed a mental break. So instead of discussing the matter at that moment, she said, "Ming, I'll talk to you later. But don't worry, I'll be fine."

Looking at Gabriella sitting on the couch she said, "Ming hopes so."

◀ • ▶

Yvonna's Room

"What's up, Bricks?" Yvonna said sitting on the bed next to him. "You still mad at me?"

He stood up and walked to the dresser. "I'm not here to talk about that."

"Well unless you wanna talk about that," she walked over to him and stared him into his eyes, "then I'm not willing to discuss anything at all."

"What is there to talk about? You fucked my mans."

"But I thought it was you, Bricks." She grabbed his hand. He snatched it away and walked back to the bed to sit down but she was on his heels. "Please, believe me I would never have given my body to your friend. You know that."

In his heart of hearts Bricks knew she would never violate like that purposefully, but he couldn't shake the feeling. "I do believe you, but it don't make what I think about the shit any different." He stood up, walked back to the dresser and sat on the edge. "I mean, how could you fuck this nigga and think it was me? What about all the nights I held you in my arms because you couldn't get to sleep? Don't you know what my body feels like against yours?"

She felt lower than low, so she walked over to him. "I was drunk, baby. And we didn't say anything when we were fucking because we didn't want people outside of the party to know what we were doing." She rested her head on his chest. "But I love you, Bricks. Do you hear what I'm saying? I love you."

"Love me like *really* love me?"

"Love you like I've *always* loved you."

"Why you just telling me this shit now? You been fucking with a nigga's head for years. Now all of a sudden you love me?"

"Baby, I was scared. But you never heard me keep it this real with you until now. I'm sorry about Kelsi, but that shit meant nothing to me, and I know you know it otherwise you wouldn't let me look into those grey eyes of yours right now. You said it yourself, *'loving and fucking is two different things'.*" He smiled but as if something else had come across his mind, he pushed her away and stood up straight. "Now what did I do?"

"Are you sure it's not because of your man out there? And your friend?"

"Are you asking me if I'm professing my love to you because Gabriella fucked Terrell?" She frowned.

"Yeah."

"You know what, don't fucking play with me!" Yvonna yelled hitting his arm. Then she gripped his shirt with both hands. "I will kill you and you better know I mean that shit." He knew she was telling the truth and when she saw it in his eyes, she released him. "I'm telling you that I love you because I do. I always have. And I love you so much that I was willing to give you up. Do you understand that this was the first time this has ever happened to me? Where I was so unselfish that I was willing to give a person up?"

"If that's the case are we gonna stop playing games and be together?"

"There's so much you don't know about me."

"Fuck that! Are you gonna be with me or not?"

"Yes. I'm gonna be with you always. Even if it's in spirit."

He didn't know what that meant so he said, "No more you love me so you gotta stay away from me shit." Then he glared at her and slapped her in the face. "And no more fucking my friends." He slapped her again. "We bound together forever, and I will go through hell just to get to you."

Smiling at him, she pushed him onto her bed and removed his shoes. When his shoes made light thumps on the floor, she removed his jeans, boxers and t-shirt. And as quickly as she undressed him she was able to undress herself quicker. "I just want to touch you first." She said. "Can I just touch you?"

"You can do whatever you want."

Starting at his feet she lightly massaged each one of his toes. And when she'd given each of his toes attention she massaged his entire foot with long smooth strokes. Then she ran her warm hands up to his ankles, his legs and thighs. Bricks was already rock hard when she finally reached his stomach with delicate smooth tongue motions. When she was done touching every inch of his body, she crawled on top of him, without sliding onto his dick. Her pussy was inches away from his thickness but she didn't let him enter her, not yet anyway.

"What you doing to me, bitch?" He asked eager to push inside of her for the first time ever.

She crouched over top of him, and slapped him in the face. "That's for putting your hands on me earlier." Then she smacked him again. "And this is for making me fall in love with you." He smiled and forcefully grabbed her, pulling her on top of his body. They engaged in a passionate kiss clawing at each other. It had been years and finally they would get what they both wanted. Fucked.

"Damn you feel so good." Bricks said. "I should fuck you up for letting that nigga inside of you. If you ever do some shit like that again I'ma kill you, Yvonna. You want me to kill you?" Sticking a finger inside of her pussy he said, "This is mine and it belongs to me. Always remember that shit."

"I'm sorry, baby," she said leaving trails of kisses along his neck. Her wet mound winded on his finger. "But I'm gonna do everything in my power tonight, to make you forget all about the past." He took his finger of her pussy and licked it. "Taste good?" She asked.

"Like candy."

She smiled, slapped her hands together, and then she rubbed them over and over until they were warm. Then she grabbed his thickness and in long glides moved her hands up and down his dick. With his grey eyes already rolling in the back of his head she took the tip of her pink tongue and played with the slit at the top of his helmet. He looked at her. "Damn, bitch. You know what you doing."

She pushed him back down. "You ain't seen nothing yet."

Wanting to taste him fully, she covered the top of his dick with her warm mouth, running her tongue in circles around the top. Then she softly suckled on his dick like it was a delicate ice cream cone and she was savoring every drip drop.

"Mmmmmmmmm." He moaned.

Wanting to take more into her mouth she removed her hands and placed her mouth on his dick, there was not one part of him that wasn't in her mouth.

"Fuuuuuccckkkkkk…"

They were just getting into the fun when horny ass Ming bust through the doors. "Oooooo, ya'll sound like ya'll having fun. Can Ming play?"

"Bitch, get the fuck out!" She said throwing a pillow at the door, running Ming away.

"Your friend is a trip," Bricks said laughing a little.

"Don't worry about her," Yvonna said crawling on top of him, placing his thickness into her body. "Worry about this pussy."

It was time, *finally*, for him to feel how hot it was inside of her. So she pushed her pussy down on his dick and rode him like a champion. Her titties bounced back and forth as her ass slapped against his thighs. He grabbed her waist and pushed into her each time savoring every motion in her ocean. There was nothing else to say, you haven't fucked a bitch until you fucked a crazy bitch, and she knew it. "Fuck this pussy, nigga. Beat that shit right."

From the corner of her eye, Yvonna could see Ming looking at them in the crack of the doorway. As long as she didn't bring her ass into the room on her first night fucking Bricks, she wouldn't revoke her exhibitionist privileges. Besides, she loved having an audience. "Fuck your pussy, baby. Beat it!"

"Damn, bitch!" Bricks replied biting his bottom lip. "I ain't know the pussy was gonna be this tight and wet."

"Now you do." Yvonna bragged.

Tiring of the shit she was talking, he threw her on the bed and wrapped her legs around his neck. Then he did something she never experienced before. Taking his hand, he pushed on her lower stomach as he fucked her over and over. Something about the pressure of his hand and the motion allowed her to feel his dick with every movement he made. It felt like it would bust out of her stomach. At that moment Yvonna stood corrected, next to Bricks, Kelsi wasn't shit. "I love you, nigga," she said looking into this eyes.

"You love this dick," he said.

"No fuck that," she said titties moving up and down. "I love you."

He flipped her over and banged it a little from the back. Then he looked at her right shoulder and saw the names *Bernice, Cream, Jhane* and *Swoopes* carved on her body.

He never saw this before because most times she wore a shirt. "Why you got that nigga Swoopes name carved on you?" He said pounding her for points.

"Because I'm gonna kill him, like I killed all them other people on my shoulder." Just thinking about their deaths turned her on. "Now you gonna keep talking or fuck me?"

Bricks turned her back over and looked into her eyes. The way she stared at him drove him crazy so he bust all his nut inside of her pussy. When they came they stopped for a moment and started again for twenty minutes, neither wanting the moment to end. "I'm about to cuuuummmmm again," Yvonna called.

"Me too, baby. Keep working that ass."

Yvonna grabbed one of her titties and ran her tongue around her nipple. Seeing her do this caused him to bust a third time. "Fuuuuuuuuucccckkkkkkkkkkkkkkkkkk!" He said. "Fuccccckkkkkk."

"I'm cumming too," she said winding her ass one last time before he fell into her chest. Out of breath she said, "I...I...really have never been fucked like that before."

"Not even last night?"

"Bricks, all bullshit aside, I made a mistake but you gotta let that shit go. Now can you forgive me or not so we can move on?"

"I'ma forgive you on one condition."

"And what's that?"

"If you be my woman, and stop playing games. Let's make the shit official."

Yao entered her mind. "I don't think we can do that right now, Bricks."

"What?" He frowned, staring down at her face. "You must want me to fuck you up."

"It's not that, baby, it's just that I got myself into something I have to get myself out of first. Once I work this through, we can work on us. And I promise," she paused, "with everything I am, that when that moment finally comes for us to be together, I'll be the best you've ever had. I'm talking about every night, I'm gonna sleep with your dick in my mouth." She grinned. "I love you, Bricks."

"I love you back." Then he exhaled thinking about her falling to sleep with his dick in her mouth. "Sounds good, but let's talk about what I came here to discuss."

"So you really didn't come here for me?"

"No." He sat on the edge of the bed.

"Okay, let's talk about it," she said sitting up straight, covering her titties with the sheets, the taste of him still in her mouth.

"First I wanna make sure you okay."

"You mean now that you fucked me and carried me?" she paused. "Yeah, I'd say I'm okay."

"Yvonna, are you okay?" He repeated with seriousness. "You know with the schizophrenia you told me about." She had forgotten about that conversation.

"I'm as good as I'm gonna be." Then she smiled. "

"Cool, now the hotel is swarming with cops. So are you clear on what we gotta say if they ask us about Urban?"

"Yeah...we were at the party the entire time." She replied secretly wanting to fuck again. "I got it. You don't have to worry about me. I've been murdering people with an unofficial immunity card for years."

"I don't know about all that but I do know we gotta be careful." He paused. "Tonight we gonna get dressed and get ready for the fight like nothing is off. Like that nigga is still gonna come downstairs and give folks the fight of his life."

"That's the part I might find hard to do."

"Why?"

"I can't do the fake shit too good."

"Well do the lying shit instead. I know you pretty good at that."

"That was low," she replied.

"Fuck low. We have to be smart. We killed a public figure. A MAJOR public figure and if we fuck up in the slightest, they gonna come for us."

"When do you think they gonna find their bodies?"

"It depends on how long he got the room for." Bricks replied. "But we can't deviate off the plan in the slightest. I told Carmen's friends that she left since me and you got back together. I'm just hoping them bitches buy that shit and shut the fuck up. I just need you to stay on point."

"I got it. Don't worry."

"Cool, let me go to my room and get ready." He stood up and looked down at her. "Once we get through this, we gonna be fine. You trust me?"

"Yeah. The crazy part about it is, I do."

Shyt List IV

Sin City

Quita

The steam from the bathroom made it hotter than Quita could stand as she sat in a tub full of water. She was contemplating cracking the door to get a little air but the children in her care would have flooded in with question after question and she needed a break. Just twenty minutes of peace and quiet, after all, what could it hurt?

She had just laid her head up against the wall and exhaled while she was thinking about the YBM. Although they threatened to do her harm, she managed to dodge them when she could. But if they kept fucking with her, she had something for that ass. She lifted Kelsi's gun and had all intentions on using it. When Bricks came to her room to look for it, she hid it in a box of menstrual pads, knowing they wouldn't go in there.

KNOCK! KNOCK! KNOCK! "Stop knocking on the fucking door!" Quita yelled at the kids who bothered her ever five minutes. "I'ma be out in a minute."

"But you taking too long!" Delilah added. "My soda is warm and I hate warm soda!"

"What?" Quita frowned looking at the closed door as if it were the child.

"I said my soda is warm and I need ice!" She paused. "What you want me to do, drink piss?"

"Wait, Delilah!" She rolled her eyes. "I said, I'm coming."

When she heard her peddling away from the door she focused on the phone on the edge of the tub. Even though she settled for a consolation prize by fucking Melvin, she hoped he'd tell Bricks how great she was in the bedroom and that he would want her anyway. But each time she called Melvin to see if he was coming to her room after the fight, like he promised while inside of her mediocre pussy, her calls landed in his voicemail. Unable to let well enough alone, she called him again, and again he didn't answer. "That nigga trying to play me like the rest of these niggas. I can't stand neither one of them mothafuckas."

Sliding the phone across the yellow tiles on the bathroom floor, she rinsed the last few suds off of her thighs before rising out of the water. She hoped leaving the kids in the living room to watch *Toy Story 3* wouldn't bite her in the ass forcing her to have to perform a massive clean up behind them.

With the white towel wrapped around her body, she grabbed her cell phone, opened the door and tiptoed toward the area they were seated, leaving a trail of wet footprints behind her. But when she did a quick accounting of the children, she noticed Delilah was missing. "Hey," she paused looking around, "where is Delilah?"

Boy's eyes were glued onto the TV along with Little Davie, Joshua, Chomps and Miranda. And not one of them gave her proper acknowledgement.

"She went to get some ice. Said her shit was hot and you wouldn't open the door so she got it herself." Little Davie said.

"Watch your mouth!"

He rolled his eyes. "Man, you ain't my daddy. Plus you asked me a question."

Shyt List IV

Quita ignored the rebellious son of a drug dealer to run into the hallway, the towel almost falling off of her body. "Delilah, Delilah...where are you?" People looked at her as if she was crazy for being half naked.

The cold air rushed against her wet skin and she could smell the scent of a recent room service order as it lingered in the air. As she approached the ice port, she did a quick prayer that when she reached it she'd she Delilah filling her bucket. But when she bent the corner, she wasn't there. Her heart pounded in her chest and her stomach made all sorts of waves. If she lost Yvonna's child, she was smart enough to know that it meant her life. Was it the YBM? Did they find out she was Yvonna's daughter and decided to take her hostage?

Rushing back to the room, Boy was the first person she saw when she entered. The door slammed behind her and he walked up to her with a serious look on his face. "Where my sister, Miss Quita?"

Quita walked around him, "She went down the hall."

"Went down the hall where?" He followed.

She turned around. "Boy, I'm the adult and you're the child. You don't question me, I question you."

"If my sister is lost I'm 'bout to call Aunt Yvonna." He went for his North Face book bag to grab his phone, only to have it snatched away by Quita.

"You can't do that!" She yelled, bag dangling in her hand. "Now go sit down."

He snatched it back. "If my mother knew how you talked to me, you would have problems. Or have you forgot who my uncle is?"

She softened the glare on her face knowing he was right and said, "Boy, I don't mean to yell at you." She got on her knees in front of the child so that she could be less intimidating. Secretly Boy hoped a tittie would pop out of her towel for nature's sake. "So how about you let me go get your sister. Okay? We don't have to worry people before time." She paused. "Can you do me a favor until I come back?"

"What?" he frowned folding is arms in his chest.

"Can you look after the other kids?"

A smile instantly appeared on his face. "Yeah...but you gotta tell them I'm in charge. Or they not gonna listen."

Believing roughing the kids' feathers was an easy price to pay to get him to remain quiet for a few more ticks, she turned around and faced the children. "Listen," all the kids stopped what they were doing and looked at her, "I'm about to go get Delilah and while I'm gone, Boy is in charge."

"Ughhh, why him?" Little Davie said. "My folks got more money than his do."

"Nigga, you wish you had more money than my family." Boy said. "My uncle is Yao. You know who that is?"

"Both of ya'll ain't got as much money as my father," Chomps added.

"First off everybody in here is broke," Quita corrected them, "because although your parents may have a little something, ya'll don't have a cup to piss in or a window to throw it out of." She paused. "Now I have to go, you all can argue about whose mother or father has the most money."

After she shut the kid beef down, she got dressed and grabbed the room key. She didn't know where Delilah was, but she knew there would be hell to pay if she came back without her. "I be back, like I said, remember Boy is in charge."

When the door closed Little Davie examined Boy. Throwing his body into the sofa he said, "He in charge. For now."

Shyt List IV

Sin City

Yvonna

People rattled on at the hotel's bar about the question that was making Yvonna so mad she wanted to throw the fuck up. It had gotten so bad that instead of saying hello when you greeted people in the hallway, it was, "Can you believe Urban Greggs is missing?"

Yvonna and Bricks looked like babies shitting in pampers they were so scared. But after his sixth drink, Bricks felt a little better. Yvonna on the other hand was on pins and needles thinking that if Yao didn't jump out at any minute on her, the police were.

Just when she thought shit couldn't get any worse, Phillip, who had held Carmen hostage for her, approached the bar. He looked like he hadn't slept in weeks, despite the fact that everything happened over a day or so. "I gotta talk to you." He said through clenched teeth. "And I gotta talk to you now!"

Bricks stepped up and said, "Fuck you want to talk to her about?"

"Nothing!" Yvonna jumped in.

Phillip mugged Bricks and then Yvonna. "Oh, I ain't got to talk to you about nothing, Yvonna? Are you sure?"

Prior to now she took him for a punk and knew at some point she'd have to break him back down. "Like I said, you ain't got to talk to me about shit!"

"Maybe I should tell everybody over here how you..."

Thinking he was about to let her pussy out of the bag she slammed down on his foot with her boots. "OOOUUUUUCCHHHHH!!" He screamed jumping up and down.

With that she jumped off of the stool, grabbed him by his ear and walked him to another area. "Look here, I don't' know who you think I am, but I can guarantee you that you haven't met a bitch like me in your life. And if you keep fucking with me, just like Carmen and Urban, you gonna show up missing."

"So you did have something to do with it?"

"Yes! And you did, too." She paused smirking at him. "Remember? You were the one who brought Carmen to Urban's room."

"So he's in there? Dead?"

"No, they're BOTH in there! And you helped me with my plan. So if you don't be quiet, you 'bout to be an accessory to the fact." She paused. "Now step the fuck off." Yvonna left him to his thoughts and walked back to her friends, but it took a few more seconds before he finally walked away.

In an effort to buy time for a fight that would never take place, Yvonna, Bricks, Ming, Melvin, Kelsi, Terrell and Gabriella decided to get some more drinks in the casino before going. "Yvonna, can I talk to you in private? Alone?" Gabriella asked.

"No."

"Please. I really just need five minutes."

"And I said no." Yvonna protested. "I got a lot on my mind right now."

Over her limit Ming said, "Ming is so excited, about the fight tonight," she continued bringing attention once again to what Yvonna didn't want to discuss. "Ming bets Urban is going to kill that Santiago."

"Ming, niggas is saying the dude ain't showing," Bricks said wishing she'd just shut the fuck up. "So slow your roll."

"Right, plus haven't you had enough to drink?" Yvonna said. "Matta fact, make that your last one."

Ming frowned. "Bitch, please! Don't get mad at Ming because Ming's the only one who remembers she's in Vegas."

"Ming, I know I asked you this before but I forgot," Gabriella said. "But why do you refer to yourself in third person?"

"Because it's *Ming's* business. Why do you do a lot of shit behind people's back?"

"What is that supposed to mean?"

Ming feeling her drink said, "I'm on to you, bitch."

"Ming!" Yvonna said. "Stop wilding out!"

"Fuck her!" She gritted. Gabriella rolled her eyes. "Now can we please have some fun before the fight?" Ming replied. "Ya'll look like you're about to go to court."

"Stop talking about the fight already!" Yvonna yelled in her face. "You make me so fucking sick when you drink! You don't know how to handle your liquor!"

Not knowing what was going on Ming said, "You just mad because you don't want your little boyfriend Urban to get his ass beat." She laughed. "Are you afraid Santiago is going to kill him in the ring or something?"

Overcome with anger, Yvonna slapped Ming in the face so hard her hand stung. A red handprint appeared on her face and Ming threw her drink in her eyes, glass included. The two ladies got to rumbling and Yvonna with her monster strength managed to throw Ming on top of the bar. Then she wiped glasses off of the bar with her body.

Ming being no slouch in the fight department grabbed Yvonna and pulled her on top of her. The two had fallen behind the counter knocking over various bottles on the wall. People screamed but could not take their eyes off of the train wreck happening. "Stop it!" The female bartender yelled. "You're ruining the bar."

Bricks and Terrell went behind the bar and brought the women back around to the front and Melvin threw five hundred dollars on the bar for the bartender's trouble.

"You're so fucking drunk and stupid!" Yvonna yelled pointing her finger in her face. "And I hate when you get like this. Dumb ass, drunk bitch!"

Yvonna stormed away from everything and everybody and Bricks was right behind her. Sensing his presence, she stopped in place, turned around and said, "Just leave me alone! I need time to think."

"Fine." He paused, putting his hands in the air before walking in the opposite direction.

Yvonna walked to the casino where there was not as much activity and no Ming. Having moved far enough away, she flopped in the seat in front of a slot machine and tried to concentrate. Her leg shook violently as she slammed her card inside of the machine and pulled heavily on the lever.

"Stupid, bitch!" She said to herself. "Always so dumb and stupid." Although she was mad, she really hated herself for having fought Ming. Like it or not, Ming was her best friend and in Yvonna's small circle that made her family.

She was on her fourth pull of the lever when she felt warm arms wrap around her neck. She could smell Beyonce' Heat perfume and knew immediately whom it was. "You really should buy your own shit you know?" Yvonna said. Ming walked around and sat in the seat next to her. The mark on her face from where she had slapped her had gone down...a little. "I'm sorry about that." Yvonna pointed. "The face thing."

"Ming knows." She smiled. "Plus you hit like a bitch." They both laughed. "You killed him didn't you? Urban. And that's what Uncle Yao wants to talk to you about."

Feeling like she needed to get it off her chest she told the truth. "He tried to kill me. I went over there to talk to him and he tried to kill me."

Sorrow for her friend covered her face. "So...where is he now?"

"In his room."

"He couldn't be. They would have found him by now."

"He rented another room in the hotel to escape everybody. I guess he must have it for a few more days because they didn't find him yet. I put the *Do Not Disturb* sign on the door on my way out so the maid wouldn't go in."

"That shit gotta be stinking by now."

"Yeah...it's two of them in the room. Him and Carmen."

Ming's jaw dropped at the revelation. "Carmen? How did that happen?"

"I tried to make it look like a murder suicide."

"Yvonna, why wouldn't you tell Ming? It's not like we haven't killed together before. Many, many, many, many times. Actually so many..."

"I get the picture!" She interrupted looking around to make sure no one overheard them. "And I don't know why I didn't tell you. I guess it happened so quickly and I didn't want to get you involved. Besides, Yao is your uncle and if you had to choose I knew you would choose..."

"You." Ming said touching her hand. "If Ming had to choose between her uncle or you she'd choose you. Uncle Yao has hurt Ming before but you never have."

"What are you talking about, I just beat your ass on the bar." Yvonna smirked.

"You mean you just got your ass beat on the bar." Ming recanted. Then a serious expression covered her face. "But after all we been through, all the secrets, you still don't consider Ming a true friend."

"You gotta be kidding me."

"Ming's not kidding. Ming's dead serious."

"You have tricked me into letting you suck my titties, lick my pussy, hump me, kiss me, rub me and all the other sick shit you've wanted to do, yet at the end of the day, I still need you around me. And you don't think you're my friend?" Yvonna paused. "You the only *real* friend I've ever had."

"Whatever."

"It's true. Gabriella asked me what was it about you I liked so much, and I told her that I know where you're coming from. Sure you're a little hornier than most, but I know where you're coming from. With you, what you see is what you get and I need that in my life."

Ming smiled. "Ming feels the same way about you." She paused and said, "Have you talked to Yao yet?"

"No. I called him but he didn't answer."

"That's who Ming's really worried about."

"Me too."

"There they go right here." Kelsi pointed. Bricks and Melvin were right behind him.

Bricks walked up to the girls and said, "We getting ready to go to the MGM Grand for the fight."

Bricks gave Yvonna a look that said, *"We know the nigga not showing up, but at least we can do is fake it."*

Shyt List IV

Yvonna looked at him intently and said, "Let the games begin."

Quita

Each step Quita took leading down the hallway felt heavy as she approached her room without Delilah. Instead of telling Yvonna that she had lost her only child, in her mind there was only one thing to do, manipulate Boy's young mind so that he would tell the story, as she needed it to be told. It was her only chance at survival.

Entering into the room she was surprised to see it torn completely apart. Capri Suns had been stepped on and the red juice inside of them was splashed against the walls, couch and carpet. Slices of cheddar cheese that she used to make their sandwiches were smashed on the TV, and even on one of Quita's black Ugg boots. What really messed her up was that she saw Little Davie hiding under the table like a bitch, while Chomps, Miranda and Boy threatened him with forks within every inch of his life.

"What's going on?!" Quita yelled temporarily forgetting that she had bigger fish to fry. "And why is Little Davie under the table?"

"Because he didn't get with the program, Miss Quita." Boy said.

Quita walked up to the scene and looked at the children. "And what was the program?"

"That I was in charge." Boy pointed the fork at himself. "And since he couldn't get with the program, he tried to take me down so he could be in charge. So we took him down instead."

"YEAH!!!!" The children cheered.

"Little Davie, get from up under the table."

Wiping the tears from his eyes and the snot from his nose he shook his head. "But they gonna poke me with forks. I don't wanna be poked."

"Little Davie, stop acting like a bitch before I tell your father." Little Davie crawled from up under the table and stood on his own two feet. But he wouldn't take another step until the children had cleared a path for him.

"I want everybody in this room to sit down!" She yelled. When they didn't move she said, "NOW!" When the children retreated to different parts of the room Little Davie sat on the sofa. "Now I don't know what you do at your house, but I will not continue to allow this type of foolery in the future. Do I make myself clear?!"

"Not really, Miss Quita. I don't understand what you mean by foolery." Boy said.

"Never mind all that, Boy, come with me." She went toward her room within the suite and Boy followed. "The rest of you betta not make a sound because the way I feel I might start fucking some kids up around here." The kids were stunned at her threat of violence.

When they were in her room Boy said, "What I do, Miss Quita?"

"Your sister was not where you told me she would be."

"Me?" Boy's expression was confused and his eyebrows were pulled together. "I don't know where she is."

"Yes you do. You said that she went to get some ice. And since that's your sister, it means you were in charge of her."

"Ahhh....Ahnnn, you the babysitter."

"Let me see what your mother will say when I tell her that you lost your sister." Quita moved for the phone hoping Boy would be scared enough to stop her. But with the handset in her hand he hadn't said a mumbling word, until she pressed the first button.

"Okay...okay. Please don't tell." Boy remembered his mother's words when she said that they should always stick together, and instead he lost his sister.

Quita smiled before turning around and then sat the phone back on the base. Then she sat on her bed. "Come over here, Boy. Hop up on the bed and sit next to me."

Boy walked slowly toward her, and sat on the floor instead. "Yes, Miss Quita."

"I know you didn't mean to let your sister leave the room. So when your Aunt Yvonna asks, I'ma say that you were sorry. And I'ma take up for you, too. Okay?"

"Yes, Miss Quita."

"You didn't mean to let her leave by herself," she continued, "but I was using the bathroom and you thought she was smart enough to come back to the room after she got ice. But she didn't. That's what we gotta say, okay?"

"Okay."

She saw tears swelling up in his eyes but this was a do or die type of situation and she needed to disconnect herself as far away from responsibility as possible. She knew at first Yvonna would blame her, after all she was the sitter, but she figured once she told her she had to use the bathroom, that no one in their right mind would expect her to take all the kids to the toilet. Her only hope was that the kids wouldn't recant how they saw her walking out of the bathroom with a towel, which meant that instead of using the bathroom, she had taken a bath. She sure hoped her version of the events would do. If it didn't she would use Kelsi's gun to protect herself.

Shyt List IV

Sin City

Yvonna

The arena was jammed pack while everyone waited to see if the fight would go down or not. Yvonna, Bricks and now Ming, were highly nervous wondering what the end result would bring.

"What's wrong with ya'll?" Kelsi asked looking at the three of them.

"Yeah, it's not even that hot in here but ya'll sweating like shit." Terrell said.

Yvonna, Ming and Bricks remained quiet as they tried to tune out the background adlib. It was bad enough knowing that unless Jesus chose to raise Urban from the dead, he would not be fighting anything or anybody tonight. They definitely didn't want to hold conversations about him. "Nothing is wrong, Terrell," Yvonna said.

While the world waited, the hotel managed to convince a few R&B celebrities who were in attendance to sing while they made further attempts to locate Urban. And although their voices soothed some, when the last verse was sung, the same question was on everyone's mind. *'Where the FUCK is Urban Greggs?'*

"Man, I think this nigga flaked," Kelsi said looking at the empty ring. "He ain't showing tonight. I'm telling you."

"It just don't make no sense," Terrell said. "All the critics said he had the fight in the bag. All he had to do was show up."

"Yeah...Santiago's reach couldn't fuck with Greggs. But Santiago has speed. If the nigga show up it's gonna be a good fight." Kelsi said. "Wait, where Melvin?" he asked changing the subject while looking around the ring.

"Not sure." Bricks said wiping the sweat off of his head. "He probably gonna be here in a minute though."

"I'll be back, I'm about to go find Gabriella," Terrell said. Yvonna rolled her eyes still mad about their union.

When he left Kelsi said, "If I knew this nigga wasn't gonna show, I'da got into something else before coming."

"Like what? My cousin?" Bricks asked trying to pick a fight to keep his mind off of the situation.

Kelsi frowned and said, "You said Greek came and got her. So she ain't fucking with me after that. Then she texted me and said she heard about what happened between me and somebody else." He looked at Yvonna. "So it's definitely a wrap."

"Nigga, please! You fucked me and got off." She yelled. "Even took some ass in the process. Be grateful and shut the fuck up!"

Everyone decided to piggyback off of that beef to stay occupied. "Yeah, nigga! Stop tripping and shit." Ming added, having no real gripe.

"Girl, I told you to stop saying nigga!" Yvonna said ice mugging her. "You gonna get fucked up."

While they spoke among themselves, Bricks looked at Yvonna and said, "You let this nigga fuck you in the ass?"

"Yes, he took some ass! But it wasn't even like that."

"Bitch, I ain't take shit! You gave it to me!"

"It don't even matter, baby because his dick paled in comparison to yours." Kelsi looked insulted and unconsciously groped himself. People around them eavesdropped. "But the fact that he acting like he ain't like it is ridiculous! If anything he need to be paying homage. 'Cause I already know not another bitch before or after me could fuck with my sex game."

The look on Kelsi's face told her she was right. "Whatever, as far as I'm concerned the shit never happened. You with my man and I still don't fuck wit' your ass."

When she was done Bricks said, "If you ever talk recklessly like that around me again, by talking about how you fucked another nigga, I'ma break your jaw. I'm not fucking with you."

The way he demanded his respect turned her on. "I got it, baby."

"And Kelsi, you my partner and all, but I ain't trying to hear nothing else about you fucking my shawty."

"Done." He said, wiping his hands before throwing them up in the air.

They managed to engage themselves in small conversation while they looked at all the celebrities around them until Yao approached with Onik and six other henchmen. "Gentlemen," he bowed slightly, "Bricks," he bowed again, "Yvonna, come with me."

Without bothering to object she hopped out of her seat. They were all proceeding to the exit when Bricks jumped up and grabbed her hand. "Yvonna, you good?" Her fingers rested softly in his palm.

Not sensing Yvonna behind him, Yao stopped, turned around and addressed the love-crazed couple. "She's with me, why wouldn't she be fine?"

Bricks gaze remained fixed on Yvonna. "Not for nothing, Yao," now he looked at him seriously, "but I'm talking to her."

Yao smiled and said, "How much longer do you think I'll let you come in between her and I?"

Kelsi stood up preparing to take a ride to hell with Bricks if it was needed.

"Uncle, please. He cares about her." Ming interjected hoping he wouldn't have Bricks killed. She knew how much he meant to her best friend.

"Don't talk to me!" Yao said. "You're nothing but a disappointment."

Ming ran away crying and this angered Yvonna even more. So much was popping off in Vegas that she wondered why she even bothered to board the plane.

"I respect you, Yao, I do, but where Yvonna is concerned, I'm gonna always be in the picture. And if we gonna do business together you need to know that."

"*If* we do business together," Yao repeated. "That remains to be seen."

Bricks was about to put the press on his ass but the look of desperation on Yvonna's face made him ease up. "I'm just making sure she's cool. That's all."

"I'm good, baby." She smiled gripping his hand tighter before releasing it. "Really."

He was about to drop the matter when out of nowhere Bricks saw a face he hadn't seen in years. It was the same dude who was in the car the day Yvonna reentered his life. And it was the same dude who was in the car when he took a bullet in the arm. "Kelsi, keep your eyes on them niggas over there." Kelsi zeroed in on the dudes. "They with the YBM."

Yvonna's heart dropped when she saw the men pile into the arena. She now realized how stupid it was to be in Vegas when the world would be there.

"Fuck!" Kelsi said out loud. "I wish I knew who the fuck lifted my piece."

One by one, members of the YBM started trailing into the arena, not knowing Bricks saw them. "Call my family and tell them we got problems."

"Well it looks like you have your hands full," Yao said, "Yvonna, come."

Yao walked off and Bricks held Yvonna back for a few more seconds. "I love you. Everything's gonna be fine. Okay?" Not caring who saw him, he pulled her to him and kissed her softly. "Now go see what he wants and call me when you can."

"Be careful, Bricks."

"I always am."

With that they walked away and Yvonna tried to ignore the buzzing of the phone in her pocket. When she looked at the phone's screen she saw that it was Bilal calling again. *I should've never given him my number.* She thought. Things were moving so fast that she forgot all about the meeting and now it was after 7:00.

When they made it to a private area in the hotel Yao said, "Where is Urban, Yvonna?" He paused. "And before you lie to me, remember that I might find out the truth. And if I find out you fucked me out of millions and lied, there will be consequences."

Yvonna thought about the consequences and then looked at Yao. Mustering up enough courage she stared intently into his eyes. "I don't know where Urban is."

Yao glared at her. "So you didn't do anything to him?"

"Where the fuck is Greggs at?" One girl yelled walking past them to the arena.

"Damn, this gonna be some bullshit tonight!" the girl's friend yelled.

"I could've saved my money and paid my rent if I knew this." The original girl said.

"I wouldn't lie to you," she lied trying to block out the women. "I don't know where he is."

He sighed heavily. "It's okay, if you really don't know then we have to hope he shows up," he said squeezing her shoulders. "Now," he smiled, "have you given any thought to my proposal?"

"You mean your demand?"

"Easy, Yvonna." His eyebrows creased. "If anybody should be upset it should be me."

She frowned. "Why? I'm not forcing you to marry me."

"No you aren't." he grinned. "But I'm the one who has to explain to my family why I married a nigger. So," he smiled again, "if I can deal with this, you can, too."

"Did you just call me a nigger?"

"I didn't call you a nigger. But I know that you are." He corrected her. "Don't worry, I'm man enough to handle anything that comes my way."

Yvonna felt all kinds of anger brewing inside of her. Part of her enjoyed the anger, because it meant she would no longer feel guilt for having killed Urban, essentially fucking him out of millions. However the other part was afraid of what she might do to Yao. As far as marriage, that was a mute point and a thought of buying that small island was becoming more appealing.

"Thanks for not calling me a nigger directly." She smiled. "That would make things awkward since you just asked me to be your wife."

"Why?"

"If I'm a nigger, what will that make our kids?"

"I don't intend on breeding with you. Once you're my wife, your tubes will be burned at once." He smiled again. "Now, I must see where this Urban is. I'll be in touch, Yvonna." He smiled. "Always in touch."

As he walked past her she made a decision. "Yao has to die."

She was just about to go back into the arena when she saw Phillip. He was on the other side of the arena talking to five men dressed in suits. They were cops and she knew because she could spot detectives if she was blindfolded. When he pointed in her direction, she dipped off before they could see her.

"You shoulda killed the mothafucka when you had the chance," *Gabriella* appeared. "Now you left a witness who could finger you."

"They gotta catch me first."

She was just about to walk away when her phone vibrated again. This time it was Quita. "I told you not to call my phone unless it was about my daughter!"

"It is!" She paused. "Yvonna, I have terrible news."

"What now? I got a lot of shit going on."

"This is important," she cried. "Someone has taken Delilah!"

Yvonna

The room seemed extra hot as Yvonna sat on Quita's stomach with her right hand pressed firmly against her throat. Her fingers squeezed her lower jaw open just enough to see the pinkness of her tongue. Behind her stood Onik and four other members of the Dynasty, and they were waiting on her command.

Tears filled Yvonna's eyes although her cries were not audible. Although she hadn't expected to love Delilah the way that she did when she first got pregnant, she now loved her more than life itself. Delilah gave her purpose and a reason to live. Without her, nothing would matter. Who was going to tell her she was the best mother in the world? Who was going to hug her and plant soft kisses all over her face? And who was going to, despite it all, love her unconditionally?

"Yvonna, please, this isn't my fault," Quita cried. "I...I had to go to the bathroom and the next minute I know she's gone."

"I don't believe shit this bitch is saying!" *Gabriella* said, kneeling down beside Quita's head. She looked over at Yvonna and pointed at Quita's face. "Look at the lies in her eyes."

Wiping her own tears away with the back of her hand Yvonna said, "What you telling me don't make sense. How could you let my daughter walk out of here by herself?"

Barely able to breathe due to Yvonna sitting on her stomach she said, "Yvonna, I swear, I was in the bathroom. If you don't believe me you can ask Boy."

Yvonna's eyes found Boy who was in the corner trembling. The other kids were held up in the bedroom because Yvonna didn't want to expose them to whatever happened next. "Boy, come here." Yvonna smiled, her eyes bloodshot red and tears rolling down her face.

"No." he said shaking his head. "I'm scared."

He held on to his backpack not sure if he would have to throw it at her or not. He'd never seen Aunt Yvonna like that, and if he could help it, he never wanted to see Aunt Yvonna like that again. Yvonna stood up. "Boy, come over here now." She remained next to Quita's body.

Boy walked slowly over to her and Yvonna stooped down. When she was at eye level with him she said, "Honey, tell me what happened."

Boy could smell the alcohol on Yvonna's breath from earlier. "Ummm....Delilah wanted to get some ice for her drink. And Miss Quita was using the bathroom so she said she'd get it herself."

"Why didn't she ask Quita?"

Jumping in to prevent him from saying any more under Yvonna's interrogation Quita said, "Because I was using the bathroom. And I couldn't bring all of them in there with me."

"Bitch, shut the fuck up!" Yvonna screamed. Focusing back on Boy she said, "Did anybody put you up to lying to me? Anybody at all?" Yvonna placed her foot on Quita's stomach. "You can tell me the truth, Boy. I won't hurt you."

Boy was crying hard. "No, that's what happened, Aunt Yvonna. I swear."

"See, I'm telling the truth," Quita mumbled.

"Kill her ass." *Gabriella* appeared. "Put your hand back around her neck...and snap it. This bitch thinks it's a game."

Yvonna thought about the fact that Quita was in charge. She could have lined every kid up and they all could have given the same story, in the end she was the adult and under her watch her child went missing. "You're right. This bitch doesn't deserve to live."

Onik and the men looked at each other wondering who she was talking to. And while their minds wandered, Yvonna grabbed Quita's neck, a trick she learned in China. She was preparing to snap it when Boy said, "No, Aunt Yvonna! Please don't!" He was crying so hard his body was shaking. Wrapping his arms around her neck he said, "Please don't kill Miss Quita. Please."

Boy's wide eyes and his innocent face immediately brought her back to reality. It wasn't until that moment that she realized how much she really loved him. At the end of the day she knew she cared about him; after all, he was her best friend's son and Delilah's brother.

Releasing her neck Quita rolled to the side to grab a few quick breaths. "If I find out you lying, bitch," she pointed down at her, "I'm gonna come back here and kill you." Then she looked at Boy and back at Quita. "And there won't be a man, woman or *child* in the world who could stop me."

"I'm telling you the truth." Quita replied. "I wouldn't fuck with you like that. I know you love your baby."

Yvonna moved to the door preparing to turn the hotel upside down in Delilah's honor when Quita said, "Yvonna, the YBM is here looking for you. I saw them in the hotel."

"And," Yvonna said figuring they were trying to get at her anyway. "What does that mean?"

"I just wanted to tell you. In case they have her."

Yvonna didn't see them grabbing Delilah although she couldn't be sure. Because she'd kill everyone in their family and she hoped they knew it.

"I saw them earlier." Yvonna paused. "In the arena, I don't think she's with them."

"Well there's something else," Quita paused. "Delilah talks a lot about two scary lines. She's seen a few while here, too."

Yvonna frowns. "That's not real. Delilah is just having fun."

"There's something else," Quita paused. "She mentioned something about a lady today."

"I know. She told me that, too."

"But this time was different. She said she knew the woman. Said she watched her when she was younger."

Yvonna's eyes widened. "Did she say her name?"

"I think she said the woman's name was Penny."

◄•••►

Hotel Lobby

Yvonna whooshed by the people in the lobby on her way to the Check In counter. She wanted to know if anyone had come asking about her, and more than anything, if any information was given. The moment she approached the counter with Onik and the rest of the Dynasty, the Agent who had been giving her shit looked as if the color had drained from her face. Although Yvonna didn't know what she knew, based on her reaction she was positive she knew something.

She stepped to the counter and put her elbows on it. The coldness of the granite counter felt icy against her skin. "I'ma ask you something and I need you to be honest,"

Yvonna paused, "did anybody come here asking about me?"

"I'm sorry, who are you again?"

"So you're actually saying after the performance I gave you when I checked in on Thursday, that you don't remember me?"

"Look, I see girls kissing each other all the time. So you ain't nothing special."

"So you do remember me?"

Getting caught in her makeshift lies she said, "Look, how can I help you? 'Cause I'm about to get off and I got people waiting."

Yvonna smiled. "Enough said."

◀ •• ▶

Parking Lot - 30 Minutes Later

The temperature had cooled down slightly when the Agent walked out the back door to her car, which was in the employee parking lot. She was so scared after her contact with Yvonna that her feet sweated profusely and moved uncomfortably around in her shoes.

She was ten feet from her car before Onik hit her in the back of the head with a closed fist. Once she was down she was dragged by her hair to an awaiting van and throw inside. Once there, she saw Yvonna sitting in the cargo part of the van with a flashlight lying down for light. Onik and the rest of the Dynasty men remained outside of the van so that they could have their privacy.

Yvonna was distraught over the loss of Delilah and had she not been so deep into murders, she would have gotten the police involved. But one call from them could have opened the doors on what she had done to Greggs and every other murder she committed. And behind bars, she couldn't find her daughter.

Wiping the tears, which crept on her face she said, "I remember sitting at a restaurant, some years back, with my daughter." She smiled although tears continued to flow down her face. "We were waiting on my friend, Ming." She giggled. "Delilah was sitting at the table playing with her fries. She always played with her food." More tears filled the wells of her eyes and she wiped them away so she could see the Agent's face. "That day... I remember making her a promise that I would always protect her. No matter what." She paused. "And I'm trying to do that now, but I need your help."

"I don't understand."

Yvonna inhaled before exhaling. "Someone has taken my daughter away from me, and I need to get her back. I need to bring her home."

"But I don't know nothing..."

Yvonna threw her hand up to silence her. "I said my daughter is missing." She said seriously. "And I need to find her." She paused. "And if you have any information that can help me make this happen, I will be eternally grateful." She placed her hand on her heart and swallowed. "I'm not a nice person all the time, and I even got a lot of shit with me, but on my life I love that little girl." She sobbed harder. "Please....*please* help me find her," she swallowed and looked deeply into her eyes. "I want to do right, but if you don't tell me everything I need to know, I will kill you with my bare hands. And I promise you, it will be the most painful thing you've *ever* experienced in your life. Now," she paused, "did anybody come into the hotel asking about me?"

Feeling Yvonna's pain she said, "Yes."

A brief moment of relief washed over Yvonna. Because at least now she was on the right track. "Okay, who?"

"Several people. A lady. Some dudes." Yvonna knew it was the YBM.

"Okay how did the woman look?"

"She was fat. And old." She paused. "But I didn't give her any information." She lied.

"Well she has my daughter, so you must've given her something."

"She seemed to be occupied by some lady who had a bunch of kids with her." Realizing her fate she started crying.

Yvonna grabbed the flashlight and took a picture out of her back pocket of Delilah. Shining the light on the picture she said, "Did one of the children look like her?"

The Agent stared at the picture and said, "Yeah. She was with them."

Yvonna dropped the flashlight and it made a loud clanking noise against the side of the van. Then she shook her head and threw her face in her hands.

"I'm so sorry. I didn't know any of this would happen. Otherwise I would have never given her your info." The Agent was beyond emotional as she sobbed.

Yvonna grabbed the light again, scooted up to her and softly patted her on the back of her head. "Stop, crying." She paused. "We both can't be both crying now can we? We need to find my daughter."

"I know." She sniffled. "I know...I'm just so scared."

"And everything will be okay. Trust me." She paused. "Now listen, I need you to tell me anything else you know. Anything at all."

"Okay, the woman who asked about you, had a napkin in her hand."

"Good. Now why is that so important?"

"Because she kept patting her face with it and left it on the counter. It had the Diamond Motel logo on it. It's at the far end of the strip. A real dirt bag place."

This is the information Yvonna needed. "Okay, do you know anything else?"

"No...no," she shook her head, "that's all I know. Now can I please..."

A blade severing her vocal cords muted any further words. Yvonna continued to pat her head until life had completely left away from her body. Removing the blade from her throat she exited the van. "Onik, get rid of the body."

"Where?"

"We are in Nevada, the desert and the largest body dump in America. You'll find a place."

"Where are you about to go?"

"I got another stop to make. And I need to make it alone."

Yvonna

A light rain fell over Yvonna as she stood in the middle of the parking lot looking at the motel room Penny was said to be in. It didn't take long to find her, thanks to some cash and her strikingly good looks. Although she was sure the room attendant didn't lie to her, it wasn't until she saw the roundness of Thaddeus body as he put a whore out of the room that she knew she was in the right place. Her only dilemma was how could she get to him to let her in?

"It's amazing, just when you think you've killed them all, you must kill more." *Gabriella* appeared. "This time make no mistakes."

Walking on the side of the motel, with the door still in her view, she wiped the water out of her face and pulled her cell from her pocket. A car passed and water from the wheel smacked against her jeans, dampening her even more. She didn't care, her focus was razor sharp.

After a few rings Ming finally answered. "Ming, I need you to come to Diamond Motel. At the far end of the strip."

"I'm on my way!" Ming got there in ten minutes flat, carrying champagne and glasses. Wearing nothing but a red negligee, a mid length rain jacket to cover it and red high heels it was evident what she thought was about to pop off.

Hopping out of the cab she said, "Which room we in?" Hope spread across her face and Yvonna could see all the nasty shit she flung around in her mind. She raised the champagne bottle in one hand, and two glasses in the other.

When Yvonna's gaze remained on Thaddeus' door Ming said, "Are we going to have a good time or what?"

"I'm not fucking you, Ming."

Dropping the items by her side she said, "Then why tease Ming like that? After how my uncle treated Ming, I thought you were going to make her feel better."

"Someone has stolen Delilah." Yvonna said, eyes glued on the door.

Playtime was not even a thought in Ming's mind anymore. "What? I mean...how? When?!!!!" Ming was immediately saddened.

"Penny stole her, and I need you to help me get her."

An evil glare came across Ming's face. "Which door?" Ming was now in "Goon Mode" and was prepared for anything.

"It's the one over there," she pointed, "but I have a plan."

◄••►

Penny's Room

Thaddeus was just thinking about the prostitute he fucked from the service he found in the phonebook. After finding out his wife had been arrested for trying to kill them, he felt it was time to celebrate. With the whore gone, he was about to bust another nut by jerking off. Lying on his back with his dick in his hand, he was startled when there was a knock at the door. "What?!" The interruption irritated him. "I'm busy!" KNOCK. KNOCK. KNOCK.

Rolling out of bed with an attitude, he walked to the door, with his dick still in his hand and looked out the peephole. Standing on the other side was the sexiest Asian woman he'd ever seen in his life. Fearing she would walk away, he snatched the door open without putting his dick away. "Uh...yes? How can I help you?"

Ming looked at his worn out old penis and said, "I'm from 'Me Love You Long Time' adult services." The gum in her mouth popped with every word. "You ordered an escort?"

Two thoughts briefly entered his mind. One, it was a little weird that she had appeared from nowhere, and second he could not afford another escort. After all, he had already spent all Old Ass Penny's money on the last whore. He quickly exited both thoughts to the left when she opened her coat and revealed her body. She was hands down the thickest Asian woman he had ever seen in his life.

"Yes, I...uh...ordered a bitch. Come on in." She handed him the champagne and the glasses and he stepped back and opened the door wider.

Once inside she grabbed the door from him said, "Get over on the bed." When his back was turned, taking the gum out of her mouth she placed it quickly over the lock to prevent it from closing fully.

Looking around the room disappointment washed over her when she saw no signs of Delilah. No little girl shoes, jacket or even a purse was present. Then there was the stench, which gave her a headache.

"Now, I'm going to run you a bath. And then you're going to come in and join me." Ming said. "We will have great time together."

Dick swinging he said, "I can't wait."

Ming rushed into the bathroom, locked the door, ran the water and called Yvonna. "Ming is in."

"Is she in there?"

Ming sat on the edge of the tub and said, "No. She's not." Silence. "Yvonna," she whispered looking at the closed bathroom door. "Are you there?"

The next sound she heard was a door being kicked open followed by Thaddeus' high pitch voice. Ming jumped up, cut the water off and rushed out of the bathroom. Yvonna was standing in the middle of the floor looking at Thaddeus on the bed. She was soaking wet and although desperate to find her child, the wetness from the rain made her look super sexy. Her silhouette due to the door remaining opened looked scary and sexual at the same time. Ming walked behind Yvonna and closed the door.

"WHAT THE FUCK ARE YOU DOING HERE, BITCH?!!!" Thaddeus yelled.

"Where is my daughter?" Yvonna took a few steps in his direction.

"What the fuck are you talking about? I don't know nothing about your daughter. Didn't you take her when you got out of that nut house?"

"Where is my daughter?" Another step closer.

"What you ain't listening? I said I don't know nothing about your daughter." He turned to Ming. "And did you fucking set me up?"

Ming tied her coat and took off her shoes and Yvonna slipped out of her shoes too. Knowing that something was about to go down, and keeping in tune with the mood, Thaddeus hopped out of the bed, cracked his knuckles, and then his neck. "What, you bitches wanna fight?" Silence. "Well, I guess Vegas about to get their show after all."

"You right about that shit." Yvonna said.

Yvonna rushed him and kicked him in the face. The floor rumbled as his weight dropping to the floor shook the entire room. Rolling over on his knees he licked the blood from the corner of his mouth and wiped the bloody drips from his nose. Quick with her follow up, Ming grabbed the phone book and whopped him in the back of his head causing him to fall face first to the filthy carpet.

Catching Ming slipping, he grabbed her by the ankle and she fell flat on her ass. The pain running through her hipbone was excruciating and this didn't do anything but piss Yvonna off. She grabbed the bottle of champagne Ming brought and cracked him on the head. The bottle shattered in a million pieces but instead of passing out, he smiled.

"I see you can take a hit," Yvonna said, kicking him in the face again with her foot. But when she motioned to place both feet back on the floor he pulled her down. It was evident that from the floor he had an advantage. "Awwwww…" Yvonna yelled holding her lower back.

The carpet on the floor provided no shock for either of their falls, they may as well have fallen on the floor. With both women down, he was able to get up and jump on top of Yvonna. His weight caused her back to press into the floor. Forcing her legs apart, he pulled down her pants with one hand and held her mouth with the other. She could smell the scent of dick and old sex on his fingers. It was obvious what was going on, he wanted some pussy and he was going to take it.

Ming still in pain, but refusing to let her friend be raped jumped on top of him and hit him in the face, back and arms. But the beast didn't seem to be phased by any of her blows. It was as if he had done this many times before. Seeing Yvonna squirming to get from up under him, Ming looked around the room for another weapon. *What can Ming use to hit this bastard with?* She thought. Having killed before with footwear she grabbed a shoe and with the heel slammed it into his bare back. He didn't budge. Instead he remained, on top of Yvonna, inches away from her hot pussy. Finally inside of her he shoved his hard dick back and forth.

"Stooop!!" She cried" Get off of me!" Thaddeus was relentless as he fucked her on the floor of the motel.

Not liking his reaction after she hit him the first time, she lodged the shoe into his back again, this time deeper.

Now she got his attention. "I'm gonna kill you, bitch!!!!" He yelled rolling off of Yvonna trying to grab the shoe from his back.

As he struggled to get the shoe out of his meaty tissue, Yvonna wiggled away from him. She could still feel his dirty penis between her legs and this enraged her. Grabbing the knife that she used to stab the Agent she hit him as hard as she could in the neck. She looked like she was stabbing at fertile soil in a garden as she sliced him over and over again. She didn't stop until Ming sat on the edge of bed and said, "He's gone, bitch." Her breaths were heavy. "Stop it already. You making too much noise."

Stopping her wild arm motions, she sat on the floor next to him, her body completely covered in his blood. "I lost her, Ming." Yvonna sobbed dropping the knife. "I lost my baby."

Ming approached her and her toes pressed into the blood soaked floor. Dropping to her knees she said, "Ming is so sorry, Yvonna. But we going to find her. Even if we have to get uncle Yao involved. Ming promises."

"I don't know what I'm going to do if I can't find my baby girl. I don't know the person I'm going to become." She sobbed.

"Listen," Ming said turning her face to her with her small hands. Blood from her fingertips marked Yvonna's chin. "Trust Ming. We will find Delilah. Even if we got to turn over the world to do it."

"What am I gonna do in the meantime, Ming?"

When she said that Penny walked into the room. Alone, and without Delilah.

"Ming doesn't know about the future, but Ming knows what we can get into right now."

Shyt List IV

Sin City

Yvonna

Yvonna walked to her room covered in blood and beaten emotionally. Before leaving the murder scene, she threw on some of Penny's oversized clothing so that no one would see the blood on her clothes after having just killed Penny and Thaddeus. The number needed to contact the people who ran the child sex ring was tucked in her back pocket. Killing Penny and Thaddeus didn't bring Delilah back, but she'd be lying if she said that it didn't bring her some satisfaction. As Yvonna tried to locate the key to her suite, the entire scene played back in her mind.

Earlier that night when Penny walked through the door, she and Ming overpowered her and pushed her to the floor. She was so shocked to see Thaddeus' dead body, that she didn't have time to ward them off.

"Yvonna, I know ya don't believe me, but I don't have Delilah." Penny said.

"Why should she believe you?" Ming said. "You've been nothing but an untrustworthy ass bitch since the day she met you."

"She should believe me 'cause I'm going ta tells her the truth."

"And what's that?"

"That I came to get ya, Yvonna. Peoples is worried. Worried that ya know more than ya lettin' on, and worried that ya will tell people about the operation. They been tryin' ta get in contact wit' ya for a minute, but ya so hard to get a hold of back home. So when we's found out ya was gonna be here, we's tried to close in on ya, thinking it would be easier." She paused only to swallow. "I was gonna snatch, Delilah. I really was, but I couldn't find the right time. She always seemed to be wit' that girl...the babysitta, I believes. So I could never get her alone. Guess I'm not cut out for this." She smiled. "I figured if I kidnapped her, you'd turn yourself over ta me. A life for a life." She paused. "Look, I know ya don't believe me, but I ain't got ya daughter. And even if I did I would never hurt her. But the peoples who have her, will probably sell her within a few days if ya don't meet with them. It's over, Yvonna, ya got to make the call."

"What does Gabriella have to do with this?" Ming asked.

"More than ya realize." The news was raining on Yvonna hard. This was the end. They finally caught her and there was nothing she could do. "I can give ya the number. All ya gotta do is meet up wit' 'em, and if they got Delilah, I'm sure they'll give her to someone you love. But I gotta be honest, it will be the end of the road for you." She paused again. "A life for a life." She paused. "Now look, afta all of the stuff I done for ya, ya think it's possible to let me go?"

"Bitch, please!" Yvonna said. "You lied to me from day one. You were never the person I thought you were and you never loved me."

"That's a lie, chile. I did love you."

"You loved me *conditionally*. And when I had the daughter you always wanted, you turned on me. And I will never forget that."

"Please, Yvonna, don't do this."

Yvonna looked at Ming and said, "Let's finish what we started."

For the next five minutes, she and Ming took turns stabbing and killing Penny until her eyes were closed and she was dead. Afterwards, they cleaned themselves up as best as she could and caught a cab back to the hotel. Once there Ming went to get Boy from Quita and Yvonna went back to the room alone. When she approached her door she noticed it was slightly opened due to the 'Do Not Disturb' sign being stuck halfway out the door. She walked into the room with caution and saw that Gabriella was sitting on the sofa with a phone in her hand.

"What are you doing here? About to fuck Terrell?" She snatched the sign out while she pushed the door closed and walked deeper into the suite.

"I'm here to see you." She put the phone down and stood up.

"About what?"

"They want me to bring you to them." She whipped out a gun and pointed it in her direction. "Now I don't wanna hurt you, Yvonna. But if you don't come with me, I'm gonna have to."

Yvonna stared at the gun with the silencer attached. She wished she didn't send Onik and the rest of the Dynasty members on their way to bury the Check In agent. "How did you get a gun? You couldn't bring it on the plane."

"I have people here." Then she paused. "Well, they have people here. Guns and anything else is not a problem."

"So, you going to kill me?"

"I don't want to."

"You know what," she paused, "for some reason I do a good job of bringing sneaky bitches into my life." She continued. "Why are you doing this?"

"Yvonna, I know you don't believe me, but I love you. I just gotta…I just gotta do what's best for my daughter."

"Your daughter?" Yvonna frowned. "You never told me you had a child."

"I didn't tell you that because I couldn't." Gabriella stepped inches closer. "But they have my child, and if I don't bring you to them, they're going to kill her. Now I'm sorry, but you gonna have to come with me. It's the only way."

"The marks on your stomach, came from a C-Section?"

"Yes. I was in a third world country, and they are not big on cosmetics for pregnancies. They practically ripped the baby out of me."

Yvonna was contemplating the best way to get out of the situation when using a key, Swoopes and Crystal entered the room. When she saw his face she felt off balance. If there was one man on the face of the earth she didn't want to see, he would be it. "Swoopes. How…how did you find me?" Swoopes and Crystal walked deeper into the room.

"I got you now, bitch!" Swoopes said. "After all of these years, I'm finally gonna do all the things to you I wanted to do."

"Who the fuck are you?" Gabriella asked.

"It don't matter. But I came a long way to get my hands on this bitch. And I'm not leaving here until I see the life taken from her body."

"I'm confused, I mean, how did you get in my suite?" Yvonna asked.

"When Bilal Jr. saw you earlier, you left your room key on the table." Yvonna remembered taking the things out of her purse, but she hadn't realized she made such a grand mistake. "And you gave him your room number. Wrote it down and everything."

"Where is he now?"

"I don't give a fuck. Somewhere in Vegas." He smirked. "Now, all you gotta do is come with me and we'll settle our beef."

"I don't think so," Gabriella said pointing the gun at her. "Now these people have my daughter, and she's coming with me."

Swoopes looked at her strangely and said, "I remember you. From the church."

"What you know about the church?"

"I know more than I should."

"Like what?" She said rapidly moving the gun between them and Yvonna.

"I was at that spot. The one where they were…selling and raping the kids." He said in a low voice.

Gabriella squinted and said, "Oh, my God! It's you. Taylor Mitchell." She laughed and said. "I can't believe my luck. If I turn both of you over to them, they'll be sure to give me my child back now." She grabbed her phone out of her purse and called them. "I have Yvonna and I don't know if you remember Taylor Mitchell, but he's here, too." She paused. "I won't let either one of them' out of my sight." The gun remained in their direction. "But now since I have them both, can you give me my daughter back?" Silence. "Hello?" She looked at the phone and back at them. "They'll be here in fifteen minutes. Everybody remain cool and stay alive."

"Do they have my daughter? Delilah?"

"I didn't know she was missing."

Yvonna felt a lump in her throat. She would willingly give herself up for a chance to save Delilah, but since that was not the case, she had to get out of the situation to find her.

"Bitch, I'm not going anywhere with you." Swoopes yelled. "And I'm leaving here with Yvonna, too."

While they were occupied with each other, Yvonna ran over to the light switch next to the door and flipped it off. Everything went black and a shot rang out in the room. Knowing her way around the suite, Yvonna moved for the door. She figured it was her only chance to get away from them both.

"Who was hit?" Swoopes yelled out into the dark. Silence. "Who the fuck was hit?!!!" He repeated.

Silence.

Instead of responding, Yvonna opened the front door and was preparing to escape but the moment she did, four armed men were standing on the other side. "We got her!" one of them said before striking her in the neck with a taser, knocking her out cold.

Shyt List IV

Sin City

Bricks

B ricks and Kelsi followed members of the YBM for thirty minutes hoping they'd lead them to Swoopes. In the end they found nothing. After all these years Bricks almost had him and it fucked him up that once again, he had gotten away.

Walking back to his room he was surprised to see Ming rush up to him with Boy. She was wearing a raincoat and looked frazzled and out of character. "Ming thinks somebody got her," Ming cried. "Ming thinks somebody kidnapped Yvonna."

Bricks felt his body fail him as he leaned up against the wall for support. Who could have done this? The first person he thought about was Swoopes. *Maybe that's why I couldn't find him, this nigga took my girl.* He thought.

Standing up straight he said, "How you know?" He stepped closer and looked into her eyes. "

"Boy go over there." Ming said pointing to a place away from earshot. When he was gone she said, "When Ming went to our room Ming saw some dead girl laying on the floor, but Yvonna was nowhere to be found."

"Who is the bitch dead?"

"Ming doesn't know!"

Bricks felt helpless in Vegas. He didn't have his guns with him. And outside of going with the hands, there was nothing he could do to defend Yvonna. He was just about to kick a few asses and worry about that later when Melvin called.

"Where are you?" Melvin asked.

"Nigga where the fuck are you? We got beef! They fucking took my girl, slim! They got her!!"

"Calm down." He said. "Because that's exactly what I'm calling you about."

Shyt List IV

Sunday

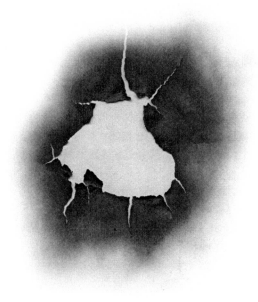

Yvonna

The room was pitch black and Yvonna couldn't see her hand in front of her face. But she could feel the presence of other people in the room with her.

"Awww," Yvonna cried out holding her bruised neck.

When she placed her hand in front of her face, she couldn't even see her fingers wiggle.

Dropping her hand to her side she said, "Where am I?" Someone in the world wanted her dealt with and had ceased an opportunity to catch her ass slipping. "I need to get out of here! I need to leave! Please! Let me out!!!"

Silence.

"You know if it was that easy…we'd be gone already." A female voice said.

"Who is that?"

Silence.

Yvonna outstretched her arms trying to touch the person who had just spoken. But the pitch-blackness provided no direction.

"I said who the fuck are you?"

"It's me. Gabriella."

"So they got your ass too, huh? After everything, you right in here with me."

"If that's what you want to call it."

"That's exactly what I call it."

Loud rumbling outside of the room caused them to swallow any upcoming words.

"Are you there?" She whispered into the darkness. "Can you hear me?"

"Yes."

"I wanna ask you something, and this time I want you to be honest. After all, what do we have to lose? Right?"

"We're both about to die, so what is it, Yvonna?"

"Why did you leave the home when we were kids? I mean, why did you leave us knowing we needed you? And why didn't you take me with you? I was being raped and tortured too. It ain't like I didn't need an escape. You were all I had."

"We are about to die, and you want *that* question to be your last?"

"Yes." She paused. "I guess I gotta know."

Irritation sounded off in her tone. "Yvonna, I can't remember that far back. We were kids, and all I wanna do now is make it out of here alive. And that should be all you're worried about, too."

"I'm worried about a lot more than that. I can't help but believe that if you took me with you, that I would've had a chance at a real life."

"Whatever, Yvonna. I'm thinking about my life right now. All that other shit you saying don't make a difference to me anymore. We adults, get over it!"

Her words hurt. "Well it should matter to you. Because for each day you were gone, during that time in my life, your absence mattered to me."

"Well it doesn't matter to me." She was cold.

"It should." She insisted.

"Why?"

"Because if we are able to get out of here, alive, I'm going to kill you myself."

"Is that right?"

"That's mothafuckin' right."

"Well what if we don't make it out of here alive?"

"Then I'm gonna meet you in hell."

Silence.

"Whatever," she said brushing her threats off, "We'll worry about that bridge if we get there." She paused. "Do you have any idea who would want you this bad?"

"You mean other than you? And them?"

"Yes."

Yvonna searched her memory and unlike some folks who didn't have enemies, there were too many people who wanted nothing more than to see her ass dead, but most of them were in their graves and unable to do anything about it. After all, she'd seen to it herself. "Could be anybody, but it's probably Swoopes. I mean, he was in the room with us, too. Why isn't he here?"

"Naw...bitch. Wrong again. 'Cause whoever wanted your ass dead got me wrapped into this shit, too."

"Swoopes?"

"What you think?"

"Wow, so after all the time we've been beefing, we are really gonna die together." Yvonna laughed.

"I guess so. And when we go to hell, we gonna be beefing there, too."

Yvonna laughed again. "I don't doubt it one bit."

"So, Gabriella, since we are about to die, keep it real with us. Tell us who these people are."

"I guess it doesn't make a difference now anyway." She sighed. "So here goes. I don't need to tell ya'll what we went through as kids. We were raped almost every day. And when some of us got out of line, like the three of us, we were beaten." She paused. "And you probably know already that the older ones, who were rebellious, were forced to have sex with church officials just to breed more kids. And if those older children got out of line, they were killed. But what you don't know, until now is that no child who was kept for breeding purposes was able to live over eighteen."

"Why?" Swoopes asked. "They still got pussies and can still make babies."

"You's about a stupid ass nigga!" Yvonna yelled within the dark.

"Bitch, fuck you!"

"Both of you be quiet. You're bringing unwanted attention." Silence. "Now, the children over eighteen, weren't allowed to live because they were legal," Gabriella continued, "and many of them knew they could live on their own. I don't know if you remember, Yvonna, but there was a lot of talk amongst the kids that, *'when I turn eighteen I'ma do this, or when I turn eighteen I'ma do that'.*"

"I can't remember a lot of things in my life at that time."

"That's because after I left you were heavily drugged. It's a wonder you remember anything."

Remembering her meds had gone missing in Vegas she said, "Before you finish, why did you dump my meds?"

"I didn't."

"If you didn't who did?"

"Terrell," Yvonna was hurt by her words.

"Why would he do that? I mean... he was the one wanting me to take them."

"He wanted you to need him. And when you didn't need him he decided to make you sick again. I caught him doing it and that's when we had sex. I guess that small secret brought us together."

"So you saying he's in on all of this?"

"No." she paused. "He didn't know my real reasons for trying to get you alone which I was never able to do. The fool was really hoping you'd love him back." She continued. "Now I had plans to try to be serious about him before all of this. I guess now it doesn't matter,"

"That's so fucking stupid." Yvonna yelled. "Everybody knows Terrell will fuck anybody in and around me just to stay connected. He would've used you to make me jealous and just like the last bitch, kill her the moment I make time for him."

Knowing she spoke truth Gabriella said, "Anyway," then she exhaled, "When the kids turned eighteen they were murdered. But the ones who were sold to parents got to keep their lives. That's how they kept so many kids in line. *'Be good and live, be bad and you won't make it to see your eighteenth birthday.'*

"That was then," she paused, "Now there are hubs in every state in America. Small churches fronted off as houses of worship. And in these places you can buy any child of any age group you want, and although most are African American children, I'm told that they just started breeding white kids, too."

"They really 'bout to make some serious cash now!" Swoopes yelled.

"Are you that fucking stupid? I mean, can you really be that crass?" Gabriella asked.

"Yeah, he can." Yvonna said. "Bilal told me how Tamal "Tree" Green and his own father Poris use to rape him. It's no wonder he's still living, especially after I put a hit on that butthole in jail."

"I'ma kill you, bitch."

"Fuck you, you one eye having mothafucka!"

"It's funny. The two of you hate each other so much, when in actuality, considering that you're lone survivors, you should be best friends. What a waste."

Silence.

"I can't stand that bitch and she can't stand me."

"You got that right." Yvonna paused before turning her attention back to Gabriella. "So, if all this is true, how come we still alive?"

"Because they wanted to see what you knew first, that's why. There's no use in killing you if you've told everybody about the operation. So the main person in charge, a man named Ernest Backer ordered to have you brought to him."

"Thought you said you didn't know who was in charge. When I asked you back in the suite."

"I lied. But now since I'm about to die I don't give a fuck no more."

"So you know where he lives and everything?"

"Yes. When he took my daughter I made it my business to know more about him than he does me. I kept all of their secrets in a lock box in a town called St. Augustine in Florida. I have the names of the kids who are now adults, and their addresses."

"So you haven't been taking down these houses? I mean, the churches. You haven't been responsible for shutting the operation down like you told me?"

"That much *was* true, but they caught up with me and took my only child. I had to stop fighting against them and start working with them instead."

"If I could get out of this mothafucka, I would find each one of them bastards and kill them." Swoopes said. "After all the shit they did to me."

"What they do to you?" Yvonna asked. "You lost that raggedy ass eye and those fingers on the street."

"Bitch, you never know what the fuck to say out of your mouth do you? Now shut the fuck up before I..."

"Before you what? Make me mad? Nigga, sit the fuck back before I unleash on your ass." Just when she said that a garage door opened and in rolled a man in a wheel chair with two armed men behind him. At first her eyes adjusted to the darkness before he became clear. Then they flicked on the lights and she recognized them immediately. It was Bradshaw Hughes who before she ran him over in a truck, use to stand five feet eleven inches tall and looks like Idris Alba. He was also both Delilah and Boy's father. What was odd was that the men with him were the same ones who fucked Ming the night she saw them sleeping on her suite floor. Niggas were always trying to get to her through Ming. And if they made it out of the situation alive, she would have to school her better.

"Did you like the note I sent you at breakfast?"

"It was you?" She said. "Bradshaw...how...did you find me?"

"Don't worry about all that," he rolled his chair into the room which they could now see was a garage. The windows, were all sealed with concrete and a used Ford truck sat toward the right. "Just know that I never forgot how you ruined my life resulting in me getting paralyzed. Just because you found out about some movie shit!"

"So you sold the people who are making that movie my story anyway?"

"Yep, and because of it I'm paid. I guess you should have finished me off after all." Yvonna laughed. "What's funny, bitch?!"

"I thought you couldn't talk." She laughed. "The last I heard you had to blink to respond to people."

"Well with the right money, and the right doctors, anything is possible. And now, after all of this time, I'll finally get to kill you."

Yvonna thought back on the day she ran over him in a truck as he was taking a jog. All because she discovered he was selling the rights to her story. Now she wished she succeeded in killing him. "So these two niggas were fucking my friend trying to get at me?"

Bradshaw looked at them and said, "You fucked her friend?"

They both shrugged. "It didn't start out like that. We were trying to wait on her. Her friend kept saying she was coming right back. One thing led to another and..."

"You fucked the bitch!" Bradshaw yelled from his seat. "You realize she's my son's mother don't you?" He paused. "You told me you couldn't find her or Yvonna."

"Sorry, boss."

"It doesn't matter." He said shaking his head. "We got her now." He focused his attention on Yvonna and rolled his chair closer to her.

"Do whatever you fucking want to me," Yvonna said. "I'm not scared anymore and I'm damn sure not about to kiss your ass. I lost everything and everybody I've ever loved." Her thoughts went to Delilah and she prayed she would be okay, and that the small lessons she learned from her, would be enough to keep her strong.

"Don't worry, I'm gonna deal with you soon enough. But before that, *MY* daughter wants to see you one last time before I kill you." He grinned. "So I'm gonna honor that request."

When he said that Delilah ran into the room and wrapped her arms around her mother's neck. "Mommy, I love you! I'm so scared, mommy! What's happening?"

Yvonna's eyes widened as she held on to her daughter with the one arm that was free. "Baby, I'm soooo sorry. I love you sooo much!"

Yvonna held on to her tightly slightly relieved that the people who were responsible for her illness didn't have her. Sure, she didn't know what kind of man Bradshaw was, but at least he was her own flesh and blood. She only hoped he would do right by her.

"Listen," Yvonna said pushing her back slightly while maintaining her hold on her arm, "I want you to know, that no matter what, your mother loves you."

"I know, mommy, but I don't want to leave you. Please don't let him take me with him." She cried. "His rolly chair makes the scary lines."

"What?" Delilah pointed at the floor and sure enough, behind Bradshaw's chair was the two track marks whenever he moved. "Those are the scary lines?"

"Yes, mommy. I told you I wasn't crazy." She hugged her mother again.

"I'm so sorry for doubting you," Yvonna cried hugging her tighter. "Even after everything I've been through I doubted you and I'm so sorry. Please forgive me."

Bradshaw, angry that the expensive chair he bought left track marks said, "She saw my tire tracks?"

"Yes, stupid ass nigga!"

Bradshaw kept his chair serviced by a local technician and whenever he would finish the work, he would apply too much black oil, which left marks. He didn't even go into his own home with his chair because of it, but it was motorized and his favorite. "Let's go, Delilah. Your mother has somewhere to be."

"I don't want to leave," Delilah held on to her mother's neck tighter.

"Please do right by her, Bradshaw. She's your daughter. Look into her eyes she's your daughter."

"I know she's my daughter! And as far as I'm concerned, she never had a mother."

The two men went deeper into the room and lifted Delilah off of her feet. In a hurry she dropped her purse next to Yvonna. "Baby you left your..."

Before Yvonna could finish speaking Delilah shot her a look. *A knowing look.* But why? Yvonna couldn't be sure but there was something in the way her eyebrows rose that made her believe that Delilah wanted to tell her something. Yet everything was happening so quickly that Yvonna's mind couldn't register. If that also wasn't weird, Yvonna saw the look she gave Swoopes. It was as if she knew him, too.

"I hope you realize this is all your fault." Bradshaw said interrupting her thoughts. "I just wanted my face to be the last face you'd ever see."

"What about me?" Swoopes said. "I ain't got shit to do with all this."

"Yeah, we innocent and wanted her dead, too." Gabriella added. "If you let us go we promise not to say anything."

"Bitch, don't be jumping in on my out!" Swoopes yelled.

"It doesn't matter," he paused. "because neither of you are leaving. In my book you're all witnesses and as a result your deaths will be charged as a product of the company you kept." With that one of the men cut the truck on allowing foul smelling exhaust to spew from the tail pipe. Then they left the room and closed the garage door taking Delilah and the light with them.

Submerged in darkness Gabriella said, "If it's any consolation, I'm sorry about Delilah."

"It's no consolation!" Yvonna yelled remembering how she just threw her under the bus.

Feeling around within the darkness again, she grabbed Delilah's Juicy purse. It was the purse she carried everywhere she went. Placing it against her nose, she could smell the scent of the kiddy perfume she purchased for her and she held it closely while breathing deeply. More tears escaped her eyes and she sobbed heavily.

"I'm so sorry, baby. I'm so sorry." Gabriella had already begun coughing due to the fumes and Yvonna could hear the car rolling away from the garage.

Although Yvonna didn't want her daughter to leave her favorite purse behind, she was grateful to have something that belonged to Delilah. And then...she felt the weight of the bag. It was heavier than it should be. When she opened the bag, her fingers moved over a knife. "Ouch!!!"

"What happened?" Gabriella said.

"Nothing."

A smirk spread across Yvonna's face. Feeling deeper into the purse, she found a gun.

"OH SHIT!" Yvonna yelled out in shock.

"Fuck is up with you?" Swoopes asked.

"Nothing." Yvonna was sure the gun was taken from Kelsi at some point. Thinking how her daughter's sneakiness may have possibly saved her life, she started laughing hysterically. Yvonna didn't know that Quita had been successful at stealing Kelsi's weapon, preparing to use it on members of the YBM if they threatened her again. She didn't know that after Quita stole it, Delilah had peeped her every move, went into the box of pads and took it from her so that she could give it to Kelsi to gain his favor. And finally she didn't know that Delilah had lifted the knife when they were at the diner eating pancakes. When Yvonna asked her what she was doing, just that swiftly she had placed the knife in her favorite purse without her knowledge. She had all intentions on killing Little Davie, as she promised. It was definitely true when they said like mother like daughter.

"Fuck is wrong with you, bitch?" Swoopes asked. "Why you so happy?"

"Yeah...there's nothing funny about being a few hours away from death." Gabriella said.

"Gabriella, what is your connection with Penny?" She said ignoring her comment.

"Nothing really." She coughed again. "They wanted us to work together to bring you to them, but the old bitch was in my way. I work better alone."

"And what about Pastor Robinson?"

"Why all the questions?"

Calmly she said, "Are you going to answer?"

She sighed and was irritated. "Pastor Robinson knows more about things than you realize and out of respect for the man, I'ma leave it like that."

"Last question, what were you doing in my suite? On the day me, you, Terrell and Ming had breakfast."

"I was coming to kill you, but Onik was in the room and wouldn't leave."

Using the knife she cut the rope from her arm. Then she waited a minute and poked some air holes into the wall, which allowed a little light to shine inside.

"What's going on?" Gabriella questioned. Remembering where Gabriella was in the room she fired the gun in her direction. "Oh my, Gawd!" Gabriella cried out. "I think I been shot."

"Ain't no thinking about it."

Silence.

"You have a gun?" Swoopes inquired. "Because if you do you betta watch that shit. That truck is spitting gas and the shit might blow."

Yvonna ignored him and focused back on Gabriella. "I know you still alive, bitch. I can hear you gasping for air like a fish out of water. So do you wanna say your prayers first or not?"

Silence.

"So you would kill me? The person who saved your life when you were younger? You would kill me, after everything we been through together?" Heavily insulted Yvonna fired again. This time she could hear her breaths speed up before finally phasing away.

"Swoopes," Yvonna sang. Swooooooooopppeeees."
Swoopes' heart was thumping rapidly.

"So I'm next huh?" He asked.

"What you think?"

"I think a proposition is in order."

Yvonna laughed. "What kind of proposition could you possibly have for me? You been trying to kill me for years. Even threatened my daughter's life at one point." She paused. "Remember that shit?"

"No, I don't."

"Well let me remind you." She said waving her gun in the direction of his voice. "I was in my doctor's office, and you said *'I wonder how far her little asshole will stretch with my dick in it.'* Just saying it made her angry all over again and her finger was inches from the trigger.

"What about all the shit you did to me? You fucking had me raped in prison. Do you know how fucking humiliating that shit was?"

"Yeah, nigga and you had your boys rape me and leave me for dead in an abandoned house! And then had a dog fuck me! You think I forgot about that?"

Silence.

"I know you didn't forget! And I admit, I did some shit to you and you did some shit to me. So why wouldn't I try to kill you? You wouldn't even have respect for me if I didn't push off on that ass." he paused. "But how many mothafuckas you killed for getting you wrong?" Silence. "If you let me go," he paused, "I can help you get your daughter back."

"What makes you think I need your help?"

"Because we in this together."

"How you figure?" She laughed.

"Because the people who sent this dead bitch over here will never let us live in peace. We gotta find out what's up with this shit and set things straight. Since she name dropped on the phone, they want both of us now."

"Want both of us? What are you talking about?"

"You heard that bitch, they won't rest until they kill you, and now me too. The way I see it, we could get much further in two's. Let's smoke some crazies together."

"I don't know..."

"If you let me go," he paused, "I'll help you get your daughter, and then we can both go find the mothafuckas who took our lives from us when we were kids." He paused. "Let's put this petty shit behind us and work together."

"It ain't happening, Swoopes. I could never trust you."

"You don't get it do you?" He asked.

"Get what?"

"THEY CAN'T STOP US TOGETHER." He said firmly.

Silence.

"Well...what the fuck you gonna do?!" He yelled. CLICK CLICK. She cocked the gun and aimed. "I would've never hurt your daughter," he revealed. "Despite what I said."

"How do I know that shit, nigga?"

"The YBM had her last night. They had your daughter and I found out about it. They said they saw her wandering in the hallway, looking for some ice or some shit like that. I made them let her go. I walked her back to that same hallway myself." How could he know about the ice if he wasn't telling the truth? "Now I'll admit, I didn't take her back to the room, because she said she knew where she was going. But I didn't sign up for stealing no kids. That's not my style. I'll kill a few bitches and a few niggas in my lifetime, but I would never fuck with a lil kid! I ain't wit' that shit so I left them niggas." The sound of the gun followed by the cold steel against his head alarmed him. "So you not gonna take me up on my offer? Even after I tried to do right by your daughter?"

Silence.

"If I let you go, and you stab me in the back, I'ma gonna finish what I started. You got me?"

"You know I don't do well with threats."

"NIGGA, I'M MAKING YOU A MOTHAFUCKIN' PROMISE!"

"I gave you my word, but if you don't trust me, kill me now. I'm not about to kiss your ass anymore. I lived a fucked up life anyway."

Silence.

Instead of steel ripping through his skin he felt tugging of the ropes holding his arm against the wall. And just like that, his wrists were free. He stood up and although they couldn't see one another clearly, they could feel each other's breath and stares. They were standing face to face.

"Are you gonna keep your promise?" Yvonna asked. Silence. "Well are you?"

"Like I said, I don't have nothing to lose. Let's do what we gotta do. I'm ready to put this shit behind me."

Shyt List IV

Sin City

Yvonna

Yvonna and Swoopes escaped the abandoned garage, which held them hostage only to find out that they were in the middle of nowhere. They tried to drive the old Ford truck but it wouldn't move two feet before it eventually shut off. The place was abandoned and held no working phones; they knew they had to kick rocks. On foot, in the middle of Nevada's dusty streets they both realized there was a long road ahead of them. Miles away from public transportation, the hot dessert air made it impossible to have any hope of survival. Yvonna herself had begun to wonder if it would have been better to die inside the garage.

Tiring of walking in silence she decided to spark a conversation. "You miss her? The girl Gabriella killed?" Yvonna asked as they walked with their thumbs out periodically, the dust covering their faces and mouth. No matter how tired she was, she held tightly onto Delilah's purse and its contents.

"You just had to bring that up didn't you?" Swoopes had taken his t-shirt off and placed it on his head to fight the sun's thick rays. Sweat covered his chocolate body and she was surprised that he was cut up like a male model, six-pack and all. To be eyeless and fingerless, he was still fine.

But it was the track marks on his arms that had her fucked up; she decided to leave that alone.

"You didn't say anything about it back there. Not even when Gabriella was alive in the garage. You never asked why she killed her and I want to know why."

"Because I know it wasn't on purpose. I charged it to the game."

Yvonna frowned. "You must didn't love her."

Swoopes was getting irritated with the soft Yvonna but he couldn't deny, it was refreshing to see her like that. Normally they throwing guns at each other and yelling hateful shit. "I don't think I could ever love another human being." Then he paused remembering Newbie and the way the small heart tattoos trailed from her ankle to her pussy. If he loved anybody, she would've been it. "Why you getting all mushy? You in love with that nigga I'm beefing with?"

"I think so." She stopped walking and leaned on her knees for support. She was exhausted beyond belief. "I don't think I can make it any further."

Swoopes frowned and said, "So you being weak now?"

She stood up and moved toward him. "I'm not weak! And don't call me that shit again." She pointed her finger in his face.

"Bitch, get your finger out of my face before I break that shit!" She did. "We fuck around and kill each other before we get at those crazy mothafuckas. So don't say a lot of shit to me and I won't say a lot of shit to you."

"Fuck all that, just don't call me weak again."

"Then stop talking shit and toughen up. Don't keep telling me you not gonna do what you gotta do."

Yvonna mustered a little strength and said, "I'm fine."

Remembering the commercial he said, "I saw they 'bout to make a movie on your life. That shit is too funny."

Yvonna stepped up to him again and said, "There are two things that's liable to make me pop off, calling me crazy and talking about that movie. You got it?"

"Bitch, please!" He yelled waving her off.

When they saw a black and silver tractor-trailer she threw her thumb out again and this time the rig stopped. Yvonna and Swoopes looked at each other in disbelief before running up to the truck's door. Over one hundred vehicles later, finally someone was willing to take a chance on them.

Swoopes opened the truck's door and helped Yvonna climb inside before he followed her. The black older male driver had an inviting smile on his face and Yvonna was momentarily at ease. "You two look like you might be thirsty."

He grabbed a cold bottle of water out of a cooler and handed it to Yvonna. She snatched it out of his hand and gulped half of its contents greedily. The man laughed heartedly.

"Don't be so fucking greedy, bitch!" Swoopes said snatching the spout from her face to finish it off. She hit his arm. Water dripped on his chin leaving trails along his dusty face.

The driver laughed again and said, "Don't worry, 'bout that. I got plenty of water."

He reached in a cooler and handed them a bottle each. But this time when he opened the cooler, Yvonna saw a picture of two kids touching each other's genitals taped on the lid. With the spout of the bottle against her lips she looked at Swoopes and he immediately followed her stare.

"So where to?" The driver asked. He still hadn't moved an inch.

"We're going to Las Vegas." Yvonna said.

"Got plans to gamble?"

"Naw, we got plans to put a few dirty men out of their misery." Swoopes replied.

"Good luck on that."

With that Yvonna took the gun from the purse and fired at his head. "Yeah, mothafucka! Good luck!"

They spent the next fifteen minutes trying to drive the rig along the road. Since neither of them was successful, they hopped out in an effort to get as far away from the crime scene as possible. They made it a few miles when all of a sudden, a black truck pulled up next to them in a hurry. Was it Bradshaw? Yvonna grabbed her gun ready to fire at will. That was until she saw Bricks jump out of the passenger door while the truck was still in motion. Melvin eventually brought it to a complete stop before he and Ming got out also.

"Please tell me you see them approaching us," Yvonna said afraid her mind and the brutal heat were playing tricks on her again.

"Yeah I see that nigga."

Yvonna ran up to him and wrapped her arms around his neck. He kissed her passionately before pushing her away to walk up to Swoopes. Stealing him in the face Bricks caught him off guard. The two of them scrapped for five minutes with no one breaking them up. When both of them seemed to tire due to hours of no sleep and the dessert heat, they stopped on their own.

"Baby," Yvonna said walking up to him as he lie on the ground, "Swoopes is going to help me with something, and I don't want him killed."

Ming and Melvin looked at each other in disbelief as both Bricks and Swoopes stood up. It never dawned on them when they pulled up that she was with him of her own free will. Dusting himself off Bricks said, "If you go anywhere with this nigga I'ma kill his ass and you, too."

"Then do it then, nigga!" Swoopes said stealing him again which resulted in another short-lived fight.

Blood covered their faces and *again* Yvonna stated her peace. "Baby, he's gonna help me find the people who raped us when we were kids. We gotta do this."

"Us?" Bricks said hearing the recollection for the first time. This caused Swoopes a little embarrassment and he walked away to give them some distance.

Yvonna stepped closer to him. "Yes. I didn't tell you all of the ends and outs with us but we were both raped as kids." Yvonna could see Bricks' chest soften a little although not a lot, because he still hated the nigga. Still, there was nothing in his opinion worst than a boy child being raped. "And if we don't take care of this problem, and kill these people, I'm never gonna be free. I'm never gonna be able to make you happy. I gotta do this and I gotta do this alone."

"But you gonna be with that nigga!" Bricks yelled pointing at Swoopes who looked back at them before looking away. "I can't have that, baby. I'll die if he hurts you."

"He won't," she pleaded, "Please, Bricks, I need to close this chapter in my life. And afterwards I need to get my daughter back."

"You found out who has her?" Ming asked feeling comfortable enough joining the conversation.

"Yes, it's Bradshaw."

"WHAT?!! HOW DID HE FIND HER?!!!"

"He's been following us for awhile. His wheels were leaving tracks everywhere he went. That's what Delilah was trying to tell me and I didn't believe her."

"Oohhhh, the two scary lines." Ming said.

"Exactly." Directing her attention to Bricks she said, "Baby," Bricks was sick over the idea of leaving her alone with Swoopes, "how did you find me?"

"Melvin, he was following Swoopes for awhile, until he saw them niggas who came to the house and took Tracy that night. You remember, they had her in the car before they let her go?"

"Yeah."

"Anyway, he started following them, until they went back into the hotel, and he lost them niggas again. But in the process he saw some other dudes leaving out the hotel. He said one dude had you in a wheel chair, and that you looked sleep and that the other dudes were walking really close to this nigga over here and Gabriella. So he followed them with the rental truck until eventually he lost them, too."

"Doesn't sound like Melvin is good with following," Ming said. Yvonna laughed, just happy to see her friend again.

"So he came back and got us and we been going up and down the same road he lost them on in the hopes that I would find you. And I did," Then he looked into her eyes, "So you see baby, I can't let you go. And if you gonna fight these mothafuckas I'm with you. I don't give a fuck about nothing anymore. But I'll kill you before I let you get in a car or anywhere else with this dude alone." That was the most romantic shit she'd ever heard in her life.

"Ming is going, too." Ming said. "So don't even try leaving me."

"You can't," Yvonna said, "What about Boy?"

"Ming already made arrangements," she said, "Quita is taking Boy to my aunt in Maryland, I told her he may have to stay for awhile. Ming didn't know how long it would take to find you, but Ming wasn't giving up."

"What about your mother? You were supposed to meet her next week."

"Its fine," Ming said sadly. "We all we got."

"And not only that, Yao is talking about killing niggas and shit." He paused. "And I think he used those words exactly. They found Urban's body in the hotel with Carmen. He thinks we're involved."

"We?"

"Yeah, the boy Phillip told him everything. He said he saw me through the crack of the door in the room. I think he even told the FBI, too. They was already asking questions once they discovered Urban, Carmen and some nigga floating in the pool. Now that nigga put us directly in the mix." Bricks said. "We fugitives, Squeeze. Ain't no normal life for us unless we want to be behind bars forever."

Yvonna was devastated. She didn't want her friends going through this shit. "Where's Kelsi?"

"He went back home," Bricks said. "But fuck all that. It's me and you against the world."

"We staying." Ming said. "With you."

Their display of love was overwhelming and then it dawned on her, despite not taking medication she was seeing Gabriella less frequently. Like Satori said, could love really conquer all?

"There's nothing I can say is it?" Yvonna asked looking at Bricks and Ming. "Ya'll coming with me whether I want you involved or not."

"Pretty much," Bricks said.

She gave them all hugs and said, "Finally after all of these years, I found a real nigga and a friend who truly loves me."

"Yeah, well, I just hope you deserve it." Melvin interrupted the love parade.

She walked up to him and said, "I know you don't get me, and you try to play hard ass all the time, but there's something about me you like. Just admit it."

"I ain't admitting shit," he said getting into the truck. Her feelings were hurt.

"He'll come around," Bricks said, "but even if he don't it don't make me no difference, I love you. That's all that matters"

"I love you too, baby."

They were walking to the truck when she said, "Wait. I got to make a call. Bricks, can I use your phone?" Bricks hands her his phone. Taking the sheet of paper out of her back pocket she dialed the number Penny gave her.

"Hello." A man's voice said.

The sun beat against her skin. "I'm coming for you. Be ready."

"Yvonna?" He said confidently. Silence. "We'll be waiting."

"Not for long." She said before hanging up.

"Who was that?" Bricks asked.

"Someone we got to get rid of."

After the call they all piled into the truck and Ming sat in the front with Melvin. Bricks sat in the back on the right, Yvonna in the middle and Swoopes on the left. Once again the two men gave each other evil stares. Swoopes looked over at Bricks and said, "I hope you know that after we get them baby rapers and find the kid, we got beef."

"Nigga, you put six slugs in me, we got beef now!" Bricks said.

As the car rolled down the dusty roads Ming flicked a few matches and looked back at Swoopes. "To be wild, you kinda cute. Eye patch and all."

For the first time that day Swoopes grinned, "Thanks, ma." He looked out the window.

"Keep that up and you just might get some." Ming continued. Bricks and Yvonna shook their heads.

He looked at her and said, "We can get into all that if you want, but for now, let's go smoke some crazies!"

Chocolate City

Yvonna

There were no praises of worship in the church today. After all, having raised enough money from the collection plate that circulated every five minutes, the church was being renovated and was closed. Smells of paint and new furniture were heavy as Pastor Robinson crept into the basement. His hair was completely silver and he had deep-set wrinkles in his face.

Singing hymns, he flipped on the light switch. And when he did the brownness of his skin was almost drained when he saw Swoopes sitting on the table picking his nail with a knife, Bricks leaned up against the wall with the handle of his gun showing under his shirt, Ming sitting down in a chair with a rope on the floor next to her black Jimmy Choo's as she flicked matches and Yvonna standing in the middle with a look that alone could kill.

"Uh…what are you children doing here?" The old preacher stuttered. "I ain't got nothing you want."

"Oh you got something we want alright," Yvonna said.

"Like what?"

Yvonna walked so close to him, he could feel her body heat and smell her strawberry scented breath. "For starters, you gonna tell us everything you know about them baby rapers you affiliated yourself with. And if you don't," she paused, "well sir, let's just say I really hope you alright with the Lord."

Chocolate City

Bilal Jr.

Bilal walked alone on a street in a small DC project. He knew he could've been killed but he was meeting his brothers for the first time. Swoopes didn't make good on his promise to handle AJ and Dirk, and as a result, he had beef and was forced to leave home.

Taking the piece of paper out of his pocket with the address, he bypassed the evil stares of many as he made his way up the street. But when he approached a green house, he saw two young twenty something year old men fixing a car shirtless. On their backs were identical tattoos that read, *"Don't Get On My Shyt List Again"*. He wondered what that meant.

When he moved closer, one of them turned around and tapped the other on the shoulder. The moment Bilal saw their faces, he knew they were related. All three shared the same soft curly hair, and their complexions were identical. He was happy to have family of his own until he felt an unwelcoming vibe from one of his brothers.

"So, you our baby brother," the nice one said. "It's good to finally meet you, nigga. I hope you ready to put in work."

Bilal just nodded, not knowing what that meant.

"Yeah, lil nigga," the other said, "Welcome home."

Shyt List V

Smokin' Crazies
The Final Chapter

CARTEL PUBLICATIONS
PRESENTS

The Cartel Collection
Established in January 2008
We're growing stronger by the month!!!
www.thecartelpublications.com

Cartel Publications Order Form
Inmates <u>ONLY</u> get novels for $10.00 per book!

<u>Titles</u>	<u>Fee</u>
Shyt List	$15.00
Shyt List 2	$15.00
Pitbulls In A Skirt	$15.00
Pitbulls In A Skirt 2	$15.00
Pitbulls In A Skirt 3	$15.00
Victoria's Secret	$15.00
Poison	$15.00
Poison 2	$15.00
Hell Razor Honeys	$15.00
Hell Razor Honeys 2	$15.00
A Hustler's Son 2	$15.00
Black And Ugly As Ever	$15.00
Year of The Crack Mom	$15.00
The Face That Launched a Thousand Bullets	$15.00
The Unusual Suspects	$15.00
Miss Wayne & The Queens of DC	$15.00
Year of The Crack Mom	$15.00
Familia Divided	$15.00
Shyt List III	$15.00
Shyt List IV	$15.00
Raunchy	$15.00
Reversed	$15.00

Please add $4.00 *per book for shipping and handling.*
The Cartel Publications * P.O. Box 486 * Owings Mills * MD * 21117

Name: _____

Address: _____

City/State: _____

Contact # & Email: _____

Please allow 5-7 business days for delivery. The Cartel is not
responsible for prison orders rejected.

NOW Available!!

ALL The Cartel Publications novels are NOW AVAILABLE for download on:

Amazon Kindle
&
Barnes & Noble Nook

Simply search by, The Cartel Publications, download the book you want and read it in minutes.

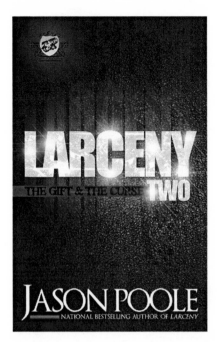

COMING SOON

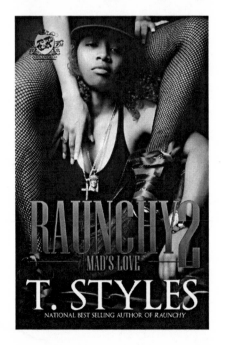

9 780984 303038